THE SWORD OF FOREVER

'Alternatively I could have your wife and daughter arrested. Conspiracy, heresy . . . I understand you think very highly of them. I understand your daughter is very beautiful. I do not understand beauty, sir knight. I understand only mathematics. Only balance. I trust my meaning is clear?'

De Chalons summoned the strength to spit at the diminutive man before him.

De Nogaret's expression did not change. 'Do you find the sight of me such a distraction then?' To the gaolers arranged beside him, de Nogaret ordered, 'Take his eyes that he may suffer no more such distractions, then bring him to me while the pain is still fresh in his mind.' As de Chalons was dragged from the chamber, de Nogaret said quietly, 'And bring his family as well.' To de Chalons he added, 'I had hoped for an easier road but now I will set my mind from such a course. You have chosen the road, sir knight, and now together we will travel along it: two humble men sharing a single horse; a single destination: the truth.'

THE NEW ADVENTURES

THE SWORD OF FOREVER

Jim Mortimore

NA

First published in Great Britain in 1998 by
Virgin Publishing Ltd
332 Ladbroke Grove
London W10 5AH

Bernice Summerfield was originally created by Paul Cornell

Cover illustration by Mike Posen

ISBN 0 426 20526 X

Typeset by Galleon Typesetting, Ipswich
Printed and bound in Great Britain by
Mackays of Chatham PLC

Contents

Then

And the Lord God said, 'Behold, the man is become as one of us, to know good and evil: and now, lest he put forth his hand and take also from the tree of life, and eat, and live forever.' And He drove out the man; and placed at the East of the Garden of Eden Cherubims and a flaming sword which turned every way, to keep the way of the tree of life.

Genesis, 3: 22–24

Now

Mankind's two most dangerous inventions, I submit, are language and the movie camera.

Grant Morrison
The Invisibles, Volume 2/14

PROLOGUE

GUARDIANS OF FOREVER

1

EGYPT: 1287

The desert festered under a dazzling, cloud-girdled sun. Ripples like those on the surface of a pond rose from the dunes, meshing the ground to the sky so that the only thing by which they could be separated was the subtle graduation between glaring white sand and burning white sky. Even the thin clouds seemed to ripple, white upon greater whiteness. Everything here took its shape and texture from the endless curve of the desert; only the pot-bellied sun defied the eternal iteration of shape.

Hughes de Chalons scraped his filthy fingers through his unkempt beard and prayed for water. It was hard to remember the sight and taste of open water, harder still to remember the proud curve of an oak or birch, the colourful spray of leaves. De Chalons scratched, digging beneath his armour to get at the ironically sun-starved flesh beneath.

Beside de Chalons his companion, Henry LeCroix, cast a leer as heavy as his armour-sheathed belly. 'You stink, my friend. You stink worse than a camel.'

De Chalons managed a toothy smile. 'My brother, we all stink in the sight of God. We fight for him and we stink for him. What a shame He is not here to join our merriment and muck out our cages!'

'It is a shame his priests could not arrange for better armour, of that I am sure. But take care with your words. God hears all, my friend, and He will strike you down if He desires it.'

De Chalons waved his arms and allowed himself to topple on to the sand. 'My Lord, methinks He has already struck!'

LeCroix pulled de Chalons to his feet and the two men bellowed with laughter. The laughter sapped energy in the dreadful heat but de Chalons did not care. He simply continued to place one mailed foot in front of the other and plod steadily across the shifting dunes, LeCroix beside him, both men leading a single stolen camel laden with enough looted gold to sink a small barge.

The knights continued to walk – plod, rather – into the white glare of noon. Their shields and helmets had been abandoned days before, their swords fastened to the camel with the packs containing the gold. It had been a long time since the attack – and things before that were more than a little hazy. It was as if the sun had driven a huge torch through the top of de Chalons' head to erase the memories of a life prior to this apparently endless experience of burning sand and burning sky, stinking camel and clatter of booty.

The attack had been a surprise, he remembered that much. Turks. Muslims. Egyptians. He could not remember, but the result was the same: four of their party – what were their names? Edward? Francis? It did not matter; they were with God now – left for dead and as many wounded. Only de Chalons and LeCroix had escaped – by the simple expedient of grabbing the first camel and running into the night. They had planned to ride the camel; they had not realized it still carried looted treasure. Now they had to walk, for the thought of losing the treasure had become as abhorrent to both of them as the unwashed smell of their own bodies – an odour which came through wearing armour continuously for the weeks and months of the Crusade in which they had until recently fought.

The attackers – he wished he could remember who they had been – had followed them of course. Three of them on horseback. LeCroix had killed two, de Chalons the remaining one. One of the horses had broken a leg as it fell and the other two had bolted. They had left the corpses to rot in the sun. It had seemed too much effort to bury them. And anyway, the enemy were heathen and did not deserve a Christian burial.

Now . . . well, some time had passed. Enough for de Chalons to have forgotten the faces and names of his fellow knights as easily as he had forgotten the smell of fresh water, the shape of an oak leaf, the wild joy of the hunt, the sensation of a full belly, the scented touch of wenches and the worried obedience of servants. All that remained now was white sand and sky, gold sun and camel. White gold. De Chalons was sure it would be the last thing he saw.

And then – unexpectedly in this land of relentless monotony – something changed.

De Chalons became aware he was sitting down on the cool sand, allowing the sweat to dry on his face, his eyes slowly cracking open as the light level fell. Slowly, his mind reached an understanding of what had happened to him.

In this land of eternal fire, he was sitting in the *shade*.

The shape looming above the sand was carved from a block of sandstone to resemble a creature combining the features of a man with the body of a lion. It was as big as a small fort. Beyond it, three artificial hills divided the sky into contrasting wedges, their sides steep and impossibly regular. De Chalons stared dumbly up at the group of objects and tried to understand how anything so strange could come to be.

His musings were interrupted as LeCroix, abandoning the camel, wrenched his sword from his pack and ran screaming towards the huge lion-like construction. In truth, he staggered and his voice was little more than a moisture-starved whisper but his intent was clear enough. 'They mock our Lord and Master. Our King! They mock the Lionheart with this abomination! I will – *ulp*!'

LeCroix fell over suddenly and lay gasping in the shadow of the stone beast, so weak from exhaustion and thirst that his own sword was now too heavy for him to lift.

De Chalons crawled laughing to LeCroix. 'You cannot . . . you cannot attack a stone monster with a sword . . . let alone a sword you cannot even lift.'

'I will kill the damnable thing ere I die!'

'But it is not alive!'

'Not alive?' LeCroix's voice affected a puzzled tone.

'No. It is simply stone. Carved stone.'

'Not alive?' Indignant anger now joined the puzzled tone.

'No, Henry. And neither is the Lionheart. He died when your grandfather was but a boy.'

'He did?'

'My brother, I fear this heathen sun has scrambled your wits like hen's eggs.'

'Oh.' LeCroix's indignant frown split into a grin. 'Well then, I suppose we had better see if there's any heathen wine to be had with these heathen eggs of which my mind is composed.'

'And any heathen meat to go with the heathen wine, eh?'

'And heathen women to go with the heathen meat!'

De Chalons sighed. 'My friend, if bad jokes were good deeds you would surely rest eternal in God's Heaven.'

Laughing weakly, LeCroix staggered to his feet and the two men moved unsteadily towards the nearest wall of the vast stone shape looming above them.

The front limbs of the stone creature spread out around them as they came closer, like an enormous cat toying with the lives of kitchen rats. It was not a pleasant thought. But neither was dying of thirst. They had to find water.

They continued towards the wall and there, at the base of a statue positioned between the great stone paws, and apparently carved to represent an ancient king, they found a door.

The door was of carved stone, heavy, apparently immovable. But such was the engineering skills of those who had built this ancient monolith that the slightest pressure of a hand caused the wind-scoured portal to swing open, revealing to the startled knights a darkened passage leading at a sharp angle downwards into the earth.

Once inside the passage the air became dry and cold. There

was no light. The passage arrowed deeper into the earth. Then it stopped and abruptly doubled back, descending even more steeply. But now there was light. Just a glimmer but enough to awaken eyes close to sleep, minds close to death. The light was flickering. Candles? Torches?

Reflections.

From water.

From a pool of *water*.

Only after they had drunk their fill and rested did de Chalons think to study the chamber in any detail. It was large. The roof was supported by rows of columns. It was like being in a stone forest. Stone flagging coated every surface. There was no ornamentation or covering of any description. The chamber was plain, faced sandstone. There was no clue to its age or function.

The pool from which they had drunk was rectangular, some forty paces by sixty. Steps led into the water, which was jet black and apparently bottomless. A stone platform within the pool and completely cut off from the chamber by the water held a maze of columns between which dim torchlight illuminated a further raised platform.

On the platform was a stone box.

LeCroix eyed the box acquisitively. 'Treasure?'

De Chalons nodded. 'What else would be hidden from the sight of God so far beneath this hellish land?'

'Then we'll take it?'

'For glory and God!' De Chalons stripped off his armour and waded into the pool. A moment later LeCroix followed him.

The platform was very large, though it apparently served no purpose other than that of a resting place for the box. The box itself was without ornamentation, with proportions which matched the platform and the pool, and the chamber beyond. De Chalons had a brief impression of patterns within patterns but the moment passed without further insight. 'We must beware heathen traps,' de Chalons muttered as he studied the box.

LeCroix's interest was more pragmatic. 'Does it have a lid? Can we open it?'

'Fetch your sword and we will see.'

'All the way from the surface? Why make that effort when a dagger will suffice?' LeCroix set the blade of his dagger to the seal of the lid and began to explore the join.

A moment later the lid fell off. LeCroix leant forward eagerly to see within but his eyes never beheld the contents of the box. Instead he fell to the ground, eyes blank, a juddering sigh the only sign to mark his sudden death.

De Chalons whirled – staggered would have been a better word – only to find himself at the bloodstained point of a sword held by the figure of a knight.

He took in the figure in a second – the armour was old and dented, bearing the scars of ancient combat, the figure stooped and obviously old – but nonetheless able and willing to dispatch de Chalons to whatever hereafter his brother knight had already arrived at.

The figure moved forward. De Chalons backed from the sword, only to find himself pressed up against the unyielding side of the stone box. The sword dug painfully into his chest. In his weakened state there was no possibility of escape.

Then, the sword stopped. The knight hesitated. The point of the sword moved to examine the Templar seal which hung about de Chalons' neck on a chain of fine gold. The seal was of plain design, two poor knights riding a single horse. It stood for charity and justice.

The sword lowered. De Chalons gauged his chances of escape by fleeing. They were slim.

'At last.' The knight's voice was old and weary beyond measure, but unmistakably that of a woman. 'The new Guardian. The new Guardian of Forever. And not before time.' The knight removed her helmet and shook out long strands of wispy grey hair. She scratched her neck. 'Wretched armour.'

De Chalons blinked stupidly. He was delirious. This was impossible. A woman. In armour! And – he now noticed – wearing the seal of thc Knights Templar.

He studied the woman more closely. Her face was ancient, lined with experience and combat scars. Yet her eyes were bright, though whether through life or madness, he could not tell. And it seemed to de Chalons as if an infinite weariness had been lifted from her at the sight of him, the realization of what he was.

He struggled to his feet, casting a look sideways at the body of LeCroix, awkwardly heaped beside the stone box, one foot draped over the stone platform and dangling in the water. He wanted to speak but there were no words.

The knight saw his hesitation and frowned. 'I left the door open for you. It's been open for years. I've been waiting here for years. Why are you so late?'

De Chalons felt his mind spin. 'Is there to be no apology then? No explanations for your words of madness? How can you know of our presence here when we did not know ourselves? And I demand that you explain the presumption of wearing the Templar Seal or as God is my witness I will take your miserable life with your own sword!'

The knight smiled. 'If you had worn the armour God provided you with as you are sworn to I'd have known who you were. As for the Seal' – her voice deepened – 'I do not wear the Templar Seal. Rather you wear mine.'

She pointed at the stone reliquary. 'Forever waits in the box. It is yours now.'

De Chalons stared into the box. It was full of scrolls. Ancient papyrus tubes each sealed with dusty wax and a single drop of LeCroix's blood.

When he looked up the knight was gone.

He never saw her again.

2

ARGINY: 2562

The woman with mismatched eyes held out her hand impatiently.

'Journal.'

Her voice was dry, impatient, slightly distracted. She did not look at her companion, trusting that he would simply obey her demand. Instead her gaze was focused on the hybrid landscape beyond the hill on which they stood, a rolling jungle of alien blues and scarlets as well as the more normal terrestrial greens and browns.

Eyes which had studied human and alien historical relics alike narrowed suddenly, darting to follow a swathe of movement within the jungle canopy. Animals screeched. A mind which had for five years eavesdropped on the whispered secrets of the earth, now wondered how many of those sounds had never before been heard by human ears.

'Was that one of the trees?'

Her companion nodded as he dug an ancient leather-bound book from his backpack and handed it to her. 'Tiger-willow. Solo hunters. We have to beat them back regularly with napalm. It's the only thing that'll touch them. Sonics are useless.'

'Mmm.' A lean hand grasped the diary, lifting it towards the narrowed eyes. One callused fingertip traced the seal of the Knights Templar chased into the leather in tarnished gold leaf. 'It's been a while, Guillaume.' Her voice was soft, the intimate caress of a lover. 'Twelve hundred years. But I've got you right where I want you now.'

Fingers crisscrossed with hundreds of near-invisible rock scars flipped open the stiff pages, riffled the crackling vellum, halted at a particular page. There were drawings here: a sketch of a landscape, a building long since vanished into antiquity.

'Arginy.' Her voice was now little more than a breath, a whisper borne out from her lips on the wind gusting fitfully around the granite outcropping which held them so high above the jungle – the last wall against which, even now, evolution was propelling a myriad unclassified terrestrial-alien hybrids. 'The Castle of Arginy. The Finger.'

Benny Summerfield lifted her eyes from the diary. She watched the hybrid jungle break repeatedly against the wall of the Massif Central like a sea and wondered how long it would be before even that immense wall broke.

Before her the Rhone Valley festered under a wine-coloured sun. Perhaps festered was the wrong word – but to her it seemed appropriate. Interplanetary war had left Earth a changed world – and the changes were hardly subtle.

She carefully rewrapped the diary in its oilskin cloth and handed the ancient book back to her companion. 'We set up camp here. Place the sonic projectors to the east and set them for thrash-metal – bloodweeds hate thrash.'

As her companion complied, unpacking a tent and hunting through his pack for some appropriate music, Benny stared at the checkered map of Europe spread out before her.

Sunset lay at their backs and the hills cast long shadows across the schizophrenic landscape to the east. Anything up to a century before Rhone had been famous for idyllic European scenery and the production of medium-poor wine. Now the valley was famous for death. Missiles had rained down upon Europe for nearly a month during the heaviest part of the war. It wasn't until a decade later that the retroviruses lying dormant in the missile casings had been discovered. The war had been well underway by then, humanity with the upper hand. But the viruses had been spread – ironically – by a military hungry to investigate the alien technology. And the legacy of the conflict grew, seeping undetected into the air and the water, insinuating itself into the food chain, producing the first of a series of changes which, by the time they were discovered, were unstoppable.

Even sterilization by nukes or antimatter would not have worked. By the time of their discovery the retroviruses inhabited 68 per cent of terrestrial DNA across more than 40 per cent of the globe. Most of them seemed harmless – physical changes affected only a small proportion of those infected. But no one knew when the next changes would begin or what they would be, or what species they would affect. The only thing anyone knew for certain was that they would be spectacular.

As spectacular as those already wrought within the Rhone Valley – one of many places on the globe where evolution had apparently gone wild, producing a hundred, a thousand, species of mutant terrestrial strains, or hybrid terrestrial-alien strains of plant, animal and human life.

The more outspoken voices of government had wanted to go ahead with sterilization anyway – so perhaps it was fortunate that Earth itself was still in a political and economical recession. More moderate voices – in Benny's opinion just as daft – thought the alien incursions into the biosphere were merely a psychological tactic by a defeated enemy, designed to show the collective mind of man what it was like from the other side of the fence. Prosecuting a racial war against non-terrestrial life became a moot exercise when you could no longer tell whether the life on your own world was strictly terrestrial any more. How could you kill the aliens if you might be one yourself?

Either way there was no solution and, in any case, Benny wasn't looking for one. She was looking for something far more important. Together with her fellow, slightly reluctant expedition member, Daniel Beaujeu, eldest son of the current Count of Arginy, Benny was conducting her own search among the mutated forests and herds and tribes of Rhone: a crusade to find the long-abandoned Castle of Arginy where it was rumoured the Holy Finger of John the Baptist had been hidden, along with a whole yummy mountain of Templar loot, more than a thousand years before, sometime in the thirteenth century.

Benny had her twenty-two-year-old sights firmly fixed on qualifying for her doctorate with a serious A-plus, an early fellowship and residency on a planet where the summers were warm, the ice-cream cool, the cashflow was good and the damnable Military couldn't make her sign away her life to the next tiresome interstellar conflict. The Finger of John the Baptist would get her all that and more.

Four weeks, seventy-three miles and one sprained wrist later she set eyes for the first time on the crumbling remains of Castle Arginy and for the first time had an inkling of precisely how large was the gulf between her dream and reality.

Castle Arginy stood atop a hill, smothered in hybrid vegetation, the stone of its walls peeling away at the insistent touch of time and the elements. Getting in would not be hard. Holes gaped in the walls where snakevines had torn nests. Bones littered the ground. No, getting in would not be hard. But getting out again. That would be the trick.

Beside her Daniel stood quite still. He seemed awed but Benny knew that was not the case. Daniel was a quiet man but that did not conflict with his determination or the basic untameable nature of his spirit. It was why she was attracted to him, of course. That and other reasons. Like his willingness to 'borrow' the de Beaujeu journal from his family without their knowledge. Well, without their consent, anyway. Now he spoke and his voice was quiet, deliberate, his words sparse and precisely chosen. 'There will be traps.'

'Of course.'

'Lethal guardians designed to prevent looters gaining access to the treasure.'

'I know.'

'We could be killed.'

'Are you scared?'

'Of course. You are not?'

'No. Traps set by human mind can be overcome by human mind.'

'You are optimistic, Benny Summerfield.'

'I am practical.'

'Is that why I love you?'

She looked sideways at him. 'Do you love me?'

'You doubt it?'

'You never say it as a statement of fact. You always ask it as a question, inviting response.'

'It is my way.'

She shook her head, running one calloused hand through her hair. 'You men, you love to be mysterious.'

He smiled. 'But you women, you love a mystery. You love to plumb our depths, to steal our secrets, to take our hearts home for booty. You loot us as you loot antiquity.'

She smiled. 'That's not very romantic.'

'Do you believe in romance?'

'And not entirely true, either,' she added, avoiding the point. 'I am a scientist. A historian and sometime anthropologist. An archaeologist. I love this work.'

'And like all lovers, you inevitably destroy that which you love.'

She hesitated, listening to the sound of the jungle moving around them. 'I'll tell you what I believe in, Daniel.' She shouldered her pack and, using her bowie knife, began to hack a path through the jungle towards the summit of the hill. 'I believe in an early start and a serious knees-up afterwards. Just the three of us. You, me and the Finger that grassed up Christ.'

'Fingers can't drink.'

'Oh really?' She smiled. 'In that case, I suppose it'll have to be just the two of us then, won't it?'

And once again, using the bowie knife and a determination which was at least as sharp as the blade, Benny Summerfield began to hack her way up the hill towards the dark enshrouded walls of Castle Arginy and an uncertain future.

3

PARIS: 1307

The most embarrassing part of the whole issue, de Chalons told himself as he was chained to the dungeon wall, was not that agents of King Philip of France had arrested him on suspicion of heresy but that they had found him in the flea-ridden bed of a cheap local whore. The charge he fully expected would be quashed within the hour – the gossip would take longer to live down.

Now, as his eyes grew accustomed to the gloom and his ears to the dank silence, de Chalons found himself not to be alone. Other men were chained in the dripping dungeon. Men whose voices he recognized.

'LeFevre? They have you too?'

'They have us all, de Chalons.' The voice was weak, steeped in pain as a good brandy might be steeped in herbs, but without so charming an effect.

'I don't understand.' De Chalons tested his chains. They were unbreakable. 'Cannot Monsigneur de Molay arrange for our release?'

A bitter laugh. 'Even the Grand Master of our Order is powerless against the King. Monsigneur de Molay has been arrested along with the rest of us, my friend. King Philip is taking no chances today. He means to see our Order destroyed. Humbled and destroyed.'

'He is insane! Mad to think he can get away with this.'

Rage filled de Chalons' head. 'I'll see him swing for this, king or no!'

Another cracked laugh from LeFevre. 'When they have taken your eyes as they have done mine, you will be unable to see anything, my friend, no matter how richly deserved.'

De Chalons felt an unfamiliar feeling stir in his breast. It was a feeling he had last seen upon the lips of Henry LeCroix as he lay dying in a reliquary beneath the Great Sphinx in Egypt. But that had been twenty years ago. A lifetime. De Chalons had never expected to feel the touch of fear himself. The treasure they had found had been too important, the station it had brought him in return for its delivery to the Templar Order too great. Now, for the first time since childhood, de Chalons knew the meaning of fear. Knew its belly-shaking intimacy. Knew its ineradicable certainty, its utter finality.

Once before he had feared he might never again see his beloved fields of England. Now he knew this fear would undoubtedly come to pass.

Death was the certainty now. The only questions were how it would come and when he would meet it.

De Chalons remained prisoner long enough to hear LeFevre go mad from infection and starvation before he himself was taken, half blind and half dead of malnutrition, by sealed carriage to another dungeon at least a day's travel away.

There he was chained and held in obeisance before a slip of a man who proclaimed himself civil servant to the King.

'My name is de Nogaret. Guillaume de Nogaret. I will waste no time with negotiations, pleas for clemency or other irrelevancies. I am here to extract from you certain information which I hope you will surrender without undue fuss.'

De Chalons found the strength from somewhere to lunge forward. The chains brought him to his knees an arm's length from de Nogaret. The clerk did not flinch. 'You have just exercised the single luxury I will permit you. Know this, de Chalons. There is no possibility of escape and no hope of rescue. You are already forgotten, as is your rather dubious Order. No one knows you are here. I could kill you now and the matter of your life would come to a neat conclusion. However, the ledger would remain unbalanced. For there is one thing you currently possess that I intend to divest you of and that is the certain knowledge of the Templar Treasure.'

'You ask me to betray God and my Grand Master. You must know I will never do such a thing. You may torture me until you drive the last breath of life from my lips but I will say nothing!'

'Brave words but ultimately futile. You see, in this matter I fear you have made a mistake. A critical error of judgement. I truly am not a torturer. They are crude lumbersome fellows who take pleasure in their craft and I have no doubt that you could outwit one such fellow easily in the manner of your own death. I, as I have previously stated, am a simple clerk. With a clerk's dedication to the facts and, much as it pains me to utter the fact, a somewhat pedantic predilection towards the balancing of books.

'You are a book, de Chalons, a ledger, a matter for balance, nothing more. Your claim to manhood ceased the moment you were brought here. Now you are an object. An object for which I have no compassion, an object whose only function will be to surrender the truth before being filed neatly with those others I have already . . . balanced.'

De Chalons said nothing.

'Our beloved King Philip is under the impression that your Order has within its grasp a great treasure. A thing from which your almost limitless wealth flows – and something which has the ability to confer such power as only kings dream of. The King feels that you may have some knowledge of this treasure. In my own humble way I must agree. I very much desire you to tell me of this great treasure. Of its location and of what it is comprised.'

De Chalons managed a weak laugh. 'As God is my witness I have sworn to protect the details of my Order against all who would threaten the security and balance of our world. I could no more tell you God's secret than I could the King himself.' Another cracked laugh. 'If only you weren't the people you are, if only you were authorized to hear my words.'

De Nogaret considered. 'You know we hold your Grand Master, Jacques de Molay, together with the Preceptor of Normandy, Geoffrey de Charnay.' It was not a question. The clerk's voice softened. 'I can gain whatever authorization is necessary for you to release the information to me.'

'Can you talk to God then, on your own private messenger service? For He alone can authorize the dispensation of His secrets.'

De Nogaret shrugged. 'Alternatively I could have your wife and daughter arrested. Conspiracy, heresy . . . I understand you think very highly of them. I understand your daughter is very beautiful. I do not understand beauty, sir knight. I understand only mathematics. Only balance. I trust my meaning is clear?'

De Chalons summoned the strength to spit at the diminutive man before him.

De Nogaret's expression did not change. 'Do you find the sight of me such a distraction then?' To the gaolers arranged beside him, de Nogaret ordered, 'Take his eyes that he may suffer no more such distractions, then bring him to me while the pain is still fresh in his mind.' As de Chalons was dragged from the chamber, de Nogaret said quietly, 'And bring his family as well.' To de Chalons he added, 'I had hoped for an easier road but now I will set my mind from such a course. You have chosen the road, sir knight, and now together we will travel along it: two humble men sharing a single horse; a single destination: the truth.'

The sound of his shoes clicking faintly against the stone corridors of the dungeon as he left was like the sound of thunder ringing in de Chalons' ears and, if he was honest, in his heart as well.

4

ARGINY: 2560

It was the flood chamber that took Daniel from her. The third trap. She couldn't bear to listen to him die so she ran, hoping the shock of her feet crashing against the stone-floored tunnels would smash the memory of his face, his broken body from her mind, but knowing instinctively that the image would instead haunt her for ever.

There were nine traps noted in the journal – one each for every hour that Christ hung upon the cross. They were not linear in nature; their order was determined by the path taken through the labyrinth. *The Mountain of God. The Well of Spears*. They had detected and avoided both these traps. It was easy once the keystone of the journal had been translated and deciphered – *for with God nothing shall be impossible* – the fact that de Beaujeu and the other Knights had designed this place to reflect the stories of the Old Testament, seeding the labyrinth of tunnels with traps for the unwary, the greedy but, more specifically, the religiously ignorant.

The application of intelligence and observation – the scientist's approach to history – that was what had brought them safely through so far. Any fool could go running around in the dark with a big gun and a penchant for fist fights. She was different. She thought her way around obstacles which would have defeated a mere adventurer.

At least, that was what happened to begin with.

Then, after three hours underground, came something she could not have foreseen – at least that was what she would tell herself in the nightmare-filled years to come – something she could no more have avoided than she could avoid breathing: an *accident.*

Castle Arginy had been built at the confluence of three rivers. The rivers burrowed under the hill on which the castle was situated. The dungeons became a warren of tunnels and flood chambers. According to the de Beaujeu journal, the Templar Treasure was buried somewhere at the heart of this labyrinth. And with it – the Finger of John the Baptist.

Erosion had caused land slippage in the tunnels. Flood chambers were scattered randomly throughout the labyrinth – chambers whose walls had been mined by de Beaujeu to create drowning holes. The triggers were ingenious, but de Beaujeu and his fellow knights had not reckoned on someone with Benny's determination, ingenuity – and the thousand-year head start she had on both the Templars' way of thinking and their technology.

But overconfidence had brought disaster. In her haste Benny had forgotten a simple truth; something passage through the hybrid jungle should have taught her: time was at work here as well. Time kills stone as surely as it kills people – in the eyes of deep time the deaths are not all that far separated.

They had worked out the task the Knights had set the unwary looter so many centuries ago, and Daniel had entered the chamber. At once stone doors had rumbled shut across the two entrances to the chamber and water had been diverted in through another channel. It covered the floor quickly, reaching knee height moments later. Daniel knew there was a trigger mechanism on the floor somewhere, a stone platform whose dimensions exactly mirrored that of the Ark of Noah. But the waters were rising quickly; soon it would be covered.

The test was simple: all he had to do was lay enough rocks on the platform to tip the trigger and close the flood gates. The complication was he had to remember how many rocks of each size would do the job. Because although the unclean among the animals had entered the Ark two by two, the blessed of God, and the birds, had entered by *sevens.* Well, Daniel knew that. They'd done the maths and worked out the number of rocks; then added a number to represent Noah and his family. Then subtracted two to represent the Raven and the Dove who had been packed off to search for dry land. Easy.

What they hadn't foreseen, what *she* hadn't foreseen, was that the rocks within the chamber, the trigger rock especially, had been eroded by water in the many centuries since its installation. The shape of the rocks – and therefore their weight – had changed. Now no amount of stones would be the correct weight to tip the trigger and reset the trap.

Bernice had used an excavating probe to try to cut through the rock and rescue Daniel. All that had happened was that she had caused a flood, a cave-in, and barely escaped with her own life.

And Daniel was gone, swept away into the labyrinth, probably drowned. The thought screamed in her head all the way back through the maze of tunnels and out of the castle. Dead. He was dead. It was her fault.

Now Benny lay outside the castle walls, head full of lightning, fingers locked around the Templar journal, mind locked on Daniel's last panicky yell, half swamped by water as he was carried away by the current.

She only became aware she was screaming when the fifty-ton tiger-willow stalking her ambled away into the jungle in search of quieter prey.

She staggered to her feet, stuffed the journal into her pocket and began to walk. She was caked with mud from head to foot, her clothes soaked, but she didn't even notice. The last thing she did was rip out the cosmetic contact lenses she normally wore and throw them away. She prayed that she would never again have to see what she had seen with those eyes.

Somehow she knew her prayers would not be answered.

5

Paris: 1314

Hughes de Chalons did not feel the sun on his face for seven years, and then it was only when they burnt him at the stake for crimes against King and God.

Grand Master Jacques de Molay and Geoffrey de Charnay, the Order's Preceptor of Normandy, burnt with de Chalons. None gave voice to a single plea for clemency or mercy from this life to the next.

With the deaths of the three men, the world's wealthiest and most famous organization had been brought to an end.

Their secrets remained hidden for more than a millennium.

PART ONE

A MAP OF SKULLS

1

Antarctica: 2595

Bernice Summerfield pulled herself deeper inside the gutted sea-lion and tried not to think of being warm.

She didn't have to work too hard. She was five hundred kilometres south of the Ross Ice Shelf, the temperature was down to minus thirty and her body was slipping quietly, without any fuss, into thermal shock. The effect made her drowsy, forgetful. Fire was a will-o'-the-wisp, glimpsed fitfully through sleep's blizzard. Even the stink of the dead sea-lion seemed easy to dismiss in the lazy haze the cold brought to her.

Somewhere deep inside, Bernice tried to remember how she got here, what she had been doing here. The images were jumbled. She remembered a book. Shattered fragments of bone. A desiccated body. A map. A man . . . no, a boy. Or had that been somewhere else? Another planet? Perhaps another time? Dellah? France? She couldn't remember. Or rather, she remembered too much, each image a jumbled mess derived from the one before, an endless iteration of meaningless form, a seven-lane pile-up of life-changing moments.

Water. Thrash metal. Cornflakes. Journal. Love. Death. Fear. Regret.

– ran every red light down memory lane –

Shivering, she drew the snow-crusted edges of furred flesh more tightly about her body. Even swathed in thermal clothing she was bitterly cold. A deep, bone-numbing cold that sapped her strength and will. She knew her fingers were turning black, she had seen them as she had worked to gut the gigantic animal which only hours before had tried to kill her. That was when she'd taken off her gloves so she could hold the knife and do the job she wanted without running the risk of slicing herself as well by accident. Some of the glove material had stuck to her skin. Or had that been the other way round? It looked a bit of a mess but at least it no longer hurt.

That was the problem, Bernice told herself. It would be wonderful if it hurt. For then she would know life was returning to her body instead of being slowly leached away by the flesh-melting cold of the ice.

But she knew. Knew she was . . . well. She knew something. What did she know exactly? Something important. Something about . . . well . . . something, anyway. At least she knew that much. Didn't she?

Didn't she?

Didn't she *what*?

Trying to remember was simply too much bother. Instead, Bernice slept, her skin cooling, her heart slowing, her mind, ever the explorer, drifting along enticing pathways, further and further from life.

The journey from Dellah had been a nightmare. Even the comfort of High Passage, bought for her by the University Governing Body, hadn't eased the memories brought to the surface by the arrival of the journal. At least Low Passage – riding cheap, as frozen baggage – at least that would have kept her mind from obsessively burning up the weeks to Earth, though she doubted it would have stopped the dreams.

The dreams had begun again shortly after the start of summer term, occurring with dreadful regularity. Dreams of France, of Daniel. Dreams of death.

Her teaching had suffered. The easy repartee established between herself and the students in the spring mutated into bitter sarcasm, until by the end of term she had accused all but one of them of inattention and sloppy work. The truth was, it was her work which had been sloppy. Heaven knew, summer should have been a time for forgetting.

And somehow she had found herself one lunchtime in the campus coffee-and-cake parlour, ordering from the wrong menu, consuming too much of the chef's special – Chocolate Skunk – and telling Stephen all about it. About Daniel. The journal. Arginy. The castle. Daniel's death.

And Stephen had listened.

And somehow she found herself crying.

And then, inexplicably, she found herself in bed with Stephen – and crying for a different reason.

But even that had gone bad. Stephen's casual assumption – to redirect her mail to the Sz'Enszisi Chateau – had come at the same time as the package containing the Templar journal and a brief telegram from a French solicitor informing her of the death of Daniel's parents during a ghost hunt in the Rhone Valley jungle, on far-away Earth. Now only Daniel's cousin Sara survived of a family she had loved, betrayed and ultimately destroyed.

And so she had applied for leave, been granted an extension, left Dellah and come to Earth.

She had spent so much of her life here, immersed in a whirlpool of different times and cultures . . . Now she hoped to take comfort from her presence here. Make it a kind of homecoming. It was an optimism she could not quite convince herself of. In any case it did not happen. Bernice did not go to France. Instead, flipping a three-headed Martian penny whilst still transiting Downbelow Station, she took passage on the first trans-orbital whose booking clerk would accept payment by her antique AmEx Platinum card.

So she had come to find herself here – nearly two thousand kilometres from the nearest baked chestnuts, huddled freezing inside the corpse of a giant sea-lion, her shivering limbs wrapped tightly around the mummified husk of an eighty-million-year-old fossil that was probably worth more money than she could earn in a lifetime – while the lifetime in question ticked quietly away.

2

Paris: 1314

Jacques de Molay awoke from a dream of fire to the sound and smell of water.

Dank, awful wetness, crawling with rats and insects.

Still, compared to the dream it was heaven.

The last Grand Master of the Order of the Knights Templar, one of the richest men in the civilized world, rolled naked on to his back. He moved carefully, wary of scraping open the sores on the scalloped stonework digging into his flesh. The pain did not bother him so much. Not now. It had become a way of life. A service to his Lord. A service he knew was nearing its end.

His dreams of fire were proof enough of that.

He coughed – produced dank wetness marginally less awful than the conditions in the dungeon. The sound echoed from rough walls, and began a spate of coughing from other prisoners. Coughing. The clink of chains. Groans of despair. Sleep-lost prayers for death. If there was a hell his God and Master was letting him experience its delights.

Something dug him in the side. Not a rat – their attentions were familiar enough. A stick.

A voice grumbled irritably, 'You there. A visitor.' Another poke. De Molay jerked, tried to get to his feet, slumped in exhaustion on the floor.

'Uncle.' A familiar voice.

'Guillaume? Is that you, my boy?' The words were uttered in a broken fit of coughing.

'Uncle, what have they –' A change of tone. 'Guard. Open these gates immediately.'

'No.'

'I am paying you enough, am I not?'

'No.'

'Guillaume.' De Molay's voice whispered out of the flame-shot darkness. 'You came.'

'Yes, Uncle. I came. But . . . these conditions. They are appalling. Not fit for an animal. I will petition the King. They cannot do this to you.'

'No. Guillaume. Listen. To me. I have dreams. Of fire. Of cleansing. The fire of heaven will cleanse me of this hell; though I have no eyes now to see it, I shall feel its purity. God is ready for me, Guillaume. But. There is something that must first be done.'

'Uncle. You must listen to me. You must keep heart. The nobles are drawing up a petition –'

'A petition. A worthy document. Five years' worth of signatures. Tell me on what bold stallion do you expect to carry this weighty tome?'

'Uncle, you mustn't speak like that!'

'Guillaume. Listen. I have seen the future. It is written in fire. Written by a finger. A holy finger. Do you understand? I would read this future before I die. Do you understand? Do you?'

Quiet. Dripping. Scuttle of rats. Gnawing. A scream. 'My finger! No! It is mine not yours to eat! My finger! Bring it here!'

De Molay uttered a sigh, felt the diseased breath rush to escape his ruined body. 'De Chalons. I fear his mind has left this world.'

'Uncle, I –'

'Listen to de Chalons, Nephew. Listen. For in his madness he speaks the truth.'

'Uncle, your friend is mad! Raving. He speaks of fingers and –'

'Listen, boy! Listen. And do as de Chalons commands.'

A moment, the ramblings of one insane then, finally, understanding.

'Yes, Uncle. I will obey.'

Satisfied he could do no more, de Molay returned to fear-clouded sleep. He dreamt.

Dreams of fire.

And fingers.

3

Antarctica: 2595

Bernice felt movement. Movement all around her. She tried to open her eyes – they wouldn't work. All she could see was veined darkness. But the movement continued. And now there was sound. A voice. A man's voice. Muffled, as if by distance. Light bloomed behind her eyelids. She heard the sounds of tearing flesh. She felt hands touching her, wiping her face. She felt herself being lifted, moved, then laid, still curled foetally, on to a flat surface.

When she finally managed to open her eyes – it felt like a million years after she closed them – the first thing she saw was an ambling mountain of a man with Eskimo features and blond dreadlocks.

'Yeah.' The voice was mountainous too, the slow, deep rumble of tilting icebergs.

Bernice tried to lick her lips. It was agony. 'Do what?'

'Yeah. You alive.'

'Oh.' Now her hands were beginning to feel like she'd immersed them for an hour in scalding water. 'Good.'

'Not unless you got insurance. You got insurance? I find you, sure, but you inside mutant sea-lion. Gut bacteria all over protein stores. Maybe twenty tons infected. I save you. You pay for damage. So if you got insurance, then alive is good – if not, well, alive is not so good.'

Bernice tried to get up, failed, lacked even the strength to fall over gracefully. 'My bones. Where . . . are my bones?'

'Yeah. You got bones. You cuddle monster. I keep for analysis. God knows what bacteria monster has.'

Bernice blinked. Things were getting out of control. 'Me Benny, Tarzan. Who you?'

The mountain smiled a grizzled smile. 'Me Butterman. World Food Surplus Storage Clerk. You nearly die in Larder of World.'

Bernice smiled – her lips cracked and she nearly screamed. 'Tell me something, Butterman. How can you tell if there's an elephant in your fridge?'

His eyes lit up with a crafty gleam. 'Is easy. Blinking great footprints in –'

Bernice slept.

Bernice did not have insurance so she gave Butterman her AmEx card. She warned him the credit was low but suggested he might get a better price haggling on the web with one of the many dealers in antiquities of the long-defunct mess of states once called America.

Butterman accepted as gracefully as a walking mountain could, and allowed Bernice to stay in the World Surplus Food Storage Facility, a gnat's whisker shy of the South Pole. ('They put surplus on South Pole so not lose, I think.' 'Oh really? When was the last time anyone dispensed any food?' '2098.')

It took Bernice a month to recover completely. As she later observed – at least she didn't want for anything to eat.

During the weeks of her recovery, Bernice learnt about her host. Conversation wandered butterfly-like from history to anthropology, pre-destination to penguins and sea-lions. Geographical feature he may have resembled, but Ikvor 'Butterman' DeLongPre was widely read and liked to *think*. Almost as much as he liked to *talk*.

One afternoon – an arbitrary designation made only by their watches, local twilight having been steadily deepening for some three weeks – her host brought up the subject of Bernice's relic.

'You cuddle monster when find. You tell Butterman. You weird? Suicide? You tell Butterman. How find?'

Bernice frowned. 'It's not a monster – it's a *raptor.* I don't remember how I found it.'

'You very cold. Your mind not remember yet.'

'That's right.'

'Tell Butterman. What of monster?'

'Well, I'm not sure . . . As far as I can tell it resembles simularities I've seen of *Utah raptor* – though what it's doing out here in Antarctica I'll never know. Anyway, it's bigger than *Utah raptor*. And proportional to its size, its brain pan is enormous.'

Butterman's eyes lit up in the by-now familiar child-like fascination. 'I read this in books. You think dinosaur smart? Like people maybe?'

Bernice shrugged, pleased she could now do so without suffering pain. 'Well. That I won't know until I can examine the body more thoroughly in a lab. Certainly its eyes are forward facing to give stereo-vision, and it seems like it might have had unusual dexterity in the digits of the forelimbs. What interests me the most are the stomach contents. Scraps of bone. Human. *Homo sapiens*. Modern man.' She carefully forgot to mention the marks on the bone fragments. The inscription – the Egyptian Ankh symbol.

Butterman considered. 'First proto-human exist only four million years ago. How explain difference? How come four-million-year-old bones in eighty-million-year-old fossil?'

Bernice shrugged again. 'Blowed if I know, guvnor.'

Once again the frenetic glow of interest. 'Oh wow. Baboushka. This cool. Like FictioNet. Smart-raptor. I like! Time travel. I like! You want lab? I call one. He come now.'

'You have a *lab*?'

'No. But expedition is. Five hundred klicks from here. Mobile lab. Survey of post-war life changes. Speak to biologist, Dottie Mars. My web-pal.'

'You have the *web*?'

Two days later an ice-skimmer hove to at the Facility dock. The storm-scarred metal hull was emblazoned with the seal of the Terran Congress and logos for Nike and Coca-Cola.

The skimmer disgorged a tall figure with ice-green eyes and a jet-black flat-top. His Eurasian face was mottled a gorgeous Hawaiian sea-blue with *ringskin* – a fashionably expensive form of bio-accessorizing. Not the sort of conceit Bernice would normally have taken notice of for a pico-second, let alone be impressed by.

Let alone be attracted to.

'Marillian,' he said. 'Got your message. Thought we'd pop by and say hello.'

'Yeah,' she said with a dazzling smile. 'I'm Benny. The lump here is Butterman. Hear you got a top lab. What's it going to cost me to rent some time in it? Oh, by the way, I haven't any money.'

He was independently wealthy, he was director of the Future Foundation Research Group, he was here with a biological expedition to chart Antarctic life changes and the price for renting one of his very well equipped labs was dinner. Five star. Penguin steaks and all the bolt-on extras. Bernice wore her best sea-lion fur and tried not to dribble at the sight of almost completely pure parsnips.

She eyed the penguin steaks with interest.

'Help yourself, they're very good.'

'Normally I wouldn't. Vegetarian. Thing is, it's easy to preach when you can pop down to the local corner shop for a tin of tofu. When you've been stuck on the ice with nothing to eat but mutant sea-lion, well . . . let's just say you tend to re-examine your ideals a little more closely.'

Marillian nodded understandingly. 'I sympathize. Moral dilemma. Never a fun thing. But look on the bright side. You're alive. You could go back to being a vegetarian.'

'I know. Somehow it feels . . . hypocritical. Silly, isn't it?'

'Not at all. Everyone falls sometime.'

Bernice picked up on the phrase. 'As in falls from grace? You're religious?'

'Does it bother you?'

'No.'

'Do you have a faith?'

'No. I have . . . some curiosity.'

He smiled. 'Standard answer. Well, let's not talk about me. Tell me how you came to be on the ice.'

She sighed and put down her fork. 'Usual story. Mid-life crisis, lover half my age, needed a bit of a getaway. Place to think and all that.'

'Why Earth? Why here?'

'To be honest, I'm not sure. Earth has always felt like a second home to me. I just needed . . . to come home, I suppose.'

'But not all the way home, right?'

'What do you mean?'

'Well, you've clearly never been to Antarctica before. Alone, unprovisioned, badly equipped. Still, you managed to survive all right.'

She laughed. 'Yes. It was a bit of bad luck for the old sea-lion, wasn't it? Still. It was him or me for breakfast and I tell you what, I'm glad it wasn't me.'

Marillian smiled. 'So am I, Bernice. So am I. Very glad.' He raised his glass. Bernice joined him in a toast.

'To survivors. And to livening up what thus far has been a very mundane expedition.'

She smiled and drank.

Not only was Marillian beautiful but he was smart. And connected. In the aftermath of the wars the political climate on Earth had turned stormy to say the least. At least three countries no longer existed and the power vacuum was being filled by a rugby scrum of pretenders. As the skimmer logos suggested temporary Congress had been set up to oversee, ratify and otherwise cloud the issue of who had most direct claim to the presidency. Congress comprised the companies who had the most power – and therefore money – and that meant Nike, whose line of infantry footwear drove all competition into the limb-spattered mud, together with Coca-Cola, whose government-sanctioned inclusion in their recipe of the drug for which their product was originally named had ensured the unswerving support of Joe Public throughout the course of the war.

Marillian exerted a magnetic fascination on Bernice. She thoroughly enjoyed his company for the week it took his science team to begin the analysis of her find. And when the inevitable pass came, Bernice came so close to saying 'Yes' that both parties mimed a Chaplinesque gulp of suprise when the word 'No' came out instead.

It was Dottie Mars – slim, elegant, with eyebrows and nails Bernice would have at least considered committing GBH to possess, together with a penchant for performing Debussy's 'Snowflakes are Dancing' on a modified snakecharmer flute and harmonizer combo – who provided conclusive evidence that both the raptor mummy and its *H. sapiens* stomach contents were genuine artifacts. What she couldn't do was explain the temporal anomaly inherent in the findings. Or why the relics had been discovered here, just a minim and a crotchet from the South Pole.

As she said, if it was a fake, it was akin to the lads who devised the Piltdown Man hoax hiding the skeleton they had made on Mars instead of in a muddy field in England.

It went without saying that no one, least of all Bernice, could come close to explaining why – or even *how* – a broken line of ancient Egyptian hieroglyphics had come to be inscribed upon the fragments of the human skull in question. That together with symbols which clearly depicted the Sphinx.

As far as Bernice was concerned there was only one way to sort it out. Translate the inscription. Check out the Sphinx.

Her only regret was that, as far as she knew, penguin steaks and non-hybrid parsnips did not form part of the staple diet anywhere in Egypt.

4

PARIS: 1314

Guillaume de Beaujeu watched from the edge of the crowd as Jacques de Molay was brought from the prison cart and bound tightly to a rough wooden stake. His companions of seven years, Hughes de Chalons and Geoffrey de Charnay were already bound. De Molay was the last. The last of an Order. The last of a society within a society. De Beaujeu had had seven years to prepare for this moment and still found himself unready. The ride from Paris to the Temple had been hard – he had ridden two horses into the ground – and another two to return with the relic of which his uncle had spoken so cryptically. Now, instead of getting more information, de Beaujeu realized, he had arrived just in time to witness his uncle's death.

Now he clutched a leather sack containing the relic, a small crystal sphere, and cursed his feet and his horses for being too slow.

He worked his way through the crowd. People were throwing fruit, rotten vegetables, screaming and cursing. Overhead the sun glared curiously down on this unimportant, somewhat absurd human spectacle. The sunlight rippled. No, de Beaujeu realized, it was tears. His tears were making the sunlight ripple.

He moved closer, the sackcloth jerkin he wore to disguise his station rubbing painfully at his shoulders. As he drew level with a black-clad guard, the fellow threw out a leg and tripped him, then spat on him as he fell. De Beaujeu rose to his knees and crawled quickly away. There were times to move openly and times to move secretly, and this was definitely the latter.

Keeping his head bowed de Beaujeu managed to get within twenty feet of the wooden trestles to which the stakes and their human kindling were fixed. Faggots were piled in heaps around the stakes. The three men were turning their sun-starved faces to catch the warmth of the slightest ray of sunlight.

Guards drew sack-cloth helmets across the heads of the three men as the last rites were delivered. Then the slight form of Guillaume de Nogaret begged each man individually to recant his evil.

The crowd were silent at this point – but they began to rant again soon enough when all three men refused to speak.

De Nogaret shrugged, a slight gesture, and signalled the executioner to light the fires. None of these men would renounce their beliefs or admit to their crimes; therefore none would receive the benefit of strangulation before immolation.

As the flames spread, the screams from the crowd grew louder and more frenzied. De Beaujeu crept closer.

'Uncle!' He pitched his voice to rise above that of the crowd. 'I have done as you instructed, I have the Relic!'

De Molay's body was now immersed in smoke and flame. His clothes were burning; his skin beginning to blacken. The stink of burnt meat filled the air. De Chalons and de Charnay were already beginning to scream, their voices ragged and intermittent as the fire gnawed like an animal at their chests and throats.

'Uncle! Uncle!'

De Beaujeu despaired. His uncle was near death. He would not be able to render any useful words.

But de Beaujeu was wrong.

Almost with his last breath, de Molay uttered a sentence. Two dozen words that would change the course of the world forever. 'The future of our world – the Templar Order – lies in my Master's tomb. The Finger that identified Christ shall once again point the way!'

The last word dissolved into a scream, a sound which lingered in de Beaujeu's head long after his uncle's body had crumbled into ash and smoke and been scattered to the four winds.

De Molay's dream of fire had become a reality.

5

EGYPT: 2595

When Herodotus visited the Pyramids four and a half centuries before His son was a mote in God's eye, they were already more than two thousand years old. The next millennium was to wreak yet further dramatic sea-changes upon the inscrutable stone-faced monuments.

There had been the minor incidences throughout history of course – for example, the political skirmish in 2234, when Heironymous Basquiat, a fashionable French artist with conveniently unverifiable ancestral connections, had first tried to wrap the Sphinx in holly-and-snowball-motif Christmas paper, and subsequently attempted to buy it. He was escorted off the Giza plateau by a number of uniformed gentlemen carrying old-fashioned uzis.

A more or less direct result of this incident was the ongoing petition from major governments that all the remaining wonders of the world be sprayed with a layer of clear glassite to protect the structures. Over the next half century this debate became fashionable with the movers and shapers, spawning no less than thirty-seven specialized companies tendering for the contract if and when it should ever be agreed, twelve economic debacles, two minor wars, a pilot episode for *All Our Yesterdays 2* and a best-selling independent comic.

The debate was settled to no one's satisfaction when war

broke out. The Leaning Tower surrendered to the inevitable when Pisa was hit by a poorly directed half-ton asteroid. Suddenly the economic focus was on weaponry and transport, and the national monuments fell into a poor second place.

Now, once again, the windswept contours of Giza were calm and peaceful, even if surrounding Cairo had increased in height by eighty storeys and the peace was due to protection from the elements by the city dome and several well-armed park wardens. And if the monuments now resided in a rippling ocean of lush meadow rather than arid sand, then at least the beauty still remained for the viewing public – subject to the regular weekly scrub with lichen remover.

Bernice sat crosslegged on the camel and hoped to God it wouldn't spit dribble at her when she tried to get off. One thing about Cairo that hadn't changed over the last five centuries was that the guides still tried to sell you the camels. It must be a hereditary thing, she supposed, passed on from family to family much like a carpenter's toolkit: the need to scam the viewing public out of every last penny before giving them a moment to realize there was no way you could get a *camel* on a commercial transport, let alone afford its upkeep once you got it home.

No, Bernice was sitting on this camel for one reason and one reason only: because the only man who had shown the slightest sign of being able to smuggle her into the Sphinx insisted that she sit upon one so that he could photograph her.

Zayad Hafiq stood in front of her now, a little man with a wiry body, bright button eyes and a sour complexion. A minor incursion – possibly a childhood infection – had resulted in a snakelike bulge across his upper back and lower neck. The ends of the bulge moved occasionally, beneath his filthy clothes. Once Bernice had seen a disconcertingly human eye peering curiously from beneath his collar.

He skipped quickly around the camel, his movements eager, if somewhat unbalanced by the weight attached to his body. His eyes flickered brightly as he moved from angle to angle, an ancient Box Brownie, whose value as an antique he could have comfortably retired on, with his family, for the rest of his life, if he'd chosen to sell it to the right dealer, clutched in his weather-beaten hands. His eyes glowed. His mouth moved silently, no doubt figuring the cashflow these pictures would get him after Bernice had left Cairo – or been arrested for posing naked at midnight in front of the Pyramid of Khufu, she added silently to herself.

'Left a little . . . no, right now . . . now lift the knee . . . yes!' *Snap snap snap*. 'And now the arms . . . if you could uncross them please . . . Ah, such loveliness!' *Snap snap snap snap snap.*

Bernice tried not to grin. Bribery was hardly the undiscovered country.

'Hey, Zayad. You know how many people tried to get me to do this before?'

'I think many. You are beautiful. You do for living?'

'No.'

'Most peculiar. You pose like pro – *good* pro. Tell me why – and tilt your head please – so.' *Snap snap.* 'And now your right leg, please –'

'It's a novelty. It's a laugh. And the leg stays where it is until you tell me how we're going to get inside the Sphinx.'

The little man froze, an expression of alarm masking his delight. 'Not here. No. Too many ears. They hear us. Not legal. They arresting come, big guns, yes?'

Bernice laughed as the fellow's English disintegrated, tapping the camel with her bare toes. 'And this isn't?'

A moment and then, in a calmer voice, 'There are those who will take bribes.'

Now it was her turn to get excited. 'There are? It's news to me – and I virtually camped out in Government Central for a week.' Bernice wrinkled her nose as a hint of the camel's breath reached her. 'Tell me where I can find these mythological creatures.'

'Oh no. No bribe will get you into Monuments. Scientists and government have all woven together.'

'Stitched up.'

'Yes. Stitched. Your leg, please? Please?'

'Zayad, hand me my clothes. And then help me down from this wretched lump of an animal. We're done.'

'No . . . the leg, please! I make much money from one so beautiful.'

'The Sphinx.'

'The leg!'

'The *Sphinx.*'

Zayad licked his lips and stacked another photographic plate into a rough leather satchel. 'All right. I tell. Then take photograph. But only to make money for my sick daughter, you understand.'

'Uh huh. Last time it was your son.'

'I have both.'

'And I have a face that launched a thousand ships.'

'Is true. Have many beautiful children. Government incentive scheme pay well for increasing population.' A quick smile, then, 'I know of jackal run. Under wall of park. Through wall of Sphinx.'

Bernice reached out one hand impatiently for her clothes. 'Oh yeah? How come no one else knows about this run?'

'You know what jackal run smell like? They brick up, forget. Not on park-keeper system any more. Anyway. Egyptian government not want anyone in Sphinx. Not for centuries. Not since Uphaut IX robot go berserk in '05. Start eating walls.'

Bernice considered. 'All right. I'll buy it.' Bernice moved her leg into an arguably more artistic pose. 'You get one shot at this Zayad, so don't –'

Snap snap snap snap snap snap snap.

Stone quiet. Dark still.

Bernice breathed dusty air and wondered how old it was.

Her feet scuffed loose stone – remnants of minor tremors. Her hands touched the ancient walls, her palms flat, the old electric thrill of the past reaching out to grab her. Funny. She'd been in more impressive monuments on alien worlds halfway across the galactic spiral arm. None ever hit her like this. Perhaps Earth would be the homecoming she sought after all.

The tunnel was dark, choked with dirt, and lichen coated the walls. The footing was hardly dangerous – each booted step sank half an inch into mulch.

Lucky there's no sunlight down here – I'd be up to my neck in weeds.

A hundred metres in the tunnel became dry rock. And it stayed that way until she hit the reliquary chamber.

Smoothly fashioned stone, pillars supporting a cracked roof, a rectangular gully – very deep – which may once have held water. Now it held something else: the legacy of fifty years of terraforming.

Worms. From about five metres down the trench was full of worms. They glistened wetly in the light from her torch.

Bernice blew out her cheeks. 'Nice.'

Looking up, she continued her examination. Within the area bounded by the gully, a glimpse of something curious, even wondrous to an archaeologist long denied permission to delve into this most compelling of places.

She stood quite still, wondering how long it had been since anyone had come inside here.

Last week probably. The Egyptian government had always been notorious for withholding permission to excavate beneath the Sphinx, even when echo soundings had located a number of possible rooms. No, said five hundred years' worth of spokesmen, what the soundings revealed were nothing more than fissures in the bedrock, and they'd backed their arguments up with smartguns just to make sure the theory stayed uncontested.

Well – even the jackals knew better now.

Bernice studied the stone platform bounded by empty space and wondered how to reach it. She moved from side to side, peering through the nests of pillars, her torchlight revealing tantalizing glimpses of artifacts, of history.

A stone box in a forest of stone columns. A suit of armour. Shreds of bone.

Answers to a puzzle posed more than a hundred million years ago on another continent – no, not answers, but perhaps the complete question.

But how to reach them?

Bernice drew a leather pouch from her money belt and took from it the scraps of human skull found in the stomach of the mummified *Utah raptor.* She shone her torchlight on the bone fragments. The hieroglyphics were incomplete, indecipherable. But the map, well, that seemed clear enough. It revealed this chamber, the platform, or part of it anyway. And what looked like a tunnel, leading away from the chamber. If her orientation was correct the map seemed to indicate a connection between the Sphinx and the Pyramid complex.

Bernice felt a familiar fire rush through her. She felt elated. The hell with teaching, this was what it was all about. Digging into history, seeking the motivation, examining the remains. Trying to understand, to know. Better to be the student than the teacher – especially when the teacher was the process of history itself.

Bernice moved around the edges of the chamber, two circuits, one quick, an attempt to detect superficial signs of tunnel egress. When this proved fruitless she made a more careful study. Those who had built these monuments – and there was evidence in the form of rainwater erosion to suggest that the Sphinx was at least twelve thousand years older than the Pyramids – had been notorious in their ability to disguise the function and placement of the obvious. Now Bernice worked her way carefully around the chamber, using a portable echo-sounder and a coarse brush to examine the walls and floor, and, wherever possible, the ceiling.

Nothing. Apparently the chamber was built into solid rock.

Another puzzle.

Bernice put away her tools and switched off the torch. Taking a candle from her toolkit she lit it and moved once more around the chamber. The flame flickered almost constantly. The air was moving down here. But was it due to her own movements, or to a passage so well concealed that it couldn't be found even with modern technology?

Bernice fastened the candle to the stone floor with a blob of soft wax, then sank into the lotus position beside it. Using the flame to focus her thoughts was something she hadn't tried for many years. And there were no distractions now.

Bernice let her mind range backwards over the oddity of the Egyptian dynasties . . . four thousand years of almost contradictory cultural references. As a student, Bernice had been attracted to all things Egyptian. The puzzle of a language which had apparently sprung into being fully formed at the time of the most ancient dynasties – and then proceeded to become corrupt and less efficient as the centuries progressed – was what first attracted her to the culture. This puzzle led to another: the application of building techniques. Egypt was home to many pyramids, an attempt by the ancients to emulate the night sky and re-create heaven on earth. This had been clear since Beauval and Hancock had first shown that the course of the Nile was intended to represent the course of the Milky Way, and that the three pyramids at Giza were precise representations of the stars in Orion's belt. What was still very much unclear was the fact that it was the earliest pyramids which had best survived the ravages of time. It was as if, like their language, the Egyptians had been gifted early with a knowledge of architecture they could never reproduce for themselves in the following dynasties.

The candle flame guttered gently and flickered out.

Bernice heard footsteps.

Lots of footsteps.

'Bernice Summerfield.' The voice had Cairo Government stamped all over it. 'You are trespassing on privately owned property. Come out now and we will not make you suffer the embarrassment and expense of arrest.'

Bernice heard guns cocking.

Scratch *government.* Read: *assholes.*

Offering a prayer of thanks that her torch was switched off, Bernice scrambled quickly to her feet. Packing her satchel as she moved, she ran quickly and quietly around the chamber to the far side of the trench. Now she was out of sight of anyone entering the chamber by the same passage she had. But she still had to get out. The problem was she hadn't been here long enough. Not even part way long enough to solve the puzzle posed by the Antarctic relics.

By now the marching feet had entered the chamber. Arabic voices muttered in low syllables. Torchlight speared through the nest of pillars separating Bernice from her would-be jailers.

And then the first voice again. A guttural sentence in Arabic.

'*Weapon fire will be heard. Use knives only.*'

Knives? Since when was anyone ever arrested with *knives*?

Bernice felt another familiar thrill surge through her – the thrill of fear. It wasn't the first time anyone had tried to kill her, but it was the first time she had been trapped in a stone chamber with no other exit by several large men with *knives* when it happened.

Why would the government try to kill her?

Why would they issue the instruction in Arabic when she had spent the past week arguing fluently with government officials in that very language?

Why would they worry about being heard?

Answer: they wouldn't. Therefore these men weren't government. Therefore they must be bandits.

Zayad had sold her out.

They weren't here to plunder the monument – they were here to plunder her wallet.

Bernice thought a nasty word to herself.

Keep quiet. Maybe they'll think you've gone already.

An eager shout. Footsteps. A flickering light.

The candle. They've found the candle.

Bernice thought another nasty word.

All right. There's only one way out of here and – hm. That's not actually true, is it? According to the map there was another egress. Another passage. But where is it?

Bernice backed away from the voices, creeping within the

shadows, exploring the walls with her hands. It had to be here somewhere.

Now the voices were silent. But she could still hear footsteps. And the torch beams were spreading out slowly around the chamber, exploring the many alcoves between each set of pillars one by one. Slow. Deliberate.

They were going to find her.

They were going to –

No.

Not if she jumped. Across the trench. Only someone insane would do that in the dark. Maybe they really would think she had already gone. If they didn't hear her. And let's face it, she had searched the walls thoroughly twice already and found no sign of an escape route. If there was another passage it debouched from the central platform.

The torch beams speared the darkness, closer and closer. Feet scuffed rock. Sharp metal glinted in the darkness. A moment from now and they'd be round the corner.

Bernice knew she had little choice. It was fish or catch worms.

Tightening her pack straps, Bernice ran towards the edge and –

– crashed into the man waiting there in the darkness.

– torch. No torch. Trap! Must have heard me. Waiting without his –

Bernice scrambled away as the man came for her, knife glinting, cold lunar edge in the torch-split dark.

– facing? Where's the trench which way am I –

A touch. The burn of metal. She fell. A shout. Hers?

The shout became a scream, ending suddenly in a thick gurgling splash, no, *slithering*, no –

– he'd fallen into the trench.

Drowned in worms.

But the shout had been heard. Running footsteps. Torch beams. Shouts.

Thunder. No – gunfire. Bullets whined and scattered across the chamber.

Bernice scrambled to her feet and without thinking hurled herself across the trench.

She landed on all fours, fell, rolled, fetched up against a pillar with a grunted exhalation.

Without waiting she scrambled to her knees and crawled deeper into the maze of pillars supporting the roof above the reliquary platform.

Bullets chased her, a maze of lead ricochets dancing between the pillars. Stone chips slashed at her exposed face and hands. Flame-coloured light flickered everywhere.

'Stupid! I said no shooting! Now they come as well! We must get her now!'

Bernice crawled across the reliquary chamber, her target the stone box she had seen briefly. A moment passed. Thc bandits were arguing about who should jump across the trench first. They obviously thought she was trapped. Well – maybe she was. Where was the box, the figure she had glimpsed from the edge? The pillars were set close together, a maze. She could see nothing. She dared not use her torch.

She kept crawling.

Shouted instructions. The sound of running footsteps. A moment of silence. A scream cut off in a turgid splash. More arguments.

Bernice grinned coldly. Another olympic failure. At least it had bought her some time.

Her outstretched hands banged against stone. Flat, not curved. The box! Further exploration brought her hands into contact with grimy armour: the remains of a human corpse placed on top of the box.

Quickly she groped for the lid of the box. A lever, a stone, something to push. Anything. A trapdoor, a way out of this, now!

Nothing.

More bullets. The flash of gunfire. She rolled across the box, fell, the armoured corpse falling on top of her as more bullets hunted the sound, more flashes split the darkness.

Something fell against her cheek. A medallion, etched by gunlight, two knights riding a horse. The Seal of the Knights Templar.

The same seal which appeared on de Beaujeu's journal!

One bullet whanged against the armoured helm a handspan from her face. The helmet clanged hollowly as the bullet punched through, the visor falling away to reveal a grimy skull, lit by flashes of gunfire.

Gaping sockets . . . grinning teeth . . .

. . . and lines, etched into the bones of the skull! A map! Another map!

Bernice grabbed the skull and wrenched it from the helmet. She felt the bone begin to crumble between her fingers. Groping in her satchel she grabbed a can of aerosol fix and sprayed the bone. A few seconds later the relic was encased in a molecule-thick glassite sheath.

– the map there's a map on the –

Bernice cupped her hand across her torch and tried to read the engravings on the skull.

A shout.

– my torch they've seen my –

More gunfire. She ducked. Bullets tugged at the corpse, ricocheted from the stone and punched holes in the armoured figure above her. Dust and bone fragments fell on to her face.

Bernice grabbed a wax crayon and a sheet of impression paper from her satchel, and began, frantically, to take a rubbing from the skull.

More gunfire. Something tugged at her hand; a breeze brushed her cheek.

The skull shattered.

She looked at the rubbing.

The tunnel where was the damn –

– trench, the tunnel egress is in the –

Shouts. Running footsteps. A grunted exhalation and crash as someone leapt across the trench and fetched up against one of the stone pillars.

A torch beam speared the darkness.

More footsteps. Another jumper. Now two bandits were hunting her.

Bernice tried to work out which way she was facing. According to the map she had made, the passage she was looking for was in the outer trench wall. But the depth. That she could not determine.

She worked her way away from the box, towards the edge of the chamber. She heard footsteps following her. Torches were zeroing in, bouncing through the maze of pillars.

Bernice stuffed the map into her blouse, licking her lips. This was it. But she couldn't see any tunnel – just an undulating mass of worms.

A noise behind her, the sound of a gun cocking.

Bernice whirled, dived away, the bullet singing across her head. Somewhere across the trench came a yell of pain.

'*Stop shooting!*'

Bernice scrambled to her feet as the man drew his knife. 'Time to blow this scene, baby.' She turned and ran towards the edge. She heard the cloth of the man's sleeve rasp as he drew back his arm to throw and imagined the blade tumbling through the air towards her back as she

fatherwhoartinheavenjustgetmethroughthisandiswear illgiveupanydamnthingyouwantjustsaytheword

closed her eyes and

exceptboozeand

leapt headlong into space.

There was an instant of suffocation, a panic attack, when she hit the worms, but by then her fingers were scraping down the opposite wall. She fell into the tunnel egress, eyes tightly closed, feeling the breath driven from her by the fall; she let out a yell, found her mouth full of wriggling flesh, surrendered to panic and spent precious seconds learning it is impossible to swim through worms.

The touch of rock beneath her hands and knees, together with the overwhelming need to draw breath, told her to *crawl.*

* * *

Bernice collapsed on to dry rock smeared with lichen and gulped air until her throat hurt. She tried to stand – banged her head on a rocky ceiling, got back on to her hands and knees and continued to crawl. The passage was very long and sloped steeply upwards. At some point the floor became flat. Shortly after that the ceiling became high enough to walk upright. Bernice stood up, muscles straining, leant against the wall and shuddered. After a while she continued to walk.

The passage remained arrow straight until it turned back upon itself, continuing to climb. Bernice kept walking. The air was dry by now, but the quality had changed somewhat. The walls were now smoothly jointed. Blocks. She was inside something. A building.

The passage ended at a barred gate. Bernice picked the lock with a magnetic hairclip and opened the gate. She found herself twelve metres up the side of the Great Pyramid of Khufu. It was still night. Cairo rose around her into the umber sky, spotlights spearing softly from the taller buildings to illuminate the Pyramid complex.

Bernice sat heavily on the stone facing.

'I think you come here.' Zayad. He was pointing something at her. It wasn't a Box Brownie.

Bernice sighed. 'Why didn't you just rob me earlier?'

'Not want to rob. Want to protect.'

'Aren't you pointing that in the wrong direction then?'

'Not protect you. Protect relics. Protect eternity. I let you in. You try steal. I kill. You just vanish. No one any wiser.'

'One more missing tourist. I see.'

'You give me relics now.'

Bernice frowned. 'You stupid . . . Your gun-happy-chappies in there blew away the damn relics! There's nothing left but dust!'

'You lie like pro – like *good* pro. You give now. Maybe I let you live.'

'And pigs'll fly.'

He shrugged. 'Oh well, not important. I kill you then take map anyway.'

'All right.' Bernice reached into her shirt. Zayad grinned. Bernice grinned too. Then grabbed a handful of worms and threw them in Zayad's face.

A moment later she was holding the Arab at the point of his own gun.

'All right. I'm tired and bleeding and covered in worm-juice – so tell me who you're working for or I'm afraid I'm just going to have to shoot you now.'

'You not shoot me.'

Bernice shrugged and took a step closer. She placed the gun against his eye, forcing him to close it. 'You want to bet your life?'

'No.'

'OK then. Talk.'

She could see him shivering. Trying to decide. He opened his mouth. 'OK. I tell you. I –'

A single gunshot shattered the silence. Zayad sagged against her.

'I –'

He blinked once and died.

Bernice jerked in delayed surprise. Lights stabbed down at her – a skimmer. Police? Government? No. She could see the Nike-Coca-Cola emblems of Congress across the side.

Zayad slipped to the ground. Something moved beneath his shirt. A glint of metal in the darkness. On impulse Bernice grabbed at the thing she could see. A medallion on a gold chain. A tiny emblem.

Two knights riding a single horse.

Bernice shoved the medallion into her pocket as the skimmer drew closer. A hatch opened to form a loading platform and a figure stepped out.

'Benny. Move it.'

A man. Marillian. She didn't move.

'How did you know I was here?'

'Bernice, the government'll be here in moments and they don't deport you for murder.'

'I didn't kill him.'

'Bernice, there's no such thing as diplomatic immunity! Now jump!'

Bernice frowned, disentangled herself from Zayad's body, shook a mess of worms from her hair and leapt on to the loading platform of the skimmer.

6

PARIS: 1314

Without dismounting, de Beaujeu hailed the Temple Guard. 'Do you know who I am?'

'Guillaume de Beaujeu, my lord.'

'And these good nobles who ride with me?'

'I know them not by name, but only by reputation, as your companions.'

Now de Beaujeu dismounted. He stood several inches taller than any member of the half dozen guards. 'An intelligent man, then. Can you tell me what we nine bring here to the Temple of the Order of God this day?'

'I cannot, my lord.'

'But you could guess.'

'No, my lord.'

'Then I shall tell you. We bear the coffer in which rests the ashes of the last Grand Master of the Order of the Knights Templar, my uncle, to be interred here by special order of King Philip of France' – *may God rot his syphilitic bones* – 'and now, unless you can think of a reason to bar us, I request again, humbly, that you allow us entry to my uncle's final resting place.'

The guard considered. 'You have authorization, of course.'

'A letter from the King himself. You can read?'

The guard shuffled uneasily. 'No, my lord.'

De Beaujeu smiled. 'I have more – appropriate – authorization.' A large bag of gold coins changed hands.

The guard weighed the bag, considering. De Beaujeu allowed his hand to fall to the hilt of his sword, apparently to rest there. The guard reconsidered. Stood aside.

'I bid you enter.'

Within the temple, sepulchral silence. Ghost beams of sunlight marked time across marbled slabs and intricately carved flagstones. Fluted columns supported an arched roof. Stained glass glimmered intimately, dappling the stonework with rainbow patterns. Shadows and dark alcoves beckoned beyond the light, fingers of night loose among the day.

The nobles moved slowly, as befitted a funeral procession. Two carrying the coffer, four flanking, de Beaujeu walking before. Two remained with the horses.

The sounds of their mail echoed distantly, rippling in the hollow darkness like water in an underground cavern.

Their measured steps struck firefly dust from the stonework. Their breath hung in the beams of sunlight with their own flickering shadows.

The nobles progressed with measured pace to the reliquary chamber. There, de Beaujeu bade the nobles set down the coffer they carried.

The men looked around in awe. The chamber was enormous, stretching, if the eyes were to be believed, almost beyond the confines of the temple walls. A place which seemingly existed beyond the confines of the real world. A place even the King dare not touch. A high, vaulted ceiling topping row after row of arched alcoves, each filled with coffers. Many hundreds of coffers. Coffers beyond number.

'So many.' The voice beside de Beaujeu was humbled by the immensity of the chamber. 'How are we to find the correct one?'

De Beaujeu glanced at the coffer now firmly seated upon the stonework. 'Would that you had been more specific with your dying breath, Uncle,' he whispered.

The noble beside him ventured, 'You said that the Master

uttered the words: "The Finger that identified Christ shall once again point the way!" '

De Beaujeu hesitated. 'The last words of a dying man. LeFevre, it is possible my uncle was mad before he died. Seven years in the dungeons can do that to a man. I venture that we put little stock in mystic thought, and more in the truth – that the Secret of the Order lies within one of these coffers. A secret we must recover and keep safe from the Holy Inquisition. A message for the future. Of our Order and the world.'

'But how are we to determine which coffer to take?'

'My uncle mentioned the Secret was interred within the coffer of his Master. We should therefore seek the coffer of the Grand Master who preceded my uncle: the Master William de Villaret. You nine shall then ride to the four quarters. I shall take the coffer to a place of safety. If you are followed or captured and interrogated, you will have no information to surrender – and the secret of our Order shall remain inviolate.'

The nobles nodded acquiescence.

'Then quickly, let us find that which we seek. The future calls – and God calls us to his service.'

7

London: 2595

If Cairo was a city built on the premise of change, London was an architectural hall of mirrors. Tower Bridge resembled the Crystal Palace; Britannia's stone face glowered down from twenty-five metres above the Royal Observatory at Greenwich; the Royal Pyramid at Shooters Hill had finally been demolished to make way for a dry ski-slope. Parliament, a medium-rated target during the war, was gone, replaced by the Republic Museum of Social and Political History. In keeping with the new political ethic, government had decentralized into a number of computer-nodes held at secure locations throughout the country and connected by the PolitNet to the Mother System within the re-coagulated Russian Federation – strictly on a need-to-know basis. Speculation was rife about just who needed to know – but then of course no one needed to know that either.

London had become a museum, an icon of history, a city of mirrors sealed beneath a pyramid of glassite. Business centres were a thing of the past, relocated to glass-ceilinged vaults beneath the detoxified, homogenized River Thames, itself now stocked with tropical species from the Pacific whose genetic purity rendered them endangered species. Replacing the offices were galleries, museums, a number of religious institutions, including the redesigned St Paul's

Cathedral, as many as twenty churches, parks, pools and entertainment centres.

Access to the various amenities and cultural centres was by application, generally birth-rating linked and strictly limited to those who could prove a genetically pure human lineage.

Population was in the region of thirty thousand, one four hundredth of what it had been in the Crush of the twenty-first and twenty-second centuries. The elite of the world lived in London. The rich. The powerful. The fashionable. As far as poverty and hybridization was concerned, there was a simple rule of thumb: *out of sight, out of mind.*

Bernice sat with Marillian in a restaurant with a perfect view of the river and watched a sandshark and a squid battle it out for the privilege of becoming the main course for a party of five Russian business executives.

Bernice studied her dinner companion over the menu. Tonight he wore nerdy wire-rimmed spectacles. On him they looked amazing. And his *ringskin* was reacting to her presence, the bio-patterns evolving serenely across his face as she watched.

She shook her head and took a sip of expensive wine. A big sip. 'Tell me about yourself. You live in London?'

'Yes.'

'Whereabouts?'

He laughed. 'I'm sorry, you misunderstand. London *is* my home. I own it.'

'Oh.'

'Yes, that's right, I . . . well, I am independently wealthy.'

'And the survey? The work?'

'I have connections with the British Museum. I sometimes do some work for them.'

'I shouldn't have thought you need to work.' It was a challenge and he knew it.

'You could say I do it for love.' A direct stare. 'Shall we order?'

Bernice frowned, deciding a change of subject was in

order. 'How can you eat from a menu like this when you know there are hundreds of tons of food going to waste in Antarctica?'

Marillian considered, 'How can you wear a dress like that when you know three hundred Somali women could be clothed for the same cost?'

Bernice bit back her answer. 'How did you know I would be there?'

'You told me you were going to Cairo.'

'But the Pyramid. That face, that exit. At that time. To know –'

'– that you needed help?' The hands holding the menu did not waver. 'That you were being held at gunpoint by a mad Arab? I imagine that takes a special . . . empathy.'

Bernice sighed. 'That's just my point. I *wasn't* being held at gunpoint. I had the gun on him. I was in no danger.' She waited for a response; Marillian let his eyes drift back to the menu. 'And yet you shot him.'

'Yes.' Still no eye contact.

'Why?' *Push him. Take control.*

'What do you think of the whale mousse? I think it sounds delightful.'

Bernice waited. 'Why is it so important?'

Bernice put on her best poker face. 'Look. You're attractive. I like you. But if you keep on talking like a berk I'll have to slap you like one.'

Marillian looked up then, and smiled. 'You are very funny, Benny. I like that.' His expression did not change. 'Yesterday I shot a man. I have only ever done that once before. It is a horrible feeling. I shot him for you, because I was frightened for your life. Is that a good enough reason?'

Bernice felt the power of his eyes and recoiled. 'All right. Tell me about the inscription.'

'No. I want to forget about such painful things for a while.' He reached across the table and took her hand. 'I want to skate with you on the Thames by moonlight –'

'– the hieroglyphics on the skull –'

'– or hunt with you in the body of a Serengeti lion –'

'– and the map? What about the –'

'– I want to sailbarge with you across the Himalaya Desert, hunt Crown of Thorns starfish with you off the Great Barrier Reef, take you dancing by Earthlight in the Sea of Tranquillity –'

'– map of Forever –'

'– or preferably make love with you – forever, since you mention it – in my tower penthouse.'

Bernice took her hand back and laughed aloud. 'Be serious.'

'But unfortunately I can do none of these things without first obtaining a licence. The same licence you need to utilize the academic facilities here.'

Bernice felt a shiver of annoyance. 'You mean I need a licence to visit a museum?'

He nodded.

'You're kidding. What kind of licence?'

'A childbirth licence. For which you have to be married.' He picked up the menu. 'Which is why I have taken the liberty of booking St Paul's first thing in the morning. You know I think I will have the whale.' His smile was heaven in the eyes of a teasing child. 'And you?'

Bernice blinked. 'You want to *marry* me?'

'Purely in order to facilitate your research. Of course.'

'Of course. And your desire?'

The smile deepened. 'Naturally.'

Bernice allowed her eyes to shift focus from Marillian to the sandshark circling endlessly in the river tank. 'Naturally.'

She put down her menu. 'I'll take the squid. Do you need a licence for pre-marital nookie? You do? Shame.'

'*That's* St Paul's Cathedral? It's got more domes than the Kremlin.' Bernice did not wait for a reply; she merely squished her black leather wedding dress, leaning into the skimmer's dome to get a better view. 'Where's the Whispering Gallery?'

'Deemed inappropriate by our new Leaders.'
'Intense.'

The Nepali priest whispered, 'And do you, Bernice Surprise Summerfield take this man to be your lawfully wedded husband?'

'Do I get membership of the local polo club as well as access to the libraries?'

The priest leant closer, unamused. 'The correct response is, "I do." '

Bernice nodded. 'Funny how some things never change.' She stared up at the gargantuan chrome and neon crucifix hovering weightlessly before the three-strong congregation. 'Innit, chum?'

When they emerged from the cathedral, Dottie Mars and Butterman – arm in arm – were crying.

The Library at the British Museum had first moved location more than five hundred years before. Now it was back where it started, a tortuous route that encompassed four museums, a secure facility, three private collections, as many compulsory repossession orders, and one medium-sized palmtop computer.

As far as Bernice was concerned, the Reading Room *was* London. It was like a mind within its body; no – like the process of memory within the mind. But even here there were changes. Minor cosmetic alterations: a slightly more hardwearing leather on the chairs, a more conservative finish to the wooden tables. The change that ran deepest was that all the books listed in the index were now kept on the premises. Thirty levels of below-ground storage had been constructed for the express purpose when regional governments – and with them their libraries – were finally abolished.

Bernice walked – *prowled* might be a better word – around the galleries of the Reading Room. The glass dome topping the circular room glowed with light. Through it, almost directly overhead, Bernice could see the apex of the

London Pyramid. Sunlight, reflected and amplified by an orbital mirror, glinted from the glass walkways, an arc of fire across the sky. Bernice pulled books from shelves, dumped them on the table she had chosen, flipped through them with an irritated *huffing* sound.

Nothing.

Beside Bernice someone cleared their throat. She ignored the someone. Continued to flip and huff. Occasionally she slammed a book shut and banged it back on to the table.

The hovering presence cleared its throat again, more meaningfully this time. Bernice looked up. The gnarled man with thinning hair who peered down at her from behind three sets of contact lenses did not even try to hide his scowl. 'Might I suggest madam tries her search through the electronic index. So much quicker – and *quieter*.'

'Unfortunately I've tried the microfiche, the CDRs, the silicon media, the mud chips and the holographic crystals. Still can't find what I'm after. Odd, when you consider the Library's reputation.'

'Indeed? Perhaps madam is attempting to access a subject matter that is *unavailable* for access by the general public.'

'Wouldn't have thought so. I want to find out about the Order of the Knights Templar and time travel. And their possible links.'

'Ah well, there you are, you see. Madam will be needing the *science fiction* section. It's in the *outer* library. The door is that way. Thank you so much for your patronage –'

'No.' Bernice allowed her voice to rise past the level of mere embarrassment. 'I don't think so. I'm pretty sure what I want is here. I just don't know where to find it.'

'That is why we have an *index*, madam.'

'Time travel isn't *in* the index.'

'I should think not. As far as I know it hasn't been invented.'

'Are you sure? It might be with all the other stuff that's considered too subversive for good old Joe Q. Public to read on his days off. The fascist periodicals, *Fortean Times*, the skinflicks and the *Beano*? Am I right?'

'If madam is correct in her initial assumption then her extrapolation is logical,' the clerk said stiffly.

'I'll take that as a "yes." ' Bernice folded her arms. 'Now if sir would be so kind as to direct madam to the relevant level, madam would gratefully refrain from utilizing her husband's personal connections within the Library and securing sir alternative employment as a public v-mail terminal cleanser.'

The clerk blinked.

Bernice waited.

'If madam will follow me, please.' She did so, through the Reading Room, past a handful of studiously incurious readers and into an employee-only elevator. A wrinkled finger touched an ivory button. 'The material madam requires will be found on level forty-one.' The clerk stepped out of the elevator.

Bernice frowned. 'I thought there were only thirty levels.'

'Madam is correct. Nonetheless the material madam requires will be found on level forty-one. A clerk will meet you there.'

Three wooden doors slid shut between them.

'We call it The Library of Things That Never Were.' The clerk was short, round, pale, boring and inexplicably cheerful. 'I suppose we should really call it the Library of Things the Government Wish Had Never Been.' The remark was punctuated by a scratchy giggle. 'I say, you won't tell, will you? I mean, you look like someone a girl could trust. I mean, well, what I mean is . . . I could, er, lose my . . . that is, *what* was it you were looking for? Oh – I'm Hanna by the way.'

'Benny.' Bernice tried on a friendly smile. It felt OK so she allowed it to stick around. 'The Knights Templar. Time travel. Any connections.'

'Oh my, did you try the –'

'– science fiction section? Yes, the Illuminati texts are out of print.'

'Oh. Well. Not to worry. I expect we can probably knock up a title or two, wouldn't you say?'

'One lives in hope.'

Two hours later Bernice found herself facing a creaking stack of volumes totalling some two hundred and three (not including periodicals). Dispensing with the obviously inflammatory, subversive, paranoid and just plain daft left a list of eighty-seven. Eighty-seven volumes – a total of more than forty thousand pages, a quarter of a million references to the relevant subject matter.

She turned to Hanna. 'I'll need a table, a chair, a gallon of coffee and a sugared banana dispenser the size of Nebraska.'

The clerk giggled, vanished, reappeared with the required items, vanished again and reappeared an hour later with an armload of heavy, leather-bound volumes whose wobbling top just concealed the clerk's wobbling chin. 'Thought you might want to check the material we have on Freemasonry.' The stack of books joined the rest. 'I brought the index.'

Bernice closed the last page of the last book and sighed. She rose to her feet, stretched, groaned and sat down in the lotus position, then began a series of stretching exercises.

She was still stretching when Hanna reappeared. 'Benny!' An eager smile. 'Morning! How are we doing?'

'Finished.'

'And?'

'Absolutely bugger-all.'

'Oh.'

Bernice stood up, threw her left hand over her shoulder, lifted her right hand behind her back, clasped her fingers and pulled. 'It's just a thought but, uh, you know the way they found the extra scrolls in the Dead Sea?'

'Yes.'

'And you know the way that extra chapter of the Christian Bible turned up in the Vatican after the Freedom of Information Act was passed in '39?'

'Er . . . yes . . .'

'Well. As I said, under normal conditions I'd rather read the collected Yellow Pages but under the circumstances . . . I don't suppose you have the missing bits of any other major religious texts, do you? Just, you know, anything you might happen to have lying around, that is.'

The Book of Things That Never Were.

Bernice held the binder with some awe. She wore gloves. She took care not to breathe on the pages. She opened the manuscript in a clean-vault.

Two hours later she had the start of it.

Two hours after Bernice left the Library Hanna was summarily dismissed from her job, interrogated and then deported.

Marillian's Telecom Tower Penthouse was as opulent as Bernice had expected, and yet at the same time there was something indefinably – and in context, disturbingly – normal about it. Amongst the Armani furnishings, the bullet-proof picture windows with their incredible views of London and a holotank the size of a subway car displaying news and current affairs programmes in fifty-three different languages, it was the little touches which lent humanity to an otherwise somewhat impersonal display of personal wealth. The set of 2145 cricket cards; the bonsai pony nibbling gently at its sock-sized bag of feed, the framed crayon drawing of Olympus Mons, inscribed 'to dady, lov Joo-Joo'. These were what caught and held Bernice's interest as she prowled the nest of rooms.

'A drink?' Marillian was dressed casually: an attractive hybrid-human skinleather patterned in sea-green to match his own skin. He looked naked but wasn't – and knew it. He directed a lifter carrying several decanters and glasses to move beside Bernice as she played with the pony – a tiny but perfectly formed Appalachian.

'Thanks. Whisky.'

'Chems?'

'I'll take it neat. Make a change.'

The drinks poured, Marillian settled himself before an

open-plan log fire and lifted his glass. 'A toast. To the happy couple.'

Bernice allowed her lips to wrinkle in a proto-smile. 'I'm not having sex with you.'

Marillian picked a sugar cube from a bowl on the lifter and held it out. The Appalachian cantered over to him and cautiously sniffed around his fingers. An eager snort, three large bites and the sugar was gone. Marillian grinned. The Appalachian cocked its doll-sized head to one side, seemed to consider the sweet it had just devoured, then began to sweat. It stamped, made a high-pitched whinnying noise, shook its head from side to side – and began to gallop madly around the room.

Bernice blinked. 'What was in the sugar?'

'Little cocktail. NA crack, some speed, a bunch of designers; nothing illegal. Trigger loves the stuff. I give it to him now and then as a special treat.'

The Appalachian charged across Marillian's elephant-skin rug, soared over the sofa in three elegant bounds – floor to seat, seat to back and back to ground – leapt through the fire, galloped along the windowsills, returned to the sofa, fell over and went instantly to sleep.

Bernice sipped her whisky. 'Don't think he'll be winning any dressage events in the near future.'

Marillian made a dismissive gesture as he drank from his glass. 'Tell me about your visit to the Library.' Was that a hint of amusement in his voice? 'What did you find out?'

Bernice rose from her cushion and moved to the window. She studied the London panorama and sipped thoughtfully. 'I've still got a lot of stuff to work out, actually.'

Marillian refreshed his own glass from the hovering tray. 'Well, until you do I've got some news you might find interesting.'

'Oh?'

'Dottie Mars made the discovery. Which is in the nature of a remarkable coincidence.'

Bernice swallowed whisky to cover her interest. 'And that is?'

'While gene-typing the *H. sapiens* remains you found within the raptor carcass, she found there was a current human match.'

'A descendant?'

'No – an exact match. Sibling parity.' Marillian took Bernice's empty glass from her and refilled it. 'It's you. The DNA in the relic matches that taken from you during our wedding application.'

Bernice blinked.

'As closely as she can tell, the human remains found in the raptor's stomach are your own.'

'Oh.' Bernice took her refilled glass. 'May I have some sugar with that?'

Night on Earth had always been a time of fairy shadows, of dim coronas, of distant sunlight bent around atmospheric corners by the laws of refraction. That had not changed with the building of the solar mirror; if anything the glorious stillness of night had been enhanced by twin arcs of dim light curving up like horns from opposite horizons, vanishing halfway to the zenith as the shadow of Earth was cast across the orbiting reflector.

Now Bernice watched the moon glide serenely out from behind the mirror's curved silhouette. Armstrong City blazed out from the Sea of Tranquillity, its light undiminished by the woven diamond sky. The reflection of the moon and the city lights gradually smeared out in a thin crescent about the otherwise dark edge of the mirror.

She felt the heat of the fire crackling against her back, the ice-frieze of glassite London beckoning from beyond the window. She had not moved for three hours.

She became aware of someone sharing the space beside her. She turned. He was carrying a silver tray worth a month's wages which held two steaming mugs of hot chocolate. When he spoke, his voice was very quiet. 'I was born in

London and I grew up here. When I was a child, looking out over the city like this made me feel like everything I could see – the buildings, the parks, the people – it made me feel like all that was a special toy my father had bought for me. Other kids had hoverbikes or pets; I had London. I would look down from here and no one would be able to see me watching them. I was anonymous. Archaeology is like that, like looking down from a mountain into a valley. You can see only so much and you have to guess the rest. And the only thing you know for certain is that the people you study will never see you watching them.'

She tried to smile. 'That's not archaeology. That's voyeurism.'

'Science as a peepshow? Tantalizing? Teasing us with glimpses of things we can never have? Maybe so.' He set down the tray. 'You are very beautiful with the moon behind you.' Anyone else and it would have been a cheap shot. With him she knew it was a simple statement of fact.

He reached forward to unwind the heavy curtain from her shoulders.

She let him.

He reached out with perfect hands to touch her shoulders, cup her face.

She let him do that too.

'Do we have time?'

She tried once more for a smile. 'The Christian Bible tells us God made the world and everything in it: but no *thing* can exist without time to define it. Did God make time as well?'

'I'll take that as a "Yes".'

She shook her head. 'Take it as an "I'm not sure".'

He sipped hot chocolate. 'You're worried about time. But you're going to live . . . well, a long time.' A moment. The moon drifted idly on, its smeared-out reflection distorting even further around the solar mirror. 'You can stay with me. I'll –'

'– protect me?' She picked at grains in the sugar bowl. 'No guarantee of that. Only guarantee is that I'll die a hundred and twenty million years ago. Eaten. Alive, probably; you know raptors. Got any more whisky?'

'You've drunk it all.'

'Oh.'

'Do you want to tell me about the Library now?'

'No. I'm too drunk.'

'I'm very interested.'

'I can see that!' Bernice allowed some anger into her voice. 'Why are you pushing so hard?'

'Look, I'm sorry. I . . . well, it's a bit odd. I mean, here we are, right, alone together in my romantic penthouse, clearly attracted to each other, but equally clearly going to do nothing about it.'

'So?'

'It's not a situation I'm used to, that's all.'

'I see. Most of your women sigh eagerly and jump naked into bed, is that it?'

He frowned. 'No, of course not, don't be so stupid. It's just . . . well, correct me if I'm wrong but there is a connection between us, isn't there? Don't tell me you can't feel it?'

Bernice frowned. 'You know I can.'

'Well then.'

' "Well then", what? It doesn't mean we have to leap into bed together.'

'No. But equally, it doesn't have to get in the way of us being friends. Does it?'

Bernice rubbed her eyes tiredly. 'No. You're right. I've been a bit . . . well, I've been married before. This personal stuff is all . . . well, it's a bit off the beaten track for me, put it like that.'

'Of course. I made an assumption. I shouldn't have done that. I'm sorry. I'll leave you to rest. I'll sleep in the guest suite tonight.'

'No.' A sigh. 'There's no need for that.' Bernice abandoned the fairyland moon. 'Yes. OK, yes. I'll tell you about what happened in the Library. Pass me that hot chocolate.'

'You want me to heat it up?'

'No.' She sipped. 'Ughh. All right then, thanks.' He took the mug from her. She followed him into the kitchen. 'I found a book. It had missing chapters from all the major religious texts. The Library acquired it when they recalled part of their own collection from a private owner a hundred or so years ago. The owner was a Freemason. Well, some chapter of the Freemasons, anyway.' She took the mug out of the heater. 'Thanks. Knowing the labyrinthine workings of the average librarian's mind I suppose it might be possible the whole situation was engineered simply in order to gain access to the book itself. I can't think of any other way such a manuscript would come to be in their hands – vaults, I mean.'

'What was in the book?'

'Missing chapters from all the major religious texts and any of the minor ones which happened to touch upon certain aspects of Christianity.'

'Ouch.'

'And certain Egyptian sects. The Ra cult, for example.'

Marillian sat beside Bernice on the windowsill, his face invisible in the non-reflecting pane, the absence of a breeze being the only indication that a barrier existed between them and the city. 'What did you find out?'

'I translated the inscription rubbing I made in Cairo. The phrase translates as a whole unit rather than individual words, and as such the meaning is not precise. But as far as I can gather, it comes out something like, "To search for the Sword of Orion: The sword that can kill death." Or maybe it reads, "The Sword that can *cause* death." Or maybe even, "that can kill *time*." '

'You're talking about immortality.'

'There was a chapter from the Egyptian Book of the Dead. Again, the text was crouched – er, *couched* – in metaphor; they always maintained their kings were immortal. Maybe they found a way to achieve literary – I mean *literal* – immortality too. As well. That is. You know. As well as the other way, I mean.'

'A way to enable people to live forever?'

'Don't know. Maybe. Maybe just their kings. What do you think?'

'Well . . . it's a lot to think about. What's it got to do with the Templars?'

'As fur – *far* – as I can tell the secret was stolen from a reliquary chamber beneath the Sphinx, by Templar Knights who were in Egypt during the third – hm, was it the third? Well, anyway, one or other of the Crusades.'

'The Sword of Forever.' Marillian considered the view of London. 'I wonder where it is now.'

Bernice sniffed and put down the sugar bowl. 'According to the Book, it's with all the other Templar treasures. Castle Arginy. Rhone. France. The hybrid jungle. Daniel. Dead. Drowned. Damn.' Bernice began to cry. 'It's OK, I'm fine.' Bernice fixed Marillian with a tear-and-drug smeared gaze. 'You want to have sex now?'

8

ARGINY: 1354

The Castle of Arginy swept upwards, its clean lines a monument to design, to the craftsmen who built it and the labourers who laid every stone. De Beaujeu considered the sweep of walls, the curve of towers, the regular battlements with pride. An old building. One whose structure was rooted as deeply in the hill which it dominated as it was in the past from which it had grown. One older than himself – and was that a comforting thought in this age?

De Beaujeu turned from his study of the keep to survey the valley, the land commanded and protected by the castle. Forty years. Forty years he had lived here now, these old, elegant stones more a home than ever Paris had been. And Marianne. Three years dead. Her memory as vivid as the day he had met her. A lifetime of love crammed into a few short years. The child she had brought him now dead also.

But for the grandchildren, his legacy would be dead.

Only rarely now, and in moments of indulgence, did Guillaume de Beaujeu dwell upon the subject of his uncle's death, of his theft of the coffer from the Temple in Paris.

Only rarely did he consider the extensive rebuilding of the basement, dungeon and sewer levels beneath the castle itself; the construction of the trap-laden maze in which the coffer, together with the Finger and other holy Templar relics now rested.

Many times over the last forty years had de Beaujeu considered opening the coffer, determining the secrets which lay inside. As one advanced in years, so one's curiosity about the future and what it held became more overwhelming. But in these moments the vivid memories of his uncle's death would return to prevent him completing his self-imposed task. The future was what it was. He had no need of it now.

No. The land had changed, moved on. War had come and gone, and come again. This day was the eve of a crucial battle. One from which he fully expected to return triumphant. And with things other than war, he was not uncontent. A life fulfilled, a secret secured and the future . . . well, the future wrested from the hands of those who would see it in ashes.

What that future would be, de Beaujeu was certain he would never know. But his position was secure within it, a part of history as indelible as it was invisible. When the time was right the Order would re-emerge into a world more willing to receive its bounty. And they would have him to thank.

In the meantime, there was the summons to arms, the matter of fitting new armour, the tempering of weapons and the training of soldiers. Arginy called and he would answer. He had answered the call of God, destiny and the future. Could he avail his people no less?

Guillaume de Beaujeu moved quickly for his sixty-two years. He went first to his rooms where he made a final entry into his journal, and thence to his mistress, the Lady Sophia, to beg her indulgence on this eve of war.

The next morning, at the head of three hundred heavy horse and twelve hundred infantry, he left his home in the defence of his land.

He never returned.

Only his secrets, and his journal, remained.

9

LONDON: 2595

Bernice awoke the next morning with only a minor hangover; nothing she couldn't deal with. She bounced out of bed, found the bathroom, showered, fixed herself up, fixed breakfast, ate it, consumed an extra two mugs of black coffee and only then realized where she had been sleeping.

She dragged Marillian from the bed and shook him awake. '*Did we have sex?*' Her voice could have scraped paint from a bulldozer.

'I think,' Marillian rubbed sleep from his eyes, 'I would have remembered.'

'That is neither a *yes* nor a *no* answer.'

'Uh . . . yes.'

'*Yes* you agree with me or *yes* we had sex?'

'Yes. I do agree with you. And no, we didn't have sex.'

'Well. Ticks in the right boxes there then. What do you want for breakfast?'

'Eggs.'

'And?'

'Just eggs.'

'Fine. I've been thinking. How good are your labs? Can we clone the *H. sapiens* DNA? Build a new me? How do you take your eggs?'

'Uh, runny. And hard. Three of each. The labs have been working for three days. No success. Coffee?'

'Can't find the milk. Virus?'

'Cell cancer. Milk's in the cow.'

'You have a *cow*?'

'And poultry. It's a good way to make sure you don't have any embarrassing genetic accidents over breakfast.'

'Outstanding. Well. What about the raptor? Can we clone that?'

'Well, the genetic organization might be simpler. You think it could give us any useful information?'

'Had a big enough brain pan. Size for size it had more brain mass than a pig – and they operate computers every day.'

'Fair point. Especially considering the potential forelimb dexterity. Mind the eggs.'

'Oops. So we clone the raptor. Hope we can communicate with it. What about memory retrieval?'

'Easy enough procedure, though we'll only get the last moments. The wealthier corporate executives have been recording their final memories for years; started off as an inheritance tax-dodge.'

'Hm. Brain dead, personality not, muddy the legal waters long enough for the heirs to collect a fortune. Neat. What about cost?'

'Nothing selling Greenwich won't cover. Consider it a wedding present.'

'Flattered. But don't sell the Maritime Museum, it's cute.'

'What about the Observatory?'

'That's nice too, but I prefer boats. They're more symbolic.'

'OK.'

'Good. If you see to that, I'll do some more research, try to find out about the Templars and their secrets before we go to Arginy.'

'Arginy.' His voice was soft but attentive. 'Do you know how many vaccinations you have to have to go to the Rhone Valley?'

'There's always aerosol prophylactics.'

'OK. Well, fine.' Marillian scooped some egg on to a fork

and chewed thoughtfully. 'Mm, cardamom; nice touch. You know, I don't want to pry but . . . Bernice, who was Daniel?'

Bernice dumped the frying pan into the shredder. 'Who was Joo-Joo's mother?'

'That's hardly –'

'Exactly. Now eat your eggs. And give me a kiss. Mm. Happy honeymoon.'

Part Two

The Breath of the Serpent

1

PANGAIA: 80 MILLION BC

Patience.

The shell was soft. It would break. All she needed was

Patience.

The nest was big but she would find a way out. All it took was

Patience.

The lesson was hard but she would learn. She grasped stones, her finger-claws retracted and moved the stones. Then pain, searing pain as Mothersmell raked her claws across her back, her downy feathers; her voice and impatient scent an undeniable presence.

–Again! Try again! Do not hurry this time. Everything comes to those with–

Patience.

The apatosaur was an infant, not yet three summers old, which had become separated from its mother and the rest of the herd. A massive grey and blue cloud moving ponderously above her head, the gigantic infant made whining noises, high-pitched, full of distress. The sound urged her to action. The infant smelt of meat, of life; a lumbering cloud that rocked the ground with every muddy footfall.

Patience.

She moved quickly, her claws blurring to grip, to tear as she leapt and climbed, swarming across the meal as it lumbered panic-stricken through the grasslands. She clung, tore at the cloud with teeth and claws, swallowing the still living flesh even as she shifted her footing, her toe-claws sinking into the meaty flank and shoulder, building a ladder from the wounds she inflicted, blood dripping from her snout and limbs, the smell of it driving her to a frenzy.

Patience.

Now her siblings joined her, rushing silently from the concealing grasses, their claws bright and eager among the sun-dappled lands. Soon the infant was smothered beneath a cloak of living, tearing hunters, eating the creature even as it ran, slowed, faltered, fell wheezing to the crumbling loam, scattering squealing siblings as it landed, its shuddering breaths propelling its meaty sides in spasmodic movements, in and out, in and out, in and . . . out . . . and . . .

Patience.

Her finger-claw searched eagerly between the infant's ribs; a cold, curved blade tucked neatly into its heart and the movement of life stilled as her snout gaped in a scream of triumph. A moment and then her siblings were carving the animal into chunks, greedily consuming the flesh, snorting foamy bubbles through the blood coating their snouts. She allowed them to play for a while and then barked, her voice sharp, an undeniable demand for attention.

–Patience!–

They watched her for only seconds before losing interest; attention turning to agitation, greed overcoming all. They continued to feed. She raised her head and screamed, knocking aside one of the bolder siblings, who fell to the ground and slunk around the dead infant with an annoyed hiss. She barked again, her voice an imperative now, one that could not be ignored.

–Patience– she told them.

–You must have *patience*–

–Now bring the baskets so that we can feed the young–

This time, reluctantly, her ravenous siblings obeyed.

2

LONDON: 2595

Bernice was discovering a curious fact about London: the future is never as fixed as you might think. Even after enduring five centuries of the warped designs of politicians, generals and city planners, little bits of the past kept cropping up all over the place. If the present-day city was a paved and greenhoused wonderland, then the past was busy pushing up between every slab of synthocrete and pane of glassite like persistent weeds. Marillian's tower penthouse, for example. No longer the tallest building in London, nonetheless the structure was at least original. And the British Library and the South Bank Aquarium. All still the original buildings. Bernice was wondering how much of the past there might be squeezed in between the chrome and crystal monument to cultural change.

She had a particular establishment in mind. Tucked away in a reclusive cobbled street, the Church of the Little Brothers of Nazareth was a small building, its faced stone worn only slightly by visitors. Bernice was not sure why she had come here. Of all the things in her life there was one that she was sure of above all others. And that was the process of faith. She neither believed nor disbelieved in the existence of God. Which was odd because on at least two occasions she could name she had actually met gods; living gods of alien species. And her experience of the many substantial deities of her own world was almost second to none.

As a scientist Bernice had no choice but to accept the cultural validity and necessity for gods. But Bernice was not thinking culturally now. She was thinking personally. And that changed everything. Because today she knew something about herself she had never before believed it was possible to know.

The doors to the church were small, in keeping with the rest of the building. Made of dark wood, they were stained even darker and worn in shallow grooves near the loop-shaped wrought-iron handles.

Bernice touched the smooth wood, the cold metal lock-plate, letting her fingers drift across the surface to the handle. She grasped and twisted. The door opened with the weary familiarity of an old man easing himself into a favourite chair.

Bernice hesitated, licked her lips, for some reason uneasy when she thought of crossing the threshold.

'It's all right, you can come in.' The voice that slipped out of the dim interior was dream-slow, lightly accented, laced with humour. 'I promise I won't try to sell you anything.'

'Oh yeah?' Bernice frowned. 'How do I know that?'

The figure that joined the voice in daylight stood a head taller than Bernice's five-five, was possessed of white-sheathed eyes in smoothly tanned skin, an impish smile and a very cool assassin's cloak. 'It's not like selling vacuum cleaners. No commission, you see.'

Bernice laughed. 'You mean you don't get a few extra brownie points for everyone you convert?'

A chuckle. 'When you're going to live forever in paradise anyway, what else can you want?'

'Fair point, I suppose.'

'You see, you're agreeing with me already. We'll have you saved, stamped, blessed, boxed and FedEx-ed to Heaven before you can say, "Jumping Jehoshaphat".'

Bernice grinned. 'Jumping Jehoshaphat.'

'Ah. You noticed the logical flaw in my proposition then.'

Bernice laughed.

'Why don't you come in and look around? Even if you don't subscribe to the religion, the architecture is quite lovely.' The man stuck out his hand. 'Priest. Markus Priest.'

'Benny.' Bernice took the hand, glancing curiously at the man. Milky sheaths hid any hint of pupil or iris. 'If you don't mind me asking, how do you know that? About the architecture I mean.'

'Right, the eyes.' Priest closed the door behind Bernice. 'You don't need eyes in the sight of the Lord.'

As Bernice watched Priest moved unhurriedly around the pews to the transept and lit a votive candle. He placed it on the podium with a number of others.

Bernice eyed the candles.

'You're wondering what they're for,' Priest said quietly. 'The Household Dog, the Douglas Fir, the Ebola Virus.'

Bernice frowned.

'On average three species of terrestrial life become extinct every day –'

'There's forty-odd candles here.'

'– and at least thirty more are created every day.' Priest's expression was unfathomable. 'I pray for all the Lord's children, known and unknown, old – and new.'

Bernice said nothing. A moment passed, the silence deepening; sepulchral, disturbing. She breathed the firework drift of candlesmoke, found herself unaccountably relishing the aroma of melting wax. She said nothing.

After a few minutes, Priest said, 'I find people come here – infrequently – to remember.'

'Loved ones?'

'Things they've forgotten. Details of a life that has passed on –'

'– before its time?'

'Who's to say? I'm not the one who works in mysterious ways.'

Another long silence.

'Would you care to pray?'

'I came here to think.'

'It's much the same thing, I find.'

'I'm not into praying, really.'

'You haven't tried it my way.'

'I smell a sell.'

Priest laughed. His voice was warm, very comfortable with itself.

'Well?'

Priest raised his hands. 'Guilty.'

'Your stock-in-trade.' Priest smiled; Bernice surrendered to the inevitable. 'Tell me all about it. Just don't try to sell me a life insurance policy.'

'Why not? Extending the term to eternity makes the repayments highly affordable. So I'm told.'

Priest tucked the ball under Bernice's outstretched hands, trickled a pass, made a double fake-out, took off from a standing jump and slammed the ball through a net bolted to the side of the church.

Bernice tried to turn three different directions at once, tripped over her own feet and sat down suddenly. '*This* is praying?'

'Every time I net one I'm nearer my God than thee.'

'I don't get it. How come you can beat me when you can't see?'

'I see very clearly.'

'You're beating me twelve-to-nothing on *faith*?'

'What do you think?'

Bernice struggled to her feet. 'I'm not buying it. You've got implants. A bodyscope. Radar. Something.'

'No.' The ball sailed over Bernice's hands and clunked into the net.

'Magnets in the ball.' She turned to retrieve it but he was already past her and homing in.

'No.'

'A secret accomplice. Stage mirrors. Telekinesis. Autosuggestion. Dumb luck.'

'No.' He threw the ball at her.

'Gullible punter?' She caught the ball.

'No.'

'Well, I give up. What's left?'

'Easy. Either I'm lying, or . . .'

'. . . you're telling the truth.'

'Want to flip a coin?'

'I'd have to steal one from a museum first. And I'd have to have a baby to get into a museum.'

'It's an imperfect world.'

'Well, we know who to blame for that.'

'Do we?'

Bernice threw the ball as hard as she could directly at his face. He spread one palm and caught it easily. 'You want to talk about it now?'

Bernice sat down, leaning back against the stone wall of the church. 'What if you knew how you were going to die.'

He sat beside her, white eyes glowing in the sunlight. 'I do know. God will call and I will answer.'

'That's a metaphor. I'm talking literally.'

'What, you mean, at 2.03 p.m. this afternoon a seven-year-old crack-head will take you out with a Hygena kitchen knife for your credit implant?'

'Yeah well, you know. Something like that.'

'All right. What if I did know how I was going to die? Are you asking how it would affect my faith?'

'Imagine you had none.'

'What, none to start with?'

'Yeah.'

'And then I found out how I was going to die?'

'Yeah.'

'Well . . . I suppose I'd give up netball.'

'And look for a reason to go on living, right?'

'Absolutely.'

'And what reason would you find?'

'Faith.'

'You seem very certain.'

'I am.'

'Is this the hard sell again?'

'No, just the truth.'

'What is the truth?'

'A hard question to answer.'

Bernice bit her lip. 'What if I said I was going to die two hundred and fifty million years in the past, eaten alive by an intelligent dinosaur?'

'What evidence do you have?'

'Fossilized bone fragments with my DNA inside a mummified carcass found on the dumb-place-to-be-without-your-woollies side of the TransAntarctic Mountains.'

Priest took the ball and dribbled thoughtfully. 'What if I told you I was dying? A tumour alongside the optic nerve. What if I said I had less than a year to live? What then?'

Bernice did not have a reply.

'I have faith, Bernice. Faith that God will find a way for me to be reborn in His eternal love.'

Bernice sighed. 'That doesn't mean *anything*. There are surgeons –'

'I said it was inoperable.'

'If it's a case of money, I can . . . I'm sorry. You don't want to hear this.'

'It's all right.'

Bernice licked her lips and closed her eyes, trying to imagine what it would be like to wake up every morning to that eternal whiteness.

'Have you ever been to the Pyramids?'

'No.'

'Inside the Great Pyramid are two chambers. The King's Chamber and the Queen's chamber. Each has two shafts connecting it to the outside surface. They're called star shafts – kind of a dumb name when you consider the ends were deliberately blocked by those who built the monuments.'

Bernice pressed her shoulders harder against the wall. 'Seven hundred years ago an English engineer named John

Dixon made an exploration of the star shafts with an extendible chimney sweep's brush handle. He found three artifacts – the only artifacts ever to have been found inside the Giza monuments. One was a rough stone sphere, another was a two-pronged hook made of some unidentifiable form of metal. The third was a piece of wood with strange notches cut into it.

'Dixon brought the artifacts back to England that same year. At the same time he transported the two-hundred-ton stone obelisk of the Pharaoh Thutmosis III from its original site at Heliopolis to the North Bank of the Thames, where it was incorrectly renamed "Cleopatra's needle".

'Upon arrival in London the record of the objects found within the Great Pyramid ceases quite suddenly. There's mention of a rumour that they were hidden beneath the obelisk by Freemasons, of which Dixon was known to be a member – then a few years later they turn up again in the cigar box in which they were originally transported from Egypt, in a drawer in the British Museum.

'The thing is – now there are only two relics. The "piece of wood with strange notches cut into it" has vanished.

"As an archaeologist you have to admit it's an odd coincidence that the one-and-only relic capable of carbon-dating the age of the Pyramids vanished so conveniently – and so completely – from the historical record.'

Bernice waited; Priest said nothing.

'But what if the relic had been deliberately misdescribed? What if it had been "a piece of *bone* with strange notches cut into it"?'

'I'm not sure I understand the significance.' Priest shrugged. 'What if it was?'

Bernice said quietly, 'The Antarctic bone fragments contained my DNA.' A breath, warm air; Bernice concentrated on the sensation of sunlight streaming in through London's sloping roof and moving across her body. 'I found a corpse in the Sphinx. A Crusader Knight. The skull was destroyed but I managed to take a rubbing. The fragments were etched.

Another section of the same map. A map of forever.'

Priest said nothing.

'The corpse was old, the bone brittle, eroded. The rubbing wasn't very good.'

Priest said nothing.

'Yesterday morning I went to the emergency neuro-clinic at Kings – told them I was getting married. Paid them cash, got them to X-ray my head for the wedding certificate.' Bernice blew out her cheeks.

Priest said quietly, 'They find anything?'

'Nope.'

'No evidence of a map?'

'Not a sausage.'

'Not even a brain?'

Bernice ventured a short-lived smile. 'The way I'm feeling at the moment, that's questionable.'

Priest waited.

' "The Sword that can kill death." ' Bernice licked her lips. 'With that we could beat the odds. Change the future. You could beat cancer; I could beat destiny. Who knows, we could both live forever.'

Priest smiled gently. 'I will.'

Bernice nodded. 'You have faith; that's fair enough. Me, I need a hell of a lot more.'

Priest took a small book from his pocket and gently placed it in her hand. 'Try this.'

3

Pangaia: 80 Million BC

Her world was warm and bright. Smells filled it. Scents to delight, intrigue, confuse and enrage. Three summers she grew and hunted. She was a good provider, highly prized by the Nest. Once every five suns she would emerge from the settlement and, with her sisters, move out into grasslands to acquire food.

Her hunts were good; the Nest thrived.

And then one day, she found the *sword* – and everything changed.

She didn't know it was a sword of course, not then and not for a long while afterwards. She thought of it as a *thing* and she found it while catching fish.

Her siblings did not catch fish as a rule; they did not like walking where the mud was. Drowning was too easy; three siblings had been lost that way. But she had devised a simple method of staying safe: stay on the rocks. Do not hunt the fish; there were plenty of fish. Let the fish come to you. Wait. Watch – then strike.

All it took was a little time and effort.

At the age of only three summers, time was something she had plenty of.

Now she had plenty of fish as well.

This morning, she lay basking on the rocks, her body

soaking up the heat absorbed by the stone. Her body was relaxed; she relished the beat of the sun, the rain-dance of water through her crest and on her skin. And also the safety – for no other predators could hunt her here: the river carried her scent far downstream and dissipated it. She doubted anyone from the Nest could smell her, let alone an enemy. But at the same time, she was alert, her body poised. She was hunting after all. Fish were notoriously slippery prey.

Then she saw something she had never seen before. The peculiar animal swam past quickly. She watched it curiously. It wasn't a fish, nor yet was it a land crawler. Yet it had legs. And it swam. And its body . . . it was round and its legs stuck out, back and legs ridged, green, like nothing she had ever seen before.

She stretched out a languid forelimb, claw extended, and scooped the animal from the river. She was a blur of motion; the swimmer jagged to the left as soon as it sensed her shadow playing across the surface. But the movement was too little too late. And she was faster. Much, much faster.

Her claw hooked in one limb and she held the animal up to her snout. It wriggled. It was a curious creature, hard-bodied with wriggling, leathery appendages. And as she watched, something peculiar happened: the animal seemed to shrink. With the exception of the leg her claw had penetrated it withdrew all its limbs and its head into its hard body.

She lifted the animal closer and bit into its back.

And broke a tooth.

Snarling, she threw the animal away. It landed on a rock and the shell cracked. She was on it in an instant, pouncing, her limbs grasping, to catch, to lift and prise.

The shell resisted her.

She considered for a moment, then hit the animal against the rock. Then again. And again. Before long the shell split completely. She hooked out bits of flesh and tasted one cautiously. It was good. She ate more.

It was while deciding whether to look for more of these strange but tasty creatures that she saw the *thing*.

It sat in the mud at the edge of the river, close to where the shellback had fallen when she had thrown it; a long spike with a crosspiece, regular, unnatural, shining in the sunlight. The edges gleamed, meeting in a sharp point at the end furthest from the crosspiece.

She moved closer, ever wary of attack while this close to the bank. She crouched to retrieve the strange object. It was heavy, made of a smooth, cold stone which looked like the silver moon but reflected the gold of the sun in threads of fire.

She held it up, sniffed it: traces, undefinable, alien, almost driven from it by the running water, clinging tenaciously to brown specks ground into the ridged blunt end.

Blood. But what sort of blood? She had never smelt its like before.

Should she take it back to the Nest, for the Older Siblings to examine? Would they praise her for her find, or berate her for wasting time while hunting?

While she was trying to decide, two raptors leapt from the greenery at the edge of the river. Aliens! Hunters!

Stupid!

Her brain shut down all higher functions immediately as she whirled to deal with the threat. She was still holding the strange *thing* when the first raptor reached her. The *thing* spun, flashed in the sun, and the next thing she knew was that the attacking raptor was lying disembowelled in a steaming puddle of its own insides, screeching furiously as it wriggled and died.

With the odds evenly matched, the remaining attacker considered, then fled, squealing in frustration.

Her mind woke up again while she was eating. She studied the strange *thing*, lying beside her, now covered in raptor blood and shreds of flesh. Then, realization dawning, she lifted it above her head and screamed with sheer delight.

Today's hunt had found something better than food.

When she got back to the Nest, she dragged the *thing* through the grass and scrub to the Inner Nest. At every step the chicks cackled at her, scraping their claws in amusement at her discovery. Their older Sibs clustered around, cuffing the youngsters and barking instructions. By the time she reached the Inner Nest she had drawn quite a crowd. Raptors leapt and chirruped around her, their attention focused curiously on every step, their claws striking bark chips and scattering leaves from the tree-limbs. Their voices were loud, interrogative, their claws reaching interestedly to touch the *thing*. She screeched at them and they retreated long enough for her to reach the Inner Nest. None would follow here. For the first time since entering the Nest she found herself alone.

Where the grassy Outer Nest ran alongside the river and smelt of water and air, the Inner Nest was close, secretive, almost claustrophobic. Built into and through a gigantic multi-limbed tree the Inner Nest smelt of loam and bark, insects and old meat. Trunks erupted from the ground to form a maze, grown to confound a larger enemy but through which she slipped easily. Light that filtered through the leaves was pale; it dappled the tree trunks and rarely glimpsed ground with shimmering patches of brighter colour.

Her audience left behind now, she moved deeper into the Nest. Here the smells were strong, almost overpowering: of birth, of food, of learning. She had glimpses of her own youth: cracking her birth shell, shedding her first feathers, breaking her first tooth, learning to retract her first finger-claws.

She stopped at the edge of a small clearing, just a gap really, overgrown with lichen and moss, a dip in the ground between and partly beneath two broken trunks.

The Older Sibs were waiting for her.

There were three; they were old beyond her ability to count. Wrinkled skin, sagging limbs, feathers sporadic and fur patchy, but eyes which blazed with ancient wisdom and arrogance. And well they might, for theirs was the most successful species yet to live upon Earth.

All that was to change.

They took the *thing* from her, took it right away and hid it.

Then they told her things, their voices gruff with age, but their ideas – oh, their ideas –

She struggled to grasp their words, fought to wake the sleeping higher functions of her mind and separate them from the primitive hunter that all her species were by instinct.

Her questions were many, impatiently barked, her mind eager for answers.

–First the Naming. Then the Learning–

–We have chosen a name for you–

–Rather you have chosen it for yourself–

–that which you must learn you will be named for–

–and never forget–

–*Patience*–

For fully two moons following the Naming she remained within the dark-scented Inner Nest. She grew fat on the work of hunters. Her mind, once awoken, was unable to sleep. She learnt things . . . such things . . . that the gold fire in the sky was called a Sun, that the silver thing in the night sky was called the Moon. She learnt of fire, of tools, of the secret names of animals and plants. She learnt to bake meat, to make dishes from turtle shells.

Holding her first turtle shell dish made her think of the day that she had found the *thing*. And she asked the question that would change everything.

–What did I find that day?–

And the Older Sibs showed her the secret place they had made. A hollow filled with silver scraps glinting with light. Plates like turtle shells, more spikes, round balls covered in spikes, smaller spikes, larger balls that were hollow like coconut shells with holes for eyes and mouth, though clearly not raptor eyes or mouth.

She was speechless.

The Older Sibs brought her into the hollow, peeled back bark-cloth coverings to reveal even more treasures.

–It cuts–

–Kills–

–It is danger–
–It is the future–
–It is called *metal*–
A pause.
–Now we will teach you of it–
–and then you will learn–
–and surpass us in knowledge–
–and then *you* will teach *us*–

Three more summers passed. All that time she lived with the Older Sibs, ate with them, learnt from them. She asked questions and they answered.

Answers that were to change her life – and her world – forever.

4

London: 2595

In her time as an archaeologist Bernice had used everything from a paintbrush to a water cannon for excavating sites of antiquity. She'd never used a road drill before, though, and was finding the machine cumbersome, hard on the ears, and somewhat lacking in fine control. She supposed it would be a problem if she were excavating for fossil remains, rather than digging through one and a half centimetres of glassite and one and a half metres of masonry. Since she wasn't, she didn't see any reason to worry.

She'd spent the entire afternoon attempting to get permission to excavate beneath the Obelisk of Thutmoses III – otherwise known as Cleopatra's Needle. The problem was not that anyone was refusing, it was just that there simply seemed to be no one to ask. At least, there was no one who was prepared to admit responsibility for the monument.

Lack of government offices was the problem. Well, it was the start of the problem, anyway. When she'd looked up Local Council Offices in the v-mail directory, the entry read, 'Moscow'. Frowning, Bernice had dialled the code anyway. A request for the deposit of one-hundred-and-thirty Adjusted Dollars for the first three minutes seemed to confirm the call was being directed halfway round the civilized world. 'I've heard of decentralization, but this is ridiculous,' she told the operator politely, and hung up.

The next obvious stop was Parliament. Bernice was intrigued to find no sign of anything more politically active than a pigeon, though she spent a pleasant half hour attempting to bribe the museum curator to let her sit on the now disused Prime Minister's chair in the Members' Gallery – only stopping when that helpful fellow confessed that the chairs were all duplicates anyway, the originals having been lost along with the original building during the war.

Bernice left the building with a better view of Little Russia's place in the world power structure but little else of value. She looked around at the glass city, its neatly presented greenery and occupants, and began to feel her options were rather quickly running out.

Then she caught sight of a neat figure crossing the lawn outside Parliament and grinned. When all else fails try a policeman.

She walked up to the policeman and smiled. He smiled back, but didn't speak.

'Excuse me,' she ventured, 'I was wondering if you could help me get in touch with whatever local council office is responsible for the maintenance of Inner London Monuments.'

The policeman continued to smile. 'Move along there, mind the traffic, thank you for your cooperation.'

'Er . . . there isn't any traffic.'

'Yes, that's right,' said the policeman. 'The time is ten fifteen. Buckingham Palace? Why yes, sir, it's over there, past St James's Park – no feeding the hippos by the way – and straight up.'

Bernice frowned. 'Perhaps I didn't make myself clear. I'd love it if you could simply –'

'Why would you be wanting the time, Sonny Jim? That's Big Ben right behind you! Best hurry now, I think your mum wants to buy you an ice-cream.'

Bernice waved her hand in front of the policeman, who smiled the same fixed smile. 'Move along there, mind the traffic, thank you for your – hey! Stop thief!' The policeman ran off, blowing a particularly piercing ball-whistle to attract help she was fairly certain would never come.

Bernice shook her head. Museum exhibits weren't what they used to be.

Leaving her friendly neighbourhood lobotomy victim to his history-book-cliché life, Bernice found the nearest internet-bar and dived headfirst into a double whisky and v-mail.

It took her half an hour to track down the contractors responsible for minor repairs to roads and buildings; five minutes to buy an industrial road drill off them, and four hours to have it delivered to an address on the North Bank close to the Needle. She was careful to meet the flatbed loader in the road, waved it down to a perfect landing, spun the workteam a yarn about digging a swimming pool, forged Marillian's signature on the receipt papers after first having ascertained that neither the woman nor man could read, agreed to dinner with either or both of them, in any combination, gave them the Moscow v-mail address instead of her own, waved goodbye, set the safeties on the rig, went back to the pub, and stayed there until chucking out time at 2 a.m. the next morning when, half cut and spiced up with enough sugar to sink a barge, she sited the drill bit upon the glassite sheathed concrete at the foot of Cleopatra's Needle and kicked in the power.

The drill screamed. So did Bernice when she realized the workteam hadn't left her any earmuffs.

An hour later she found the box. It was made of stone and engraved with the Seal of the Knights Templar. The lid was fixed. Detaching the drill bit she used it to crack the lid. The halves fell open to emit a breath of stale, cold air. That and the smell of cigars. Inside was a smaller, wooden box. Bernice reached for the box, then hesitated. Even skin oil could be lethal in her game. She touched the box with one fingertip only after first pulling on a pair of surgical gloves taken from her satchel.

The shell of the box was brittle, the lid sheathed in flaking paper, blackened with age, upon which she could just make out the words,

Thomson and Thomson

'Cigars of the Pharaoh'

Est. 1832

Bernice took the can of aerosol fixative from her satchel and carefully applied a thin coating to the surface of the box. She was careful to mask the edges of the lid to make sure she could still open it afterwards: she had worked too long and her ears hurt too much from the drill to replace one near-impenetrable box with another. A few moments and the job was done. Her ears ringing with the sound of the drill, Bernice carefully lifted the box and opened the lid.

Which was exactly the moment she felt something uncomfortably like the barrel of a gun dig into the side of her neck.

She glanced around – slowly.

It had felt like a gun – and it was one.

There were two guns and they were being held by two grey-clothed figures. Guns and figures were identical: medium tall, medium broad; short, neat hair, grey Soochi suits, grey Nike business shoes, ties, and full-width mirrored contact lenses. Their faces were identical too – as close as was possible when considering one was male and the other female – each composed of neutral features set in identical unreadable expressions. Bio-accessorizing toned visible skin surfaces to match the suits. Each wore precisely the same amount of eye-shadow – or each had been burning identical amounts of midnight oil.

Still kneeling, Bernice began to turn. She used the movement to conceal the cigar box as she slipped it into her pocket.

The woman spoke.

Bernice thought about tapping her ear to indicate she was still having problems hearing, then remembered the proximity of the guns.

The figures exchanged glances. The man spoke.

Bernice licked her lips and remained motionless.

Another exchanged glance.

Bernice said, slowly and quietly, 'I can't hear properly – the drill. Didn't have any earmuffs.' The words sounded like badly muffled echoes in her own ears.

The figures exchanged looks. The man signalled her to rise. As she did so he reached out a hand to help her. Bernice took it automatically – and felt him slap something cold and hard across her head.

There was a sharp pain in her ears and then her hearing came back.

The man stepped away from Bernice. 'Nerve stimulator.' His voice was like his body, calm, neutral, controlled.

The woman added, in identical tones, 'We normally use them to overcome neurological shock produced by our handguns.'

The man, 'We wouldn't want to kill anyone.'

The woman added, 'That would be counterproductive.'

Bernice blinked. 'Counterproductive to what?'

'Our job.'

The man smiled ingenuously. 'Perhaps we'd better introduce ourselves. Special Agent Kepler –'

'– Special Agent Newton –'

'IFB.'

Bernice pursed her lips in amusement.

'The Institution for Freedom and Benevolence.'

Bernice's smile faded as she caught sight of a ring on the man's finger. A ring with a familiar seal. 'You're linked to the Masons, aren't you?'

Newton and Kepler exchanged looks. Suddenly both guns were out again.

'Uh huh.' Bernice licked her lips. 'Just a wild guess – sorry.'

'Give us the artifact –'

'– here and now –'

'– and we'll let you live –'

'– and you'll never see us again.'

'I see. You'll be benevolent towards me and I'll retain my freedom if I do as you say.'

The woman smiled – the change of expression was frightening.

The man said simply, 'Yes.'

Bernice frowned. 'Why do I get the feeling there's something wrong with this picture?'

The agents exchanged quick glances.

'You are eternity,' said Newton.

'You must die so the future past can live.'

Bernice tensed herself to run. Clearly these two were raving lunatics. 'Yes. Well. It's a good plan as far as it goes but what if I offered you an alternative?'

Newton and Kepler exchanged looks – and that moment, Bernice whipped out the can of aerosol fixative and sprayed both gunbarrels solid.

'It's called *save ass*!'

Grabbing her satchel, Bernice ran to the drill rig, kicked in the fans and banged her foot down on the throttle.

The rig scooted forward at slightly faster than walking speed.

Newton and Kepler made their guns vanish in perfect time and began to walk towards the rig. Bernice found the dashboard release, ripped off the cover, scrabbled inside for some kind of override. Newton and Kepler were seconds away. Both were reaching inside their suits. Bernice didn't think they were reaching for underarm deodorants. She grabbed a wire, ripped the covering off it with her teeth, repeated the process, twisted the wires together, convulsed from a minor electric shock and hung on to the steering wheel as the rig suddenly accelerated along the North Bank towards Westminster Bridge at ninety kilometres per hour.

A hundred metres from the bridge the road was blocked by a grey limousine with mirrored windows. The limousine dropped to the road broadside on to the rig, its bumpers hanging over the slidewalks on either side of the road.

The windows began to wind down.

She saw guns. Lots of guns.

Bernice swung the wheel, allowed the rig to plough through the embankment wall, teeter for a moment on the edge of falling into the river, then right itself and career in the opposite direction, back towards Newton and Kepler.

The two agents did not move – except to aim their new guns. Bernice hunkered down behind the dashboard and thought really hard about praying. She was trying to decide whether or not it would be hypocritical when the first shots ricocheted from the drill housing.

Bernice slammed her palm down on the drill pad, firing up the motors and engaging the forcefield containment. Ammunition sprayed against the drillfield, whickering away into the night to the accompaniment of crumpling metal, breaking glassite, and a cat's indignant scream.

Newton and Kepler leapt aside as Bernice gunned the throttle and the rig surged forward. She glanced back long enough to see the agents rise gracefully from identical breakfalls and dive into opposite doors of the grey limousine, which then accelerated along the embankment in near-silent pursuit.

Bernice turned left, away from the river, hoping to lose herself in the crowds of people visiting the theatres on the Strand.

There weren't any crowds.

The various theatres and entertainment centres proclaimed their wares in holographic glory to an empty street.

Bernice gunned the engine and roared up the Strand. Behind, the near-silent *oooohhhhhhhhmmmmmmmm* of the limousine's fans hummed as it charged along behind her.

Cursing the lack of rearview mirrors, Bernice risked a glance backwards. The limo was closing fast.

Bullets *whanged* off the rear casing. One spattered against the drillfield a handspan from her face.

The hell with this!

Bernice wrenched the wheel; the rig angled left and then

right, taking out a jeweller's shop front and the window display in Ace Tanner's Classic-Heavy-Metal Music Emporium. Bullets followed closely. Too closely.

Thank Heaven they're too tight to use smart 'munition –

At that moment a shell passed beneath her arm and tucked itself neatly into the engine cowling. Horrible noises came from under the hood, together with more than a hint of smoke.

Bernice wrenched the wheel again; the rig blew a torque buffer as it angled right, demolishing the corner of the Bank of North Africa before accelerating in lurching arcs along the approach to London Bridge.

Behind her, the limousine did not slow as it took the corner, slipping under the demolished bank before fifty tons of masonry dislodged by the rig fell into the space it had occupied just seconds before.

Bernice fought to control the rig as it careered along the approach road. Demolished during the war, London Bridge had been rebuilt in glassite. A three-tiered structure containing shops, restaurants and entertainment centres, the bridge towered over the glassite-sheathed river, seeming to extrude upwards from it, a delicate curve of palisades and columns and two high observation domes at either end.

Bernice took this in during the thirty-second approach to the bridge, before ducking as the rig took out the toll barrier and ticket machines. Her eyes were firmly closed when the rig jagged to the left, plunging into the pedestrian colonnade through a large revolving door, smashing through pillars and a shrubbery, crashing through both walls of a NewsNet parlour, a sweetmeat vendor and a bio-implant surgery, and scattering several dozen people before regaining the road and accelerating again.

Bernice plucked a sugared snail from her hair as the limousine cruised after her into the bridge. Figuring she might as well be hanged for a pound as for a penny, she swallowed the snail whole – and the rig suddenly jagged right, demolished five ionic columns, scattered a number of strolling couples, plunged through a VR Multiplex where about forty teenagers were scrambling each other's nervous systems in a game of Neur-O-Tag, took out Screen Three (the restored, extended *Hammer and Sickle*), Screen Five (the first legal showing in five hundred years of Kubrick's *A Clockwork Orange*) and Screen Seven (*Indiana Jones: Final Genesis*) before plunging through the outer wall and falling amid a shower of debris more than thirty metres into the River Thames.

Falling.

Smooth.

Rush of air.

Slow tumble of moon and stars.

Dizzy.

Sick.

Crystal shatter of bridge against glass sky.

At least the water will be –

The rig hit the surface of the Thames and, drill and driver screaming, smashed through the protective glassite and plunged beneath the surface.

The limousine followed the rig from the bridge. Bernice had a bubble-obscured view of it settling without any fuss beside the hole the rig had made in the glassite roof.

The rig settled on to the machined riverbed. A tiger shark nosed the wreckage as Bernice kicked her way clear of the cabin and struck out for the surface. The shark came a little too close to the drillfield and lost a fin. Thrashing angrily, the animal swam in frenzied circles, leaking blood.

Bernice reached the surface, kicked even harder, anticipating air – and banged her head against the glassite roof.

The water came right up to the glassite.

There was *no air.*

She pressed upwards, trying to find the edges of the hole made by the rig. She caught sight of movement – feet moving on the water, centimetres from her face. A grey face peered close, smiling, then a hand swam into view.

A dull thump. A flash of light. Glassite cracked a hand's width from her face.

Gunfire.

Bernice jerked back, swimming upside-down beneath the roof, trying to keep her attackers in sight as they pumped more ammunition into the glassite.

They had her bearing now; more ammo smashed into the glassite, tearing a hole, chopping the water into deadly lines of bubbles. Bernice waited out of the line of fire until the agents had to reload and then gulped a mouthful of air from the hole. She dived as more bullets were fired into the water after her. She swam straight down, trying to put distance between herself and the agents, hoping the depth of water would conceal her until she could find some way out of the river.

She noticed the water dim around her and changed direction. Oil from the rig?

No.

Blood.

From the shark.

The animal circled her now, swimming close, bumping its razor-skinned belly along her side, scraping clothing and skin away in a rush of blood. Bernice could not repress a scream – a mass of bubbles erupted from her mouth and nose. Half her air gone. *Stupid!*

The shark, driven to an even greater frenzy by the scent of human blood, circled even closer.

She dived. Maybe there would be something on the rig – a breather mask for the operator, something, anything. Maybe she could lure the shark back into the drillfield and kill it.

If wishes were fishes –

The only good thing was that the blood in the water concealed her from Newton and Kepler, though it didn't stop them loosing random shots into the murky depths. If they couldn't see her maybe she could find some way out of –

Light bloomed in the water.

A restaurant; the light was streaming upwards from its roof.

They could see her.

Everyone could see her.

The stream of bullets stopped. The shark lurched lop-sidedly away.

Maybe the light would work to her advantage – if she didn't drown first.

Bernice peered into the restaurant, had a glimpse of staring faces, smiles, pointing fingers. Diners and the maître-d'.

We'll have the octopus, if you please.

Of course, madame.

A moment and then a hatch in the seabed opened. A robot handler reached for the octopus in question. Bernice grabbed hold of the mechanical arm and was dragged back down into the airlock.

Two minutes later, gasping with breath, dripping water on to the Armani upholstery and carpets, Bernice squished her way from the kitchen into the main dining area. She ignored the astonishment on the faces of the diners, sat heavily in one elephant-leather upholstered chair and waited for the inevitable confrontation with the maître-d'. He arrived after she had wrung out her hair and before she had quite finished using her shirt to bandage her side. Bernice dripped water on to his shoes and smiled disarmingly. 'Table for one?'

The cigar box was intact though the contents, at least the organic contents, were nearly ruined. It took her fourteen hours of hard work with a microscope and brushes before she reconstructed even part of the phrase engraved upon the fragment of bone – for bone it was, not wood; she had at least been right about that.

As for the markings, they seemed to refer to something called the Box of Ra. According to record, the markings resembled those observed in the latter half of the twentieth century in a Masonic temple near the shores of Loch Ness, in Scotland.

5

PANGAIA: 80 MILLION BC

–Today we will learn of humans–

Patience watched as Raptor Old unsheathed his finger-claw and used it to draw back a cloth covering which had been draped over a wooden table.

Raptor Old was wrinkled, his neck folds loose, his feathers grey-brown and lacking the lustre of youth. But his eyes were sharp, and held a piercing brilliance. If his claws were becoming blunt, at least his mind was still as sharp as it had ever been. Old was arguably the most dynamic member of the Elder Siblings. Many deferred to his experience; others considered him an outspoken radical. Patience respected him for his ideals and his ideas.

On the table between them, revealed as the cloth was removed, was an animal. It was strange looking, strange smelling. Dead, yes, but still somehow . . . alien.

–Animals such as this have been observed living in settlements throughout the colder regions of the Great Nest, far to the north–

She moved closer, studying the features as Old pointed them out. A flat face, a round skull, muscle mass low, fat mass high, limbs peculiarly straight, eyes forward-facing like her own, but so much smaller – and such a strange colour: blue. It had hair upon its body; she supposed that acted much as her own feathers, though it was clear the hair was not vestigial. This was obviously a much more primitive animal than her own kind.

–It is clearly not evolved from a true hunting species such as our own. It seems weak, and obviously cannot run very fast. One obvious difference is the size of the brain. Relatively speaking, this animal has a large brain. There is evidence to suggest it may have some level of sentience. It is clearly a tool-user; observe the construction of the digitals on the forelimbs, the potential for the application of leverage, and the existence of an opposable thumb–

Raptor Old snorted and barked his way through a more detailed description of the animal's physiognomy, then unsheathed his finger-claws and disembowelled it.

–As you can see, the internal organs are superficially similar to our own. It has a heart, lungs, stomach, and so forth–

Raptor Old motioned Patience forward to assist him remove, catalogue and classify the organs.

–How did this specimen die?– she asked curiously.

–I do not know. Bite marks on the hind limbs suggest it may have been attacked by a predator–

Patience watched closely as she helped. It was a fascinating day, the start of a fascinating year.

A year that changed everything.

–They cover their bodies. How peculiar–

Patience and Old were hiding among a scatter of rocks on a hill overlooking one of the settlements. It was a curious place. They lived in nests made of dried mud shaped into regular bricks. They had fire. They cooked their meat. They wore coverings. Sometimes the clothes were made of the shiny metal of the same type as the sword Patience had found so many years ago.

Old nodded, grunting a quiet reply. –That is not all that is peculiar about them. Their use of tools. It is very sophisticated. Though their bodies are not as efficient as ours their ability to manipulate their environment far surpasses our own–

–And they can talk–

–Indeed. They have oral and written language; they know how to grow crops, build. I have seen them pray: they have philosophy, perhaps even a religion. They are not the primitive creatures we once thought–

Patience wrinkled her snout in a frown. –In that case, there is something I do not understand–

–And what is that?–

–If they are as sophisticated as you say – how can it be that we have never encountered them before?–

Raptor Old tilted his head to one side, considering the question. Before he could answer there came a number of alarmed shouts from the small valley beneath them.

–They have seen us!–

Patience and Old leapt from the rocks and bounded at speed from their hiding place. Though the mammals followed for some while, there was no way their feeble bodies could keep up. Even Raptor Old, way past his prime, had no trouble evading the curious, slow creatures.

It was three days' travel to the Nest. On the eve of the second day, Raptor Old told Patience, –There is something you must know–

Patience finished off a mouthful of hadrosaur, following the meat with a long snort of water from the nearby stream.

Old let her finish and continued, –Something important– He settled beside the fire they had built, scraping patterns in the loam with his claw. –Ours is still an emerging society. For example, only in the last few generations have individuals been born who struggle to understand what time is and how it applies to our culture–

–But the concept of time is fundamental to everything! Without it there can be no growth, no development. Time shaped us – but without time there can be no evolution–

–True enough. And a perfect example of what I call the New Mind. It's a different way of thinking. It is the ability to plan, to reason, to make assumptions and then test them. It is the basis of all scientific reasoning. Do you agree?–

–Of course–

–Good. Over the years I have been watching carefully for minds such as yours. Minds with the abilities I have spoken of. I want you to know that I have been watching you. Watching you since you were a chick fresh-hatched from the egg. I always thought there might be something special about you. It was the way you asked, 'When?' not, 'Why?' The way you looked at things. I knew your mother very well. She indulged your need to play games in the dirt as a chick. You are high born, Patience. You could have aspired to any office in our culture. Instead you have defined a new science – one which looks at the past. It is something most of our species think of as playing chicks' digging games with odd sticks in the dirt. But you and I know better. Whereas the instincts of society are driven by their past as hunters, your instincts are driven to search the past for clues to shape society's future. Do you understand?–

Patience felt her head spinning. Old was right. He had just defined, in a few breaths, what she had struggled to understand about herself for a lifetime. –Yes. I understand! I do! But . . . why did you not tell me this earlier?–

Raptor Old considered. –Your mother taught you to hunt and I let her. You were a good hunter, one of the best the Nest has ever had. Do you know why?–

–No–

–Because you did not chase prey. Instead you observed their movements, learnt their behaviour, anticipated their responses. When you hunted you knew what any given animal in a single herd would do, where they would run when under threat. Without you there were seasons when the Nest might have starved. You could not have done any of this without possessing the type of mind I have described. Patience, you are thc future. That was why we Elder Siblings removed you from the hunt and brought you into the Inner Nest. It's why we have spent so many seasons teaching you and in turn learning from you– He hesitated, then continued,

–It is why I want you to join me on an expedition–

Patience waited. Raptor Old scratched the back of his neck with his claw; shook his head, blew flakes of skin into the fire, where they burnt brightly, drifting upwards to meet the stars they so resembled. Finally he spoke again.

–I am a scientist. For many years, I have been investigating the presence of this particular species. Recently I have determined them to be a more efficient survivor species, principally because of their aggressive psychological make-up and agricultural skills. However, unfortunately my findings have been interpreted by the Ruling Family as a threat to our society. For the past five years, the Ruling Family has been studying the mammals, assessing the likelihood of being able to wipe them out or domesticate them–

Patience said nothing, though her scent glands reacted instinctively to Old's words.

He continued, –As you have so correctly observed, their society is out of time. Something that should not exist. Their civilization – language, agriculture, science, social structure – are already fully established. It is as though their culture has skipped entire generations of learning to appear, fully formed, in the *now*–

Patience waited, her heart hammering in her chest, for Raptor Old's inevitable conclusion.

–I want you to help me find out why – before you and I are forced to provide information which will destroy them–

6

The Midlands: 2595

Bernice bought tickets for Nairobi on her own credit implant, persuaded Marillian to accompany her to Victoria monorail terminal, and hit the rest room; changed her clothes, hair and face; emerged from the rest room within two metres of her husband, who did not recognize her; bought a ticket to Japan with gold, munched conspicuously on some jellyfish-savouries from a dispenser, belched, hit the rest rooms again; emerged as an expectant mother with no luggage and stowed away in the freight compartment of the first train heading north.

Let the nosy oiks try to sort that lot out.

Bernice waited until the linecar was underway, then removed her bloated stomach. She made herself a mattress from a number of pieces of luggage and settled down. The linecar accelerated through the London Wall, across the thirty kilometres of withered green belt and through two hundred metres of tropical jungle. It slammed into the tunnel system still accelerating, finally entering the country-wide maze of pipes, smoke and blast furnace heat connecting the perimeter factories of the Worldwide Chemicals Manufacturing Facility to its mother-node in the Orkneys doing better than a hundred and eighty KPH.

Ten minutes after that Bernice took out a small toolkit and set to work on the compartment's inner door.

* * *

Special Agent Kepler found her an hour later, eating lunch in the dining car, beside TV windows that looked out on to lush countryside several centuries past its sell-by date.

She sighed. 'Table for two?'

'That depends on the quality of the after-dinner conversation.'

'Nice view, isn't it? Specially generated for the delectation of our paying customers.'

'You know what I mean.'

'I'm sure I *don't* know what you mean.'

'You have something I want.'

Bernice grinned. 'You and every other red-blooded male I know.'

He allowed her to glimpse the gun carried beneath his jacket.

'Oh. *That* something.'

'Yes.'

'Well . . . I don't know how to tell you this but . . .' She took a deep breath. 'I don't have it any more. It was destroyed, you see, when I fell in the river. Sorry. But it was your own fault for chasing me.'

Kepler's face did not change expression. He simply reached for his gun, stopping only as the waiter approached to take their order.

Bernice said, 'So. I assume that you'll be alighting at the next stop. Well, please don't let me detain you. In the meantime, shall we order?'

Kepler looked at the waiter. 'We haven't decided yet.'

The waiter moved away.

Bernice waited.

Kepler said, 'I don't believe the artifacts were destroyed.'

Bernice shrugged. 'Tell me about the Masons. The IFB.'

Kepler considered, tilting his head slightly to one side – it was the only concession to body language she'd seen him make. 'First I get the artifacts.'

Bernice shook her head. 'First I get the information.'

'No.'

'Then shoot me.' Bernice waited. 'Though of course if you do that you'll never find out where the artifacts are.'

Kepler thought this over. 'You have nothing to lose by telling me their location. You cannot possibly understand what they mean.'

'Oh. About the Sword of Forever, the Box of Ra, you know, all that stuff? Yes, you're probably right, I'm just a woman after all. I wouldn't know a Templar Order Seal from an ABC Minor's badge.'

'What do you know about the Sword of Forever?' Kepler's voice was sharp.

'Oh . . . this and that, you know. Stuff.'

Kepler leant forward. 'You're treading on dangerous ground.'

'Is that a threat or a geographical supposition?' Bernice affected nonchalance. 'It's just that the one indicates marked lack of observational skills and the other indicates a marked lack of witty-but-threatening conversational gambits.'

'Ms Summerfield, this is –'

'Summerfield-Marillian. And it's *Mrs.* If you please.'

An impatient sigh. 'This is no time to play the fool. You're dealing with concepts you cannot begin to understand. Ideas are dangerous. They can change the world. Is that what you want?'

'I'm a scientist and a woman. How could I want anything else?'

'Don't play games with me.'

'No games. Fine.' Bernice leant forward. 'According to legend the Box of Ra contained a number of objects including a rod, a lock of hair and various other objects. When the box was opened before the Egyptian Pharaoh Geb a bolt of fire, described by scholars as "The breath of the Divine Serpent", emerged, killing Geb's entire court and gravely burning Geb himself. With me so far?'

Kepler said nothing.

Bernice said, 'How does this Ark-equivalent tie in with the Map of Skulls and the Sword of Forever? Not to mention the

Needle relics? Not to mention my own eighty-million-year-old DNA? Are you trying to find the box? Conceal the box? Destroy it? You know –' Bernice hesitated. 'Is it just me or have people in high places been watching the wrong sort of movie?'

Kepler said nothing.

Bernice shrugged. 'Fine. No games. I'm getting hungry. Either tell me what I want to know or shoot me. Either way I'm going to order now.' She signalled to the waiter. 'I want whatever the chef's special is, I want two of them, I want a bottle of the most appropriate wine – no ceiling – and I want you to charge it all to him.'

'Very well, madame. If sir would be so kind?'

Kepler extended his arm. The waiter ran a blood sampler along the skin of his wrist and then gathered up the menus, before departing.

For long moments neither Bernice nor Kepler spoke.

Eventually Bernice said, 'Let's start with something easy. How did you find me?'

'I'm very good at my job.'

Bernice pinched the bridge of her nose in a tired gesture. 'All right. Here's what I think. I think that you and Newton are Freemasons. I think you belong to a Masonic Chapter existing within the organization but separate from it. I think your brief is to protect ancient artifacts such as the one which I found beneath Cleopatra's Needle from accidental discovery by anyone not "in the know". I know the Masons evolved out of the ruins of the Templar Order after the Inquisition. It's safe to assume the two organizations may have similar aims – there are certainly connections between them. I think you think you're protecting the public. I'm pretty sure you don't want to kill me but you have to isolate the information you think I possess, keep it from public knowledge. Am I close?' Kepler said nothing. 'I'm close, aren't I?'

The waiter returned with several dishes, a bottle and two glasses.

'Bet you your starter I'm right.'

Kepler pushed aside his dish. Bernice poured two half glasses of wine and freshened both with a sugar lump from a complimentary bowl. She knocked back her drink in one gulp. 'I'm waiting.' She poured another drink.

Kepler said nothing, but she felt the agent's eyes on her as she raised the glass and sipped.

'Look, I'm sick of this macho brinkmanship crap. Let's just eat, OK? The salted flamingo knees look great. Talk to me or not. I really don't care.'

Bernice finished her wine, then began to eat. Twenty minutes later she called for another bottle. By this time her movements were more than slightly wobbly. She filled both glasses, spilling at least as much as she filled, and added sugar lumps.

'You know,' she said carefully, 'you're being *rude*.' She added, 'Don't you?'

'I don't drink on duty.'

' "No wine, no women, no you, no wonder it's dull." ' Bernice blew out her cheeks. 'Great poet wrote that. Long time ago. Obviously knew about men like you. I bet –' Bernice burped. 'Sorry. I bet you don't do anything. Do you? On your days off, I mean.'

'I don't have any days off.'

'Don' have t'tell *me* twice! S'obvious! Say,' Bernice chomped on a particularly crunchy bit of flamingo leg, 'you married?'

'No.'

'Girlfriend?'

'No.'

'What about, you know, whassername? Newton? You two . . . you know . . . are you?'

'No.'

'Oh. Well. You like blokes then? That it?'

'No.'

'No need t'be aggressive. M'only asking.'

Kepler said nothing.

'Good.' Bernice crunched alone for a moment, then said brightly, 'Hey. Know y'r being rude, I s'pose?'

'Rude.'

'Watching a girl eat on her own. S'rude. Bad mammals – *manners.* Bad manners.'

'Sorry.'

'No you're not. You're rude. Plate of food here. You want me to eat yours too?'

'If you want.'

Bernice suddenly snorted with laughter. 'Hah. Got you sussed. You just want to get me sloshed. Think you're going to have your wicked way with me. S'true, innit?'

Kepler said nothing.

'Think you're gonna get me drunk, so I'll –' she burped again, loudly '– so I'll spill the beans about the – ooh, I feel sick – the stuff I found. Right?'

Kepler said nothing.

Bernice blinked, hiccuped, then let out a deep sigh. 'Trapped wind,' she said with a dazzling smile. She added, 'No, but I'm right, right? About what you're up to, you crafty old bugger. You think I'll tell you all my secrets. Don't you? All of 'em.' Bernice giggled, letting herself slump on to the table. 'You must think I was born yesterday.' Her hand reached, almost of its own accord, for the wine bottle. 'Well, listen up, buster, 'cos I've got some hot news for you. You listening? Good. 'Cos it goes like this –' Bernice leant closer across the table, lowering her voice to a conspiratorial whisper. 'I wasn't born yesterday.' In a lightning swift move, Bernice flipped open Kepler's jacket and took his gun, reversed it and slammed the barrel against his eye, forcing it shut. 'And I'm not drunk.' She hiccuped again. 'But I *am* going to puke – ooh. Sorry about the shoes.'

Bernice was aware of the other diners rising from tables and backing nervously away. Kepler didn't move.

'There, that's better. Now. Two things are going to happen. First – I get to keep the gun. Second – you get to tell me all about –'

'I don't think so.' Newton's voice. Hard. Decisive.

Bernice had one second to make a decision. She turned, saw Newton, the gun she held. She loosed a number of wild shots. Diners threw themselves to the floor. Newton ducked, fired back – the window behind Bernice cracked. Bernice threw herself across the table shooting, blew the glass from the frame a moment before she reached it.

The pastoral view disintegrated and was replaced by a blurred stream of oil-dark metalwork, a glowing lattice of flickering lights and the deafening screech of displaced air.

Sliding across the tabletop towards the window, Bernice decided leaving the train by such an unorthodox method was probably not such a good idea. She scrabbled for a grip on the tabletop but found nothing beyond the condiment tray, itself already sliding towards the jagged opening. Plates and other small items bashed against her as they vanished through the broken window. She felt hands at her ankles – Newton and Kepler. Were they trying to save her or push her out? It didn't matter. Not now. If she was going so were they.

She reached back and grabbed both agents, one hand each, and the pressure differential dragged all three from the dining compartment, through the window and out of the train.

7

PANGAIA: 80 MILLION BC

The expedition progressed northwards for many weeks, its movement slow and methodical, charting each anthropological find made in as much detail as was practical for such a far-ranging quest.

The expedition consisted of Raptor Old and Patience together with a number of students, younger specimens some two to three seasons old. Old was responsible for setting policy and decision-making, Patience determined which observations would be made at any specific site and how those observations would be tested. The students were responsible for recording the observations, making suggestions of their own, as well as the care and feeding of the food animals the expedition brought with it. Game was much scarcer here in the north than in the lush southern lands of their home.

One of the younger Ruling Family members accompanied the expedition as an independent observer. Raptor Fast was, as his name implied, a fine specimen of adult male raptor. By comparison with Old his body was lean and brightly coloured, his scent unobtrusive but compelling. Patience, drawn often to conversation with him, found him a curious individual. He apparently displayed none of the arrogance, misgivings or paranoia she had come to associate with the Ruling Family, via the stories that Raptor Old had related.

She wondered if Fast was the exception to the rule; young enough still to be open-minded, or if he was simply a renegade thinker; a true scientific mind who had been tactfully excused a political role within the Nest until he was mature enough to see things the way his Family wanted him to see them.

That question was not going to get an easy answer so Patience never brought the subject up. She was an observer. She would do what she did best. Raptor Fast would reveal himself to her eventually, by his actions if not by his words.

The expedition continued into the cold lands in a routine that was dull but at the same time exciting. Students would range ahead, scouting for food and signs of habitation. If signs of the latter were found, Patience would accompany the student in question to the location while Old supervised the construction of a Nest. If Patience deemed the settlement worthy of further study then the Nest would be concealed and protected, hunters would be set to guard the perimeter and observers would take turns watching them and making notes.

Once a week, all would join in a hunt for food. This was a popular time among the students: of all the things raptors liked to do, eating and playing were number-one favourite. The hunt indulged both needs and provided for the release of any latent aggression or tensions which may have built up over the course of the previous days.

So far, personal interaction with the humans had not been deemed advisable. This was Old's idea and it was supported without argument by both Patience and Fast. Some of the students were eager to get up close and test them directly in terms of strength and agility. A near miss with a human hunting party which resulted in three minor wounds and a hasty retreat from the area, convinced everyone that – where the humans' swords and armour were concerned at least – discretion was, without a doubt, the better part of valour.

So the expedition progressed further and further into the cold lands. With its strange vegetation, unfamiliar animals and constant ground tremors, the cold lands were something of a mystery to the raptors. Raptor Old suggested that the students also note general observations about the changes around them, including particular references to specific animals, vegetation, composition of the air and ground, amount of sunlight, and the landscape. The workload increased as the temperature fell. But Raptor Old was delighted with their progress, ever eager to move on, to see what lay beyond the next hill or valley.

As far as the specific objective of their expedition was concerned, the settlements they investigated seemed to grow in sophistication and complexity as the land got colder; another thing which provoked Old to snorting paroxysms of scientific enthusiasm.

Progress was smooth and relatively uneventful for three months.

The attack came during preparation to observe a new, even larger settlement. At the time it was a tragedy – though when she thought about the circumstances later Patience would come to think of the word *destiny* as more precisely applicable.

The discovery of the new settlement came first during a hunt.

Food was scarce this far from the Nest. The lower temperatures generally drove game further south. The animals they had brought with them for food had succumbed to the cold several weeks before. They had taken what meat they could from the cooling bodies and carried it with them. It was all gone now; had been for several weeks. The spoor of a lone apatosaur had brought them to a bluff overlooking a small valley, through which a river wound in shining loops.

Halfway along the valley, the river was straddled by a number of large constructions.

A nest.

A vast human nest.

Leaving the incredible view to follow the trail of the apatosaur, three of the students were attacked – not by humans but by another tribe of raptors. The attack came swiftly; the hunters were older, more experienced, with yellow snouts and blue feathers. In the cold, on unfamiliar ground, the students did not stand a chance. They were attacked without warning and killed within moments, their bodies cooling, their blood staining the frost-glazed earth. The attackers snorted and screeched in triumph, pawing over the remains, burying their snouts in the carcasses and quarrelling over the choicest titbits.

When they had eaten, they began to follow the students' trail back towards the Nest which Old and the rest of the team were building as a base.

The invaders came upon the camp and attacked immediately, disembowelling another student and wounding Raptor Old as he turned to face the challenge.

At the sight and smell of the attackers, Patience went a little mad. Her mind seemed to take a step backwards, to regress, until the primitive hunting instincts she had possessed came once again to the fore. She moved, not as elegantly as Fast, but with much deadlier purpose: tracking, anticipating, striking. Of the seven attacking yellow-blue raptors, three were killed by Patience. Another was cornered by the remaining students and ripped squealing into shreds, while a fifth was disembowelled by Fast and left steaming on the ground to die.

The remaining two attackers turned tail and bounded from the Nest, screeching and hissing with frustration.

Patience took stock of the fallen bodies, nudged the student to make sure she was really dead, then turned her attention to Fast, and to Raptor Old. Her mentor was on the ground, propped against a tree stump, blood leaking from a wide gash in his flank. It wasn't fatal but it was extremely painful – and it meant he could move no faster than a slow amble. Fast, like herself, was uninjured.

For a long while there was silence, broken only by panting breaths and hissing anger. Then the panicky scents and chittering of the three remaining students took over.

–They will bring others–

–We must leave–
–If we run they will follow–
–If we do not they will kill us–
–Either way we will die–
–What are we to do?–

Patience considered. –We must find running water. That will mask our scent. We will go to the river. Then we will hide, and decide what to do– She indicated the fallen student as they began to move. –And bring raptor dead. We will need food–

The river walk was a nightmare of semi-frozen rapids. Lumps of ice battered them. Patience tried to catch some fish but her customary dexterity deserted her in the aftermath of the attack. She found the knowledge distressing. It had been many years since she had been on the hunt – she suspected that she had survived by sheer luck.

On the outer slopes of the valley, they found a cave. The cave stank of dead meat – its occupant having recently died from the cold. They dragged the corpse into the river, having first ascertained that it was inedible. Then they retired to the cave and built a fire.

They discussed throughout the day and into the evening, at first in reasonable tones and then in heated barks and scents. Put simply the expedition was divided. The three remaining students wanted to terminate the quest and return to the southern lands with the information they had already gathered. The single opposing voice was Raptor Old, who not only could not journey south until his wound was healed but *would* not. His determination to stay, to rest and in the spring thaw to return to his investigation only fuelled arguments which escalated to screams. Patience found herself undecided but supported Raptor Old out of loyalty. Also, while she was scared of death, she was also eager to finish gathering the information which was the purpose of their expedition.

Only Raptor Fast seemed to have no opinion. He listened

carefully to the escalating argument, making no sound, offering no counsel.

But when the students, tiring of what they now clearly considered to be the rantings of an enfeebled mind, simply marched out of the cave and began to run homeward, he stayed.

It was a solution of sorts.

8

Glasgow: 2595

Gold.
Silver.
Copper.
Iron.
Caesium.
Thorium.
Uranium.
Beryllium.
Pitchblende.
Monazite.
Cavorite.
Silicon.
Carbon.
Cobalt.
Lead.
Pigs.
Scotland.

Bernice sat up, groaned, spat mud and straw, stood, slipped and promptly sat down again. Using small, cautious movements she scraped muck from her face, blinked, opened her eyes.

She was in a pig-sty.

In a pig-sty in the middle of a factory the size of a small country.

There were about thirty pigs staring curiously at her. They had obviously all been eating a moment before – until she had sat up and emerged dripping from the goop. Then they had stopped. Now they were looking at her. Bernice licked her lips, scowling at the taste. She tried to remember whether pigs were dangerous. These pigs were very big – as big as small ponies. Their expressions were unreadable.

But they were very quiet for pigs.

Suspiciously quiet.

Being careful to make no sudden movements, Bernice felt herself all over. No damage. No real damage, anyway. She supposed she had the mud to thank for that. She tried to remember what had happened after being sucked out of the train. She had a vague memory of whirling sky and land, all composed of gunmetal piping and thumping pistons, oil-black and stinking of sulphur and metallic compounds. She remembered the sensation of falling – it was becoming quite familiar actually – and the astonished expressions of pigs. These pigs? Maybe. Then there had been nothing. Not for some time. How much time? Where was she? Why were the pigs staring at her?

'Jeez.' Bernice managed to make the word come out vaguely recognizable. 'Where am I?'

The nearest pig snuffled closer. She caught a glimpse of an open mouth full of neat teeth and shuffled backwards until she slipped in the muck.

The pig leant over her until its face was a handspan from her own.

'Glasgow,' said the pig.

His name was Anson and he was five years old. He was the gang boss for this area. The other twenty-nine pigs' jobs consisted of operating a basic level of computerized technology in response to certain conveyor belt stimuli, for which their reward was a regular dose of vending-machine-dispensed, performance-linked candy treats. Their conversation, though ribald, was limited to the word *yes*, the word *no,* and the phrase *fuck you.*

After a while, Bernice realized the only difference between these pigs and most of the human population of the world was that the pigs could spell the words they knew.

When Bernice asked Anson how far she was from Loch Ness and how she might get there, Anson snorted with amusement. 'Lady Boss want Loch Ness. Loch Ness out of work purview. But not matter. Anson smart. Anson got initiative. Anson got leadership skills. Anson got *certificate.* You want see Anson certificate?'

'Uh . . . yeah, sure. Why not.'

Anson ambled over to the entrance to the pen, unhooked the gate and tugged on a chain hanging from an old-fashioned computer keyboard. A whistle blew. 'Come on, you oiks. You want to eat forever? *Up-an-attem-let's-go-let's-go-one-two-three-four-fire-in-the-hole!*'

The pigs stirred to a chorus of good-natured *fuck you*s. Anson snorted in amusement. 'Pigs are so stupid,' he confided to Bernice. 'They work for sugar-coated peanuts. Could get enhanced. Grade Two like Anson. Fast track to management. Got certificate to prove. Anson show.'

Bernice nodded as the last pig shuffled through the gate. Anson nudged the gate shut and latched it.

'Get moving, you lazy oiks! Anson show Lady Boss to where she wants to go. You better be working when Anson get back or no candy!'

Anson's quarters were what you might expect from a pig: neat, precise, with inordinate amounts of straw and a daylight lamp turned on and off by a chain hanging almost to the floor. A v-mail terminal squatted near floor level in one corner, the keyboard and mouse replaced by a snout-sized joystick and touchpads. Bernice was interested to note the straw here was of a higher grade than that in the pen. Maybe management did have its perks.

Anson fished with his wrinkled snout in a touch-drawer,

extracting a wooden box of treats, a grubby cloth doll covered with teeth marks and a piece of laminated plastic inscribed with the words,

This is to Certify that

PORKER 32997-ANSON

Having passed GRADE 700 Management

Is Hereby Awarded the Rank and Privileges of

GANG BOSS

For

SECSHUN NINE-FIFTY-THREE-A

The capitals were handwritten, the writing so sloppy it could only have been human.

Bernice admired the certificate roundly for a few moments, until Anson took it from her, placed it reverently back into the drawer and gentled the drawer shut with his snout.

'Lady Boss want eat? Lady Boss want check quota? Figures all sound. Anson knows.'

'No, Anson. I just want to get to Loch Ness.'

'Anson show. You go fast. Loch Ness section seven-eighty-three. Nine levels down. One hundred and fifty kilometres.'

'A hundred and – bugger me, that'll take forever.'

'Lady Boss travel like pigs. Horse-and-cart. You get there real fast. Up-an'-attem. Two days, tops.'

'Anson, you're a genius.'

'Anson know. Anson –'

'– I know, I know –'

'– *got certificate!*' Bernice joined in with the inevitable last phrase and they both snorted with laughter.

The stables were automated, the horses better cared for than some people she had seen recently. The carts were wide enough for two pigs, were covered in a layer of Astroturf and held a tiny water dispenser. Directional control was via a snout-sized touchpad hooked up directly to the horse's neural jack.

Bernice raised an eyebrow. 'All mod cons.'

She thanked Anson, swapped v-mail addresses and climbed into the cart. Five minutes later she was once again heading north.

She could only wonder where Newton and Kepler were – and how close – and what they would do if and when they caught up with her.

9

Pangaia: 80 Million BC

The cold worsened. The river became solid, the water so hard she had to cut it with claws and bring the pieces back to melt by the fire.

Game became very scarce.

One day when she left the cave to hunt, Patience was amazed to see the earth had changed colour. White lay across the ground in a thick carpet. Patience had never seen such a thing before. She took a few cautious steps, felt the ground bite her – it was cold!

She had a moment to digest this amazing fact before losing her balance. Her legs slipped out from underneath her and she went skidding and sliding down the hill to collide with a tree-trunk, panting, hissing and – incredibly – snorting with laughter.

Raptor Fast had appeared at the entrance to the cave at her initial cry of alarm. Now he snuffled with interest and amusement. A moment later he too slipped, a long ungainly slide which resulted in him landing headfirst in a freezing drift beside Patience, who threw back her head and cawed with laughter.

They spent the rest of the day playing in the snow, hunger temporarily forgotten.

When they returned to the cave it was to find Raptor Old much worse. His wounds had not healed well through the winter. He had rarely left the cave, instead spending his time making notes on his observations of the expedition so far.

When Patience and Fast returned to the cave, Raptor Old was lying still upon the floor, his skin a dull grey, all colour leached from it. His feathers were lank. He was shivering, even though the temperature in the cave was comfortable, due to the fire at its mouth. His eyes were wide open but obviously could not see them. He made no move to sit or defend himself, or even acknowledge that anyone had entered the cave.

There was a peculiar scent in the air – the smell of age and sickness.

Patience and Fast snuggled close to Old, using their bodies to keep him warm. As they lay there, in the cave, listening to the sound of meltwater dripping from the icicles at the cave mouth, Patience said, –He is dying–

Fast snuffled agreement. –His scent will bring others to us–

Patience shuddered. One encounter with the rival tribe had been enough. –We cannot let him die–

–He is too weak to move–

–We could take him to them–

–Do you think that's wise? We don't know how they will react. Perhaps it would be better to kill him here and now, then return to the Nest–

Patience considered. Fast was right, she knew it; still, some shred of loyalty still lingered. To Old, to the Expedition, to the idea of meeting the humans face-to-face.

Fast seemed to know her thoughts. –Do not be led by the future – Old was and he will die soon. Come back south with me. We could stay together. Raise a family–

–And give up my life to care for squealing chicks? I don't–

–Not if you don't want to. You're important to the Nest, Patience. We need you. My Family knew that when they sent me with you. It's why I have stayed with you. My loyalty is to the Nest, true – but to you also. You are indivisible–

The statement made Patience rumble in annoyance. Fast sensed the change in her attitude and shuffled uneasily. Patience felt her anger subside slightly. It was good that Fast respected her. But would he do what she said?

–As yours is to the Nest, my loyalty is to Old. I must try to save him. I will go to them and try to get help–

–They will kill you–

–You do not know that–

–And you do not know that they won't–

Fast shuffled in agitation. –I cannot let you–

Patience was on her feet quickly, her lean body trembling, her claws outstretched. –I am bigger and stronger. How will you stop me?–

–How will you take him without *me*?–

–I will go alone–

–And what if I kill him while you are gone? You will have no reason to stay then–

–I will have a reason. I have another loyalty. Something you do not understand. A loyalty to what will come–

–Scientists' nonsense!–

–It is the truth–

–It is nothing but chick's cackle–

Patience took a step closer to Fast. –If you kill Old you will never know what it would be like to start a family with me–

She waited. Her companion made no move to oppose or argue with her further. After a moment he looked down at the ground.

Hoping she had guessed correctly about Fast's interest in her, Patience leapt over both him and the fire, left the cave and began moving towards the settlement.

She did not look back.

10

LOCH NESS: 2595

There was a monster in Loch Ness and its name was World Chemicals.

Bernice stared down across the valley from the mess of pipework which had once been known as the Grampian Mountains, fascinated by the changes wrought here by time and man.

The landscape had changed. Inverness was gone, replaced by a deepwater channel connecting the loch to the Moray Firth. Beyond this Bernice was surprised to see little change. She had thought perhaps the grey-purple-green of the hillsides and blue-steel of the loch itself had been replaced by oil-black metal, hills of chemicals, gigantic cracking plants and refineries sucking minerals from the North Sea.

Not so.

Granted, there was little or no real sky to be seen between the refinery towers roofing the loch; granted also that the grass growing abundantly upon the hillsides was tainted a sickly yellow and that the water itself had an oily brown sheen to it; true also that the temperature here was somewhere between temperate and tropical – but these things aside, the loch and surroundings were remarkably intact. Only as Bernice urged the horse to descend the hillside did she realize why.

She saw beach huts, small prefabricated buildings, a community. A holiday community for the working proletariat.

Loch Ness was Brighton Beach for pigs.

Bernice spent the night in an unoccupied beach-front apartment, listening to the sound of lapping water and wondering whether the legendary monster was still in the area and what it thought of its new neighbours. The light never changed. There was no night or day beneath the gunmetal sky. Just the multiple stars of arc-lights and sunlamps streaming down on to the lightly oil-streaked hillsides. Giant fans sucked most of the pollutants from the air. When it rained – which it did around four in the morning – the droplets were greasy to the touch and smelt faintly of petrol.

In the morning she explored the apartment in the hope of finding food. She had not eaten for almost two days. All she found was some porridge-like substance dispensed in plastic bowls from a vending machine. It tasted disgusting but she guessed it would probably keep her alive. At least the water from the dispenser was relatively clean-tasting. She used more of it to wash and then went outside to look for the horse.

She didn't find the horse. She did find two rather worse-for-wear special agents with large grey guns pointing, respectively, at her head and her heart.

The temple didn't look much like a temple. It looked more like a twentieth-century country house. Inside it was a bit different though: sandstone faced the walls, pillars supported the ceilings . . . in short, it seemed as if a little slice of ancient Egypt had been re-created, or perhaps moved, here to Scotland.

The agents ushered her into the house and then seemed content to do nothing. Bernice suffered a few minutes of this and then shrugged and got up.

'You can look at anything you want.'

'But if you try to escape . . .'

'I'll never get to dig up another bone, right?'

The agents said nothing. Bernice shrugged and began to mooch around the ground floor, her interest caught and held by the inscriptions carved upon the walls and pillars. There seemed to be references here to the Temple of Solomon, the legendary resting place of the Ark of the Covenant. Was the Box of Ra really the Ark? Did it contain part of the Map of Skulls? What was the connection? Was there in fact a connection?

Newton and Kepler simply watched her, seemingly with amusement, wander quickly around the rooms, touching the walls, tracing inscriptions, muttering obscure archaeological references aloud to herself.

As far as Bernice was concerned, she didn't care whether the agents were humouring her or not. It wasn't like she had any options; they had the artillery. So she made the best of a rum do, skanking along the pillars and panels, letting her eyes drift from one resting place to the next, soaking up information like a sponge.

She saw vague references to the Map of Skulls – not by name but by symbol, the Ankh – the Egyptian symbol for life, bounded by an infinity sign. The mixed reference told her something as well: it told her that the concept spanned generations, perhaps centuries.

There were a series of pictagrams, illustrations showing a man dressed as an Egyptian king using a sword to fight a great battle against another great king. Closer examination showed the king was fighting against himself. Fighting death? Fighting his own death?

Other pictograms showed a box, some kind of force emerging from it, a crucifixion. That in itself was odd – the artifacts and engravings seemed far too old to contain Christian references, unless of course Christianity took its symbology from hitherto unknown Egyptian sources.

Bernice sighed. 'You did that deliberately, didn't you?' she said accusingly, directing her words equally at both agents. 'You brought me here and let me look around. You knew whatever information recorded here is so obscure as to be practically meaningless.'

Newton said, 'Obscuring meaning is a job requirement.'

Kepler added, 'And we're –'

'– *very good at our jobs.* You said.'

There was a moment's silence. Bernice drank in the dusty calm of the house, the weight of its architecture, the meaning sealed into every arch and pillar and flagstone. 'What now?'

'Knowledge and meaning are divisible.'

'You know everything and understand nothing.'

'This is as it should be.'

Bernice blinked. 'You guys ever thought about doing vaudeville?'

The agents exchanged glances.

'If she dies here it won't matter how much she knows.'

'Or where she has hidden the Needle relics.'

'Then you agree, we should kill her?'

'I agree.'

Bernice stuck up a finger. 'Excuse me. What if I've told someone?'

Newton tilted her head on to one side, considering. 'Like the pig you mean?'

She threw a pig's trotter on the floor beside Bernice. Bernice looked at the foot and shivered. 'Anson . . .' She looked up, her expression thundery. ' "The Institute for Fairness and Benevolence",' she said bitterly. 'You hypocritical bastards. You killed a pig with a vocabulary of less than five hundred words, the intellect of a babe-in-arms, and the interest in history of a frog. I could have told Anson the truth and he wouldn't have understood one word, nor how to apply it. You better hope your affairs are in order because when I get the first opportunity I'm going to send your bodies to an early grave and your pathetic souls straight to hell!'

Newton picked up the trotter, fished out a large bunch of keys and attached them to what Bernice could now clearly see was a key-fob. She breathed a sigh of relief. Anson was obviously still alive. She exchanged glances with Kepler and then both Masons put away their guns.

'She'll do.'

11

PANGAIA: 80 MILLION BC

The first time Patience tried to approach the settlement she was driven off by a number of hunters with swords. Fearing for her life, she turned and ran; even in her weakened condition, she bounded across the river at a speed the humans simply could not match. The second time she approached they were waiting for her, and tracked her for a long way back into the hills. She was nearly cornered in a box-canyon, but managed to leap clear at the last moment along a rocky bluff that was too steep for the humans to negotiate in number or at speed.

She waited for three days and then tried again, this time with a different approach. This time, she took the carcass of an infant brontosaurid with her. She dragged the corpse across the river and as close as she could to the settlement, then waited.

This time when the hunters came she did not run. Instead she pushed the corpse towards them and then stood back. And waited again.

The hunters prodded the corpse for a while, conversing amongst themselves in peculiarly soft tones; tones, Patience was curious to note, that matched their bodies. When the hunters turned towards her she leapt away and ran. Three days later she returned with another corpse. This time when the hunters approached they did not draw their swords.

Patience waited long enough to make sure they knew she was not going to attack, and that she had left the food for them and then, as gently as she could, she barked a request for help.

They looked at her stupidly. They didn't understand.

It took the best part of another three days to make them understand she wanted them to come with her. Then, a party of five accompanied her to the cave. At first they thought the supine form of Raptor Old was more food, for they moved forward with swords drawn. Patience got between them and hissed – gently. Then she stood aside to let them approach, so that they could see Raptor Old was sick and that he needed help.

Raptor Fast was outside the cave, hidden in some foliage, watching everything that happened. If anything went wrong, he would try to help. She hoped.

They studied Raptor Old, made their curious soft noises, then picked up the Elder Sibling and began to carry him back to the settlement. Patience followed them, and Fast followed her.

Halfway to the settlement, they changed direction. They did this at the command of one of their number who unaccountably reminded Patience of Raptor Old, despite the dramatic physiological differences. This human was obviously ancient; his skin was wrinkled and reddened, his hair thin and wispy, his eyes bleached by the harsh conditions; yet his movements were sure and his voice was firm. Patience decided that she would trust this one. As if she had a choice.

The party walked for several hours towards the end of the valley, and there Patience was astonished to see a building such as she had only seen before in ruins. It was a large construction with pillars supporting a sloping roof. It was built into the side of a hill. Inside was darkness.

The humans made it clear that Patience and Fast were to remain outside – in any case Fast was still trailing the party at some distance – and then they took Raptor Old in.

A short while later they emerged without him.

Patience began to get agitated; she made scents and barked

in concern. The human she thought of as the leader, made curious gestures: approaching with his forelimbs outstretched, making soothing noises similar to those a mother would make to her chick if the infant was alarmed or scared.

Patience controlled herself with an effort. She calmed down, allowing herself to be led away from the temple. She could not save Raptor Old – but if these humans harmed him they would regret it.

Patience stayed with them for three days. At first, Fast would not stay with her. He remained at the edge of the settlement, sleeping in the wild, hunting for himself and leaving food for Patience, which she shared with the humans.

During the first day, Patience saw almost nobody other than the half a dozen hunters who had moved Raptor Old and their Leader, whom she came to think of as White Hair.

This human spent almost all of the first day with her, sharing food, trying to imitate the noises she made. Neither had much success duplicating the sounds made by the other, but both found there was some common ground in the use of symbols, at first scrawled in the dirt, then written in books. Patience was surprised to find that the humans' written language apparently contained more characters than her own. It was as if they were more sophisticated than her – at least, as if they saw themselves that way.

Patience slept little that first night, tormented as much by bad dreams as she was by the curious presence of many human infants, whose presence she felt constantly around the small building they had given her to sleep in.

Communications continued the following day, long into the night, with no real progress. Tension was high. Patience could feel hostility from some of the mammals. And fear. Did they think she was going to attack them?

Soon after the midday meal, White Hair had a number of hunters stand near to Patience's hut. Was she under guard? Or being protected?

The next day, her third within the settlement, Raptor Fast

approached the settlement, causing a minor commotion at the river, but White Hair soon smoothed the way and Fast joined her in a growing crowd of curious onlookers.

–Do you know what has happened to Old?–

–No. Their speech is hard. Talking with pictures is clumsy and crude–

–I have been watching the temple. No one has gone in or out since we were there–

–I know– Patience grunted in concern. –If they have killed him, or allowed him to die–

–Then it will be your fault!–

The curious onlookers moved backwards at the sharp tones in Fast's voice.

–Be quiet. You will scare them. They die easily. They are frightened of us–

–Good. Then we have the advantage–

–We want their help!–

–We cannot even talk to them! They are stupid. This was a stupid idea–

–No. It was necessary. And they are not stupid–

–It was an indulgence. A stupid indulgence that has cost Raptor Old his life!–

–You don't know that!–

–Then where is he? I have seen no one take him food in three days. He is dead. We must leave here or they will kill us too–

–I refuse to believe that–

–Then ask your friend–

White Hair, as ever, was standing near by, observing the conversation. He could not understand the words but had no trouble picking up the angry overtones. He approached, arms spread, still making those soothing noises. Fast snapped at him in irritation. The hunters approached quickly, but White Hair stopped them with a gesture. Then he approached Fast, who was swaying, balanced, poised to run or attack.

Patience felt powerless to interfere. Fast did not trust these strange creatures; he must learn that trust for himself. But would he?

White Hair stopped a good way from Fast, hesitated, then continued forward. He must know that Fast could be on him in an instant. Many of the humans had seen Patience hunt – they knew how fast the raptors were, how quickly they could kill. But White Hair seemed to know something. His manner now displayed irritation, or perhaps frustration. It was as if he wanted Fast to wait just a short while longer. He kept looking at the sky, noting the position of the sun. Patience was sure that was what it was.

But Fast had missed it. Patience could see his muscles bunching for a leap. He planned to attack – perhaps planned was not the right word. He felt threatened and instinct was taking over. Did White Hair realize that?

Patience moved towards White Hair, trying to make him understand that he should move back, allow Fast some room to think. But the hunters misinterpreted the gesture, responding to Fast's aggressive body language even though it was Patience who approached.

Fast noticed this right away, and crouched, mouth open, hissing gently, a sure sign of attack. His eyes were fixed on White Hair. There was no way the human would escape with his life if Fast was not stopped right now.

Patience changed direction suddenly, pounced on Fast, bore him to the ground. The hunters drew their weapons, but did not move to attack. Good. Patience stamped on Fast hard, keeping him down, off balance, nipping at his flanks and using her claws to keep him at bay. Fast was confused; he blinked, barked in confusion and then hunkered down on the ground as the truth of the situation began to sink in.

The hunters put away their weapons at a sign from White Hair.

And that was when Raptor Old sprang across the river and ran into the settlement, cawing for attention, his wounds miraculously healed by some method that defied all understanding.

12

Loch Ness: 2595

'So this is the bit where you tell me the plot and then kill me, right?'

The agents had not replied. In fact they had not said a single word since pronouncing her eligible for . . . well, whatever they had planned. Faced with the obvious alternative, Bernice had no choice but to allow herself to be blindfolded. She had been taken down some steps. Wine cellar? Basement? Rocket silo? Secret underground headquarters of SMERSH?

There was no way of knowing.

All she knew was that it was cold. And quiet as the grave. Hm. Maybe that wasn't such a good analogy.

She was allowed to sit; the floor was cold stone. There was a long moment of silence. Then Kepler's voice. 'I told you there are some secrets which would change the world if they ever got out.'

'"He said, cocking his gun."' Bernice tried to keep the shake from her voice.

Newton said, her voice quite neutral, 'You know things we need to know. We like you. We don't want to kill you. But we would if we had to. To protect the greater truth.'

'The Sword of Forever?'

Newton sighed. 'I'll be honest with you, Bernice – may I call you Benny? – I'll be honest with you, Benny. There are those in our organization who would sanction your death at the drop of a hat and think no more of it than tearing up a betting slip. That's all you are to us at the most. A gamble. We know you have information; we don't know how much. It's too dangerous to let you go and the alternative is we kill you and never find out ourselves the information we need.'

'So?'

Kepler said, 'So we have devised an alternative. A trade off.'

'Tell you what you want or I'll never play the piano again?'

'Not exactly.'

'There's a better way.'

'Neater.'

'Stronger.'

'And that is?'

'We tell you everything,' said Newton.

'And then make you one of us,' said Kepler.

'And then there'll be no secrets because we'll all be on the same side.'

'How do I know you won't just kill me like you tried to before?'

'Because you'll be of the Order. The Order does not kill the Order.'

Bernice laughed. 'You guys could offer candyfloss to a baby and make it sound like a death threat, you know that?'

'Oh yes–'

'– we know–'

'– it's what you might call–'

'– a once in a lifetime offer.'

Bernice blinked. 'Well . . . I'll need some time to think it over.'

The guns reappeared. 'There is no time.'

'Choose now.'

'Or eternity dies.'

'And so do you.'

13

PANGAIA: 80 MILLION BC

The raptors stayed in the human settlement for several more weeks, learning more vocabulary and more of their culture, interacting on a daily basis.

Patience was amazed at Raptor Old's apparent resurrection. Now that he was back with them she was even less inclined to acknowledge the secret fear she had felt all along, that Fast had been correct and Old was dead and it was her fault for involving the mammals. Now all that was proved false. Old was alive, in the highest spirits she had seen him for some while. The only thing that clouded the perfect reunion was that he remembered nothing of his stay within the human temple beyond a few disjointed images.

This was what drove a wedge between Fast and the others. Patience could tell he was scared, even though he hid it well. He was nervous all the time, feathers raising at the slightest excuse, his colour and scent unmistakable. It was clear to Patience that Fast was scared by what had happened to Raptor Old. And Patience knew why, too – it implied the humans had a power greater than the raptors, a power they seemed willing neither to acknowledge nor explain.

Old wanted to explore this power, investigate it. He saw the potential for almost indescribable growth and learning, a meeting of two cultures, human and raptor. He tried to communicate his ideas to White Hair but was frustrated by the lack of common ground in the language.

And then Raptor Old began to have dreams. Strange, recurring dreams. He told Patience and Fast about them, as much as he could remember. He dreamt of a box. A human dressed in armour. He dreamt of a world destroyed, broken into pieces and scattered. He dreamt of the future, he said, and it was a world that terrified him. Not his comfortable future of cooperation and learning.

–It's wrong, something's wrong, something's going to go wrong–

Patience awoke one night to those words being repeated over and over again by Raptor Old as he slept, writhing upon the loam bedding.

Fast thought Raptor Old was beginning to go mad. Privately, Patience wondered if Fast might be right.

When he awoke in the morning, Raptor Old showed no signs of the previous night's distress.

–Breakfast?– Patience enquired.

Raptor Old just stared, his ancient eyes alive with memories. –I remember what happened to me– he said. –There was a human in the cave, with a box. She opened the box and there was a light. Oh, yes, I know what you're going to say: primitive fantasies, a delusional brain looking for meaning in its madness. I was delirious, I grant you. But I am convinced of this: this species has access to an advanced form of science which is lifetimes away from our grasp. I was dying. You both said so. Something in that cave brought me back. Not only as I was but better than I was. I feel younger. Newer, somehow. My memories . . . they are clouded sometimes . . . there seem to be blanks . . . but I am here, alive. How do you explain that?–

Patience growled softly. –I cannot–

Fast added in a stern bark –And should not. This power. It is beyond our understanding. We must leave here. These creatures are dangerous to us. A threat. We must go back to our own lands and recommend–

Patience heard the words in her head a moment before Fast uttered them.

–To the Ruling Family that they be utterly destroyed–

Silence, deep, broken only by the sound of infants playing nearby.

Raptor Old hissed softly. –These beings have a cultural heritage which is older than I can determine. Thousands, perhaps millions, of years–

Fast shook his head from side to side. –Then why have we not seen them before?–

–I do not know–

–I do. They have been hiding from us. Building up their strength and waiting to attack us. To wipe us out–

Patience growled. –That is the thinking of chicks! You are better than that–

–We will see– Fast snorted, barked his annoyance, sprang up from the floor and left the dwelling place.

Patience rose to follow, to argue. Raptor Old stopped her with a soft growl.

–Let him go. He is not stupid. He will see we are right–

Tragically, Raptor Old's estimation was far from the truth, a fact borne out the next morning when the two raptors were awoken by angry shouts and the thud of rocks being hurled against their dwelling place.

Patience emerged from the hut to find a crowd gathered around, hurling stones, screaming abuse.

Then White Hair pushed through the crowd, a number of hunters with him. They were carrying what looked like two sacks of meat. They laid the sacks at the door of the hut and Patience could see they contained bodies. Humans.

They were dead, disembowelled by raptor claws.

Patience made gestures of submission, trying to communicate that she knew nothing about what had happened. White Hair ignored her. He was furious, his anger almost palpable. Try as she might, Patience could not communicate with him. Or he would not listen.

Raptor Old emerged from the hut, curious about all the

commotion. He saw the bodies, sniffed at them.

–Raptor Fast–

–I know! He killed these to provoke a conflict!–

–No, he is too clever for that. He killed them so we would be killed. That will give him the evidence he needs to start a war–

–We have to stop him. Get back to the Nest–

–Without evidence that he is wrong, that will be useless, even if he did not have a twelve-hour head start–

–What shall we do, then?–

Raptor Old eyed the ugly crowd, which was for the moment held in check only by the presence of White Hair. –We must get to the temple. Find evidence to refute Fast. Only then can we follow him–

–But the humans–

–We are faster and stronger. We must try not to kill any more of them than is necessary–

A rock flew out of the crowd and struck Patience on the shoulder. She squealed, felt her mind acknowledge the undertow of her primitive self: the hunter, the killer. She struggled to rise above the impulse to respond to the aggression with killing blows. –We must go. Now! Before they attack. Before we are forced to defend ourselves–

Raptor Old nodded. –Break through the crowd there. Head for the river. If you can cross that you will be able to outrun them–

–Me? What about you?–

–I am going to stay to talk to them. I may be able to–

–No! You can see what they are like! They'll kill you–

–They saved me. They will not waste that effort. They are intelligent beings–

More rocks flew out of the crowd. And now the hunters were approaching, weapons drawn.

–Go now!–

Raptor Old took a few steps closer to White Hair, his claws sheathed, head bowed in the pose of submission. White Hair stepped back quickly, his eyes flickering nervously from side to side. The crowd was beyond control now. He began to shout orders at them. Raptor Old approached even closer and then . . .

And then . . .

One of the hunters ran forward and plunged his sword into Raptor Old's flank. Old screamed, whirling to send the human falling, his guts churning from his slashed-open stomach. The rest of the hunters and the crowd moved as one creature. Patience felt blows land, rocks, swords. The pain did not register, though, for the primitive intelligence which controlled her hunting skills had subsumed her will. She was truly an animal, whirling, kicking, slashing, leaping, screaming; a hissing nightmare of bone and muscle, claw and teeth. She smelt blood, her own and that of the humans, and entered a frenzied state of shock from which, afterwards, she was to remember only fragmented glimpses of the carnage.

14

Loch Ness: 2595

Bernice was taken into the cellar of the house and told to undress. Then she was given clothing resembling a pair of white pyjamas and was told to put it on. A few moments later, Newton and Kepler came in holding a white cotton hood, a hangman's noose and a stone goblet full of aromatic liquid.

Bernice eyed the noose suspiciously. 'Just because you've got me dolled up like Wee Willie Winkie doesn't mean I won't black your eye if you try to put *that* on me.'

Newton spoke softly, the words unfamiliar, though the language – Egyptian – was easily recognizable.

Bernice frowned.

Kepler said, '*Ma'at*. "Righteousness, truth and justice".'

Newton added, 'This means you.'

'It is also a word symbolic of Freemasonry –'

'Therefore, you are also symbolic of Freemasonry –'

'Since the concept of *Ma'at* clearly applies to you as well.'

Bernice chewed thoughtfully on her lip. 'You wouldn't be trying to sell me a line, now, would you?'

'Of course we are –'

'It's your only alternative –'

'– to death.'

Kepler held out the stone goblet.

Bernice shrugged and grinned. 'Times like this I'm glad I

didn't stay a nun.' She downed the drink in one. A moment later the hood and noose were secured around her head and neck, and she was led from the cellar.

Bernice reviewed what she had read in London of the Masonic initiation ceremony. It was a ceremony designed to emulate the ancient-Egyptian king-making ceremony, carried out traditionally in the Pyramid of Unas. A candidate was presented to the sky, symbolized by the chamber roof, and adorned with two crowns to symbolize Upper and Lower Egypt, and was then made to drink a powerful drug. The candidate then lay near death through the night, to awake the following morning with stories of a near-death experience, which confirmed him to the people as the new king.

Her head began to spin as she thought this. Fear? Too late to worry now. She took a few more steps and found herself stumbling.

She fell to her knees, supported by the two agents, one on either side.

A voice she did not recognize began to speak.

'Almighty and eternal God, Architect and Ruler of the Universe, at whose creative fiat all things were first made, we the frail creatures of Thy providence humbly implore Thee to pour down upon this convocation, assembled in Thy Holy Name, the continued dew of Thy blessing. More especially we beseech Thee to impart Thy grace to this, Thy servant, who seeks to partake with us in the secrets of the stars. Endue him with such fortitude that, in the hour of trial, he fail not but, passing safely under Thy protection through the dark valley of the shadow of death, he may finally rise from the tomb of transgression to shine as the stars, for ever and ever.'

As the words rumbled on, Bernice felt her head begin to spin. By the end of the prayer she remained upright only because she was being supported. Then the support was removed and she fell. She seemed to take forever to reach the ground, didn't even feel the impact which shook the side of her head. As she lay motionless upon the ground Bernice wondered what had been in the ceremonial goblet she had drunk from. She would've bet a thousand dollars against an overripe banana it hadn't been dry white wine.

She told them everything, of course. And then they told her everything. Afterwards, she felt herself laid on a slab of cold stone, still hooded, and waited to die. Obviously they were going to kill her now. Nothing happened. She waited. Nothing continued to happen.

She became aware that something in the cellar with her was breathing.

Hissing.

She could hear the scrape of

(claws against)

metal against stone as she held her breath, tried to identify the sounds. No chance. She glimpsed grass. Felt hot sunshine. She tried to raise her hand to shield her eyes but her arms were bound, held straight out from her sides by a wooden pole. Her legs hurt, too. She sat up, then found she was already standing. No, not standing, but tied in an upright position. She struggled. The wooden pole to which she was bound shuddered and swayed.

How much had they given her to drink?

She tried to speak. There was no sound. No breath of wind save that which she caused by her own movements. She hung awkwardly, her back and shoulders in agony. The effort to draw breath against the weight of her own body made her want to scream. The sun drove molten spikes into her head. The sun – and the knowledge that no king-making ceremony should cut this close to the bone. This was carrying the near-death experience too far. *I mean, the whole thing's a scam, right*? Unless, of course, the drink was –

– was –

– poison, what if they'd given her too much bloody –

– something moved at her hands. A hammer blow. A silent shriek of pain.

Christ! Her hands! What were they doing to her – ?

The raptor crouching at her side rose to its full height and pushed the spear it held between her ribs.

15

PANGAIA: 80 MILLION BC

She was dying. She knew it, felt the truth in every lurching step, in every fractured breath; her flanks heaving and blood bubbling at her snout, her breath wheezing through teeth blunted and broken from killing. Her right forelimb was broken at the wrist, the claw torn out.

Her scent mingled with the scent of humans until she could no longer tell them apart. There was just a metallic taste of death which filled her head and scraped her mind clean of all willpower.

She ran all day, limbs pumping, muscles screaming, reached the temple half-drowned from the river, half-dead from sword cuts and stone wounds.

Inside, the cool darkness did not soothe. Her mind was busy shutting down, death bringing to the fore once again the primitive urge to survive, the imperative to run, to breathe no matter what the cost, no matter how bad the pain in her limbs and chest.

She controlled the impulses coursing through her. The primitive mindscream that told her to run and kill. Instead, she walked, slowly, methodically, through the temple, observing inscriptions and pictures and great openings blazing with coloured glass which formed pictures. She was searching, hunting for evidence, for proof. Something to deny Fast his legacy of war.

If she couldn't save Raptor Old, she could at least do that much.

She could save those that had killed him.

All she needed was a sign. Something to prove Fast wrong. Then she could get out, get away, try to heal, return to the Nest.

All she needed was a sign.

She found Raptor Old's body instead.

It was many days dead, the wounds unmistakable, as impossible to heal as she remembered them. Her mind reeled. Fast had been right. They had brought Old here to die and die he had. And yet he had been alive, too!

Or was she going mad?

How could there be two of him? Two individuals with the same body, the same life experiences, the same memories?

Patience emitted a mournful howl, backing away from the stone resting place of Raptor Old with dragging steps. Her jaw worked and she screamed, loud and long, and every remaining bit of energy, every drop of fear and regret she possessed, went into that scream.

Patience opened her mouth as an intelligent being; she closed it as a hissing animal, her intellectual processes overcome by shock and anger, the hunter-killer now firmly in control again.

When the mammal appeared behind her dressed in armour and carrying a sword, Patience was as incapable of thinking rationally as she was unable to prevent herself leaping on to the figure and slashing at it with claws and teeth, ripping through helm and head and face in a single terrible blow, before burying her snout in the bloody mess and beginning to feed.

Food in her belly bought her some time to think, though it did nothing to alleviate the pain. By now she could hear the sounds of mammals entering the temple. She sprang further into the maze of pillars and chambers, the mammals in close pursuit, hunting her by the trail of blood she left behind.

Her wounds brought Patience to her knees deep within the temple, in a chamber containing a wooden box covered with engravings. One of the engravings showed the world – obviously after a terrible cataclysm had occurred – sundered into many different pieces. Something about this image caused Patience to falter – and in that moment the room was full of humans. Screaming humans. Humans with swords and daggers, the killing metal.

Patience struggled to her feet, remaining claws extended, breath a bloody hiss through broken teeth. She looked around for a weapon, a shield, anything. There was only the box. She grasped at the lid and wrenched it off. Perhaps she could use it as a –

silent concussion of light erupted from the box, its force stilling screams, erasing fear and anger and pain, sundering flesh and mind and untold megatonnages of rock, rendering half a world lifeless and splitting the rest along faultlines already stressed for millennia as –

her last memory was of the temple collapsing under tons of ice. Darkness and cold a killing weight upon her until even the light from the box, her world, her life itself, were all finally, utterly extinguished.

16

London: 2595

Two minds remembering cold.
Remembering pain.
Dreaming of dying.

She awoke to the face of her husband and rescuer.

'Watch out for the cocktail – it's a killer.'

'I shouldn't wonder. It stopped your heart beating for nearly a minute.'

She shook her head – then gasped at the pain. 'We can't keep on meeting like this. It's bad for my self-image.'

She awoke to the face of a dead human, a younger version of the one she'd killed and eaten a world away in time, a flashfrozen image of murder and destruction surrounded by the warm-nest chick-fuzz of other, less immediate, less perfect memories. Memories that faded quickly, even as she barked a hoarse interrogative that made her throat hurt like fire.

'Take it easy.' The human female's voice was mother-comforting, though the words were the usual human fleshy-tongued nonsense. 'We couldn't adjust your vocal chords and anyway it would take too long for you to learn English. We'll start on sign language as soon as you're fit. I'm Benny by the way. And you are?'

She struggled against restraints, felt liquid slosh around her. She barked, screeched, made the scent of fear. Her claws snapped restraints, smashed against a wall she couldn't see. Images of herself breaking out of the egg assaulted her, panicked her. The invisible material cracked, then smashed, then fell away and she coughed up more liquid.

'Uh huh.' The human's words were still nonsense. 'Guess we're going to have to teach you some patience, right?'

Part Three

A Labyrinth of Ghosts

1

Arginy: 2595

Arginy was at Mardi Gras when they burnt the ghost.

It was night, of course; the village lit by oil-lamps carved from hybrid fruit. The hundreds of shimmering pumpkin faces put even the moon to shame. Thousands of candles illuminated hundreds of villagers; faces painted, clothes a wild cacophony of colour and movement. A dozen different sorts of music played from thrashmetal to Charleston, the sound blasting from equipment ranging from modern boom-busters to ancient wind-up gramophones.

Everyone from the youngest child to the oldest adult seemed to be dancing that night. Dancing to celebrate death and dancing to celebrate life.

The life in question was nearly over, a hybrid who had wandered from the wall of jungle alone and who, removed from the nurturing environment in which it had been created, now lay dying upon its own funeral pyre.

Bernice moved within the bustle and laughter of humanity, looking for room and board for two people, a dozen crates of equipment and one intelligent reptile. She encountered the *ghost* surrounded by a milling crowd and thought he (she? it?) resembled a skin-textured spider, the extra limbs arching above the back and then down, the extra joints on otherwise normal human limbs provoking a sense of profound unease.

To the crowd he was a curiosity, a danger, but no threat if tended properly.

'Oh look at him, isn't he precious?'

'He looks like a big bug!'

'Don't be rude, dear.'

'But he *does*!'

'The children don't understand; have some more mead.'

'Is he dying?'

'He looks like he is.'

'Is it a *he*?'

'Hush, dear, it's not *respectful.*'

'How can you tell?'

'Well, what is he then if he isn't a he?'

'Certainly not *human.*'

'It's sad.'

'Don't be like that! It'll be happy soon.'

'Yes, happy!'

'Happy and warm.'

'Oohhh *warm*!'

Bernice eased her way through the crowd, ignoring the children jostling eagerly for the best position to watch. She turned away from the flames when she saw the hybrid was still moving feebly in the pre-immolation heat, and bumped into a younger woman dressed as Death in neon-splashed crow's tatters. She realized as she apologized that everyone was wearing breathmasks beneath their costumes, even the children; and now she looked for it, the telltale glitter of aerosol prophylactic.

Despite the gaiety, no one was taking any chances with the hybrid.

Bernice moved further from the fire. Even drowned in happy laughter as they were, the sounds there were becoming unpleasant. Arginy was a town too full of ghosts already to witness another added to their number.

She felt the eyes of the woman dressed as Death follow her as she turned to go, and was unable to resist another glance. Something about her eyes, the way they sat within her mask, hard inside the ragged cloth, hard and cold as stars seen from remotest space.

'Hello, Bernice.'

Bernice hesitated. The eyes held her for a moment – the moment stretched. 'Do I know you?'

'You ought to. You killed my cousin.'

'Sara?'

She lay outside the castle walls, head full of lightning, fingers locked around the Templar journal, mind locked on his last panicky yell, half swamped by water as he was carried away by the current.

Bernice felt her head cloud with the fumes of alcohol and smoke and burning meat.

He was gone, Daniel was gone; swept away into the labyrinth, probably dead. The thought screamed in her head all the way back through the maze of tunnels and out of the castle. Dead. He was dead. It was her fault.

'Sara Beaujeu?'

'I'm surprised you remember me.'

'You were . . .' *The farmhouse had been large, rambling, the rooms caught in a maze of history; her presence ghostly; skipping feet and excited laughter preceding her merrily, her smile as warm as the fires that kept out the night.* 'You were so small.'

'I was six when Daniel died.'

'You had the attic room. You wanted to show me your butterfly collection.'

'Over a hundred species – more than half of them pure.'

'You were so proud.'

'As I was of Daniel. To catch someone like you.'

Bernice gulped air, tasted smoke, gave no thought to the alien DNA which might be drifting within it.

'He loved you, Bernice.'

'Sara. I'm so sorry.'

'He loved you and you killed him.'

'It . . . wasn't . . . Oh hell, who am I trying to fool.' Bernice blew out her cheeks, rubbed the bridge of her nose, looked around for somewhere to sit; every space was occupied by whirling bodies, leaping children, fluttering pennants, flickering pumpkin faces, sweetmeats, smoke, fireworks; a cacophony of colour and movement.

Sara peeled off her Death mask; the face beneath was deeply tanned, eyes and skin a generation beyond her twenty-six years. 'Come back to the farm. Mother will want to see you.'

'I don't know if that's such a good . . . I mean I'm here with, well, some friends . . . I'm . . . well, I'm going back. To Arginy, I mean. To the castle.'

'Of course you are. And I'm going with you. Why else do you think I sent you the journal?'

The farmhouse was just as she remembered it, half an hour's travel by horse and trap from the village, snuggled against the foot of a cresting wave of rock, the Massif Central, unbroken since her last visit by the creeping strangeness inching its way out of the Rhone Valley.

Cold stone, grey and purple in the starlight, the scattering of low cloud warmed by the flickering lights from the village. Ivy (unclassifiable) crawling across the walls. Windows warmed through with apricot firelight. Bernice caught the hint of animals, the smell of cows and dogs as she and Sara stabled the pony (hybrid – sterile). Later, when Marillian arrived, they unloaded the load-lifter.

There had been a minor panic when the dogs caught scent of Patience as she sprang clear of the lifter and had to be locked in the barn. They howled all night. Other than that things went smoothly – as smoothly as Bernice might have expected while introducing her husband to the only surviving relatives of the first man who ever loved her, and whose death she was responsible for.

Like the farmhouse, Sara's mother, Daniel's aunt Françoise, was also much as Bernice remembered from the past. She had put on a little weight but was as handsome as ever she had been. With her glasses perched owlishly upon her tilted nose and her hair cropped short and tucked away beneath her habitual cap, she could appear to a stranger as either the distant academic or the robust farm owner – Bernice had seen her play both roles to the hilt. The truth was that Françoise Beaujeu was neither academic nor farmer. She was an engineer. She designed machinery. Domestic and industrial: light machinery designed to hold down a ploughed field against time and the odd incursion by snake-vines; heavy machinery designed to tear down the encroaching jungle, to hold a line against the inevitable legacy of the war.

Now she and Sara watched as Bernice brought Marillian and Patience into the farmhouse kitchen. Her face was calm, the twists of light from her glasses slipping across her cheeks as she moved.

'You must be hungry.'

It wasn't a question; the table was loaded with food. Bernice wondered how long they had been expected.

'Françoise. This is my husband, Marillian. And this is Patience. She's –'

'– a dinosaur. So I see.' Françoise Beaujeu turned to her daughter. 'Sara, get the prime beef out of the freezer, zap it, mark eight for ten minutes, then chuck it in the tin bath, the one we use for the horses.' Sara vanished into the pantry and Françoise turned her attention back to Bernice's party. 'And I'm Françoise Beaujeu. Bernice and I have . . . some history.' No one spoke for a moment. 'Well, Benny. It's been a long time. You'll want to eat. We can talk later.'

The meal was delicious. Bernice remembered all the food here being delicious. Afterwards, on her mother's instructions, Sara took Marillian and Patience through to the lounge, leaving Bernice alone with Françoise.

'Walk with me, will you, Benny? We should settle the dogs.'

Outside the night had changed; the low cloud had vanished

to leave a clear sky filled with stars and the faint ribbon of the solar mirror. The dogs whined, scratching at the door of the barn as they sensed their mistress approach. Françoise unlatched the barn door and opened it. 'Heel!' The dogs came without any bother. She crouched and made a fuss of them. Bernice took a step closer. One of the dogs growled softly. 'Friend,' Françoise said softly. The dog – as mixed a breed as you could get without actually introducing non-terrestrial DNA – came over to Bernice and made a fuss of her.

'He's gorgeous.'

'Make no mistake. They're killers. Both of them.'

Bernice glanced at Françoise, wondering if there was an unspoken threat attached to her statement.

Françoise stood, ushered the dogs back into the barn and latched the door.

Bernice wondered whether she ought to say something about the dogs being locked up on her account – then thought better of it. 'It hasn't changed much here, has it?'

'You think not?' Françoise walked around the barn, setting a fast pace across the field towards the hills, black and silver in the starlight. A few minutes passed in silence. Great square animals loomed patchily out of the darkness. Cows, conversing in mellow tones, chewed over the day's events, the new arrivals, the sense of the past catching up with the present.

'You still have cows.'

'It's the only way I know to ensure uncompromised dairy produce. Beef, milk, you name it. I could retire comfortably on the sale of breeding DNA alone. Anything else is a bonus.'

'That's good.'

'You think so?'

Bernice bit her lip. 'I assume so. I'm not really qualified to judge.'

'No.' Françoise shut down the electricity supply to the five-bar gate with a whispered command and climbed it easily. Bernice followed her into the field, her feet sinking into mud. Curious, the cows ambled closer. Françoise ran her hands along the flank of the nearest animal. 'You were at Mardi Gras.'

'Yes. They were burning a hybrid.'

'They were burning a *ghost.* We call them that. Mostly they're sad, even pathetic creatures. It's a ceremony. It shows respect. The hybrid would have died anyway, away from its tribe, away from the other ghosts.'

'Tribe?' Bernice struggled to maintain her balance in the mud. 'How many people are there in the jungle?'

'Human? None. Hybrids? There's never been a successful census. Twenty-five years ago a man from the government went in with a palmtop and an environment suit. We found his suit six months later. It wasn't damaged.'

Bernice considered. 'He took it off?'

'Obviously.'

'Voluntarily?'

'The seals were opened from the inside.'

'Oh.' Bernice followed Françoise in squishy near-silence across the field. 'We never talked about it, did we?'

'Daniel? Or the jungle?'

Bernice was glad Françoise could not see her blush in the darkness. 'Either.'

'As I remember you were too eager to get off on your treasure hunt. You came here, a city girl, and used my nephew to get to his family's heritage.'

Bernice bit her lip. 'It wasn't like that. We were kids. We loved each other. It was an adventure. A stupid adventure. I know better now.'

Françoise said nothing for a while, then turned, heading towards the next field. Her words were almost lost in the night and the wind.

'When Sara told me she was going to send you the journal, I argued with her. Not the first argument we have ever had but certainly the most heated. When my brother James and Daniel's mother were killed I wanted to destroy that book. Burn it, the way they burn the hybrids. It's a hybrid. A symbol of the past and the future. It has secrets, Benny, secrets that kill. Do you have it with you? – No, don't show me, I don't think I ever want to see it again. No. You keep it; Sara gave it to you – the responsibility is yours now.'

Bernice hesitated, began to speak, changed her mind, and said, 'I don't know what to say to you. You're not making this very easy for me – not that I think you should – but . . . it hasn't been easy for me either these last twenty years. I . . . well, my life changed, you know that. I qualified, I became an archaeologist. I've done good work. I've opened up the past, brought dead civilizations back to life. Some of that is down to Daniel.' Footsteps squelching in mud. 'Wouldn't you say?'

Françoise made a sound – a sob or a laugh, Bernice couldn't tell. 'Your choice was made before you met Daniel. He wouldn't be dead if it were otherwise. Don't fool yourself, Benny. Lie to anyone else you like, but never yourself.' She hesitated, then added, 'I hope you're never betrayed by someone you care about as much as Daniel cared about you.' Then she turned and headed back to the farmhouse, leaving Bernice motionless, her mouth open, shocked as if she had just been slapped.

Bernice stayed out in the fields for another hour, snuggled inside her poncho, gazing up at the stars. She watched the moon creep slowly across the sky, watched it play tag with the gigantic oak looming over the farmhouse, watched the silver light spread out across the branches in concentric circles, trying hard to empty her mind of all thoughts.

Impossible, of course.

Doubly impossible was returning to the farmhouse. All that awaited her there was a lifetime of guilt and a man she did not love.

Bernice hunkered down inside her poncho, arms wrapped around her knees, crying when the cows mooched closer.

An hour later the cows moved away as a dark shape sprang lightly over the fence, moved silently through the mud, to crouch, breath hissing slightly, beside her.

'Hey, buddy.'

Patience swung her thickly muscled neck against Bernice's head, butting gently. Bernice wrapped an arm around the raptor's neck, drawing the surprisingly warm body closer still. She took the offered thermos of hot chocolate, and dumped a generous dollop from her hip flask into it.

'My dear; your very good health.' She drank.

Patience growled; the cows shuffled uneasily; Patience uttered a series of yipping barks.

'Oh yeah? Me too. Want to hang out?'

2

ETHIOPIA: 2575

Marillian had not seen Lake Tana from the air; there were no direct vision ports in the sub-orbital which had finned down at Adis Ababa three days earlier; but the virtual vision system had shown the lake as it sat in the Ethiopian Plateau, more than a thousand metres above sea level. He'd thought the tiny stretch of water resembled the pupil in a large grey and purple eye that was the mass of mountains between the Sudan and Somalia. The image had been a disturbingly accurate iteration of the All Seeing Eye which was the central symbol of the Masonic Chapter to which he belonged. The image served only to reinforce his personal belief that God was at best a moot concept even if there were larger, possibly unseen patterns of order at work in the universe. His own Chapter, for example, dated back more than fifteen hundred years – to a time when there was no such thing as flight or aerial photography. Yet there he was, just hours before, looking down at the Ethiopian Plateau with its steel grey eye which seem to gaze into his very soul, and the resemblance was uncanny.

Of course it could all have just been nerves. It wasn't his first mission by a long chalk – though only twenty-six years old Marillian was an accomplished Mid Level Mason – but one thing that hadn't changed over the decade since his father introduced him to their local Lodge was that he always got jumpy when out in the field. He supposed in a way it was lucky. That jumpiness had saved his life on more than one occasion.

An hour had passed, the sub-orbital had finned down and the Jennings-Bankhurst Expedition had got smoothly underway.

Now, from the creaking deck of the load-lifter skimming the surface of the lake, Marillian began to appreciate how extraordinarily large the seemingly tiny expanse of Lake Tana really was – more than ten thousand square kilometres. A tiny inland sea, bordered by mountains, with more than forty islands of its own. As he passed across its surface – the surface of the Eye – he felt its gaze even more strongly upon him, both reminding him of his purpose here and making him wonder about the results of failure should that purpose be discovered.

The Jennings-Bankhurst mission had a simple, overwhelming objective. It was his purpose to ensure that objective was not achieved.

Marillian leant against the load-lifter's deck rail and watched the water ripple past. He wondered what alien toxins drifted beneath the dazzling surface. As was becoming commonplace throughout Earth, the war had brought an end to the centuries of internal struggle. For many generations Somalia had been torn by internal conflict between neighbouring clans, as well as by the imposition of a supposedly unifying government by outside agencies such as the USA and, after that was lost, the UN. By the time the clans had decided it would be better to unite against a common enemy rather than use the greater war as an excuse to continue their own internal conflict, a direct hit from orbit had not only rendered the decision irrelevant but also resolved all the remaining clan-warfare for good – by effectively rendering all parties concerned bio-hybrid – and therefore threatened most directly by the agencies which had until then tried hardest to help and support them.

Two decades later Kenya and Somalia were both still sites

of massive bio-infestation – mutations were spreading south across the equator, towards Tanzania as well as, more slowly, north across the Ethiopian Plateau. Nairobi was gone, inundated by hybrid jungle. Adis Ababa, once with a population of more than five hundred thousand, was now home to an ever-shifting population of hybrid humans and a sanitizing force of the Russian Conglomerate Military Red Cross intent on purification of local areas. It had cost the Museum of Natural History in London most of its public display rights advances to bribe the Military to give safe passage to the expedition. It was a huge risk – but as Jennings-Bankhurst had said, if it paid off, it would do so in some considerable style.

Henry Jennings-Bankhurst joined Marillian at the rail. Strands of silver hair rippled in the alpine air, a marked contrast to Marillian's own tightly bound, jet black topknot. Jennings-Bankhurst stood with a stoop and walked with a limp, the former due to an age far in excess of the biblical norm and the latter acquired through a 'disagreement' with a hungry hippo along the Congo some years before. Marillian studied the reddened skin of hands and face, the tiny broken capillaries in the cheeks and pouches of skin around the piercing eyes, and wondered what he himself would look like if he survived the forty-odd years necessary to reach his mentor's age.

Jennings-Bankhurst gazed out at the expanse of water, eyes sliding across the horizon, from sky to water and back to sky. The colour was not markedly different; there were no clouds. ' "The jewel of Ethiopia".' His voice hardly carried above the wind.

Marillian smiled to himself. Jennings-Bankhurst was never above an appropriate quote; Aeschylus was a particular favourite. ' "A copper tinted lake that is the jewel of Ethiopia, where the all-pervading sun returns again and again to plunge his immortal form, and finds solace for his weary round in gentle ripples that are but a warm caress." '

Jennings-Bankhurst shivered, and not with the wind.

'They had a way with words in the fifth century.'

Marillian drew in a breath of damp air. 'Do you think we'll find it?'

Jennings-Bankhurst allowed his gaze to move forward, in the direction the load-lifter was travelling, and let his eyes travel the distance to the mass of rock and trees curling up from the dazzling waters. 'Tana Kirkos,' he said gently, his words almost lost in the wind. 'It has to be on Tana Kirkos.'

The island was rich in vegetation, a supersaturated wonderland of smells and noises. Moist, freshly turned loam, sun-baked rock, the scent of tropical flowers and cactus plants and water. Bees and hummingbirds with dragonfly wings alternately blurred and froze, droplets of brighter colour among the earthy richness. A kingfisher dived, sudden death, into the water, to emerge dripping with its next meal wriggling in its beak.

The load-lifter drifted slowly into dock at a wooden jetty and the members of the expedition debarked. Marillian followed Jennings-Bankhurst and the translator, a middle-aged Somali gentleman with incredibly wrinkled skin, a cataract covering one eye and ears that stuck out sideways from his bald head like jug-handles; his name was Ondemwu.

As he stepped down from the dock, leaving the load-lifter pilot to secure the platform, Marillian felt strange. Two and a half hours on the platform moving at the beck and call of the waves made the ground seem dizzyingly steady. He walked slowly from the jetty and then stood quite still upon the beach. Sand and tiny pebbles and shell fragments scrunched as he moved, grinding minutely together at his feet when he stopped.

The monks had seen the expedition while it was still afloat; a number had come to meet them. They stood now some metres distant, silent, cowled figures, faces covered by hoods, bodies swathed in robes that made all gauge of characteristics impossible. Marillian squinted against the sun and considered the figures. Bearing in mind the proximity of the Somali bio-infestations, the monks might all be hybrids under those robes and no one would ever be the wiser. It would be bad luck for them if they were. Especially when the Military Red Cross arrived to sterilize the island.

One of the figures stepped forward; Jennings-Bankhurst matched the movement, Ondemwu at his side. Marillian edged closer as they met on the edge of the sand, close to the tree-line; there the ground was dappled with splashes of sunlight and drifting shadows from the palm leaves.

Looking directly at the monk, Jennings-Bankhurst said, 'Greetings.'

Ondemwu's translation was much more elaborate than the single word.

The monk uttered some words in response.

Ondemwu said, 'The Brother Yariam welcomes us to Debra Makeda.'

Marillian looked up sharply at the sound of the name. Jennings-Bankhurst seemed to have been electrified. His hair was standing straight out on end and a glow filled his eyes. He pointed a shaking finger, trying unsuccessfully to conceal his eagerness as he said, 'Debra Makeda? Did I hear you correctly? Debra Makeda? Not Tana Kirkos? The Queen of Sheba's Mountain?' Jennings-Bankhurst waved a hand impatiently at Ondemwu, who translated for him.

The monk replied in broken Amharic. The words *Debra Makeda* were unmistakable.

Jennings-Bankhurst blinked, shuffling agitatedly for a moment. Marillian waited for the explosion of enthusiasm. Behind him came the clunk-and-splash of the load-lifter being secured to the jetty. Overhead, among a storm of wings, came the disturbed cries of tropical birds.

Jennings-Bankhurst eventually said, 'Oh my. It's here. It has to be.' To the patiently waiting Ondemwu he added, 'Ask them. Ask them if it's here.'

Ondemwu spent a few minutes talking to the monk, who then turned away. The other monks also turned their backs.

Jennings-Bankhurst turned eagerly to Ondemwu. 'What? What did he say? Have I offended them? Is it here?'

Ondemwu shrugged. 'They cannot say. They have invited us to meet the Abbot.'

The members of the expedition followed the monks through a neat banana plantation and along a steep, winding track towards the summit of the island. Marillian took off his jacket as they walked – the air still had a bite to it but the exertions were making him sweat. Ahead of them the monks glided, apparently effortlessly, along the track, their feet hidden beneath the all-concealing robes. No man (were they all men? It was impossible to tell) uttered a single word during the journey. With their robes the colour of deep forest and their faces and hands concealed by hoods and sleeves, the monks were like spirits, extrusions of the very land itself, and almost indivisible from it. The birds made more noise than these human chimera. The only footfalls to be heard were those of the expedition members. Even Ondemwu's bare feet were louder upon the track than the monks' sandals.

Marillian walked faster in order to catch up with Jennings-Bankhurst. 'Is this it, do you think? The Queen of Sheba's Mountain?'

The old man shrugged, apparently unaffected by his rapid ascent to more than a hundred metres above the lake. 'Can't you feel it? There is power in this place. How else could the island and its ecological system be so pure when surrounded on three sides by such hostile bio-infestations?'

Marillian folded his jacket into its purse and slipped the purse into his pocket. 'I have no answer.'

Jennings-Bankhurst allowed his wrinkled skull to drift into a nod. 'A good place to begin.'

A short while later they passed the first of a number of low, round buildings covered with thatched roofs. The monks must live here, Marillian thought, though there were none in sight at present. Perhaps they were all out working. Or praying. Whatever it was that monks did on a tiny island in the middle of nowhere like this.

They moved on, passing beneath an arch set into a high stone wall. The arch opened on to a large, grassy clearing in the centre of which stood the Church of Kirkos. This was a long rectangular structure, curved at each end, made of stone blocks. The roof was of thatch-covered timbers. A wooden walkway completely surrounded the building.

Jennings-Bankhurst said quietly, anticipating Marillian's comment, 'It doesn't look that old, does it? Then again, there have probably been churches on this site for more than fifteen hundred years.'

Yariam led them round the building. Here the clearing rose to a high point on the cliff edge near the summit of the island, overlooking Lake Tana. Here Marillian could see a hooded figure moving near three rock pillars which, even from here, were clearly artificially worked. The robes did not conceal how tall and thin the figure was. Yariam held back now, allowing Jennings-Bankhurst to make his way forward towards the figure. Marillian followed, with Ondemwu. The expedition leader leant in close to Marillian and whispered, 'Look at those monoliths, the way they are cut. They are old. The Axumite period. I'm sure of it. Perhaps older.'

Marillian absorbed the words. If Jennings-Bankhurst was correct, the stones indicated they were another step closer to the expedition's objective.

They slowly approached the figure, who remained with his back to them. He was making gestures with his hands, flinging droplets of moisture from a shallow bowl into declivities in the upper surfaces of the stone pillars. As Marillian watched he dipped the forefinger of his right hand into the bowl, swept the hand above his head and commenced a new up-and-down motion.

Jennings-Bankhurst's voice was an excited whisper. 'Look at that! "And the priest shall dip his finger in the blood, and sprinkle the blood seven times before the Lord, before the veil of the sanctuary." ' The old man was almost quivering with excitement. 'The Book of Leviticus. Chapter Five. "And he shall sprinkle the blood of the sin offering upon the side of the altar, and the rest of the blood shall be wrung out at the bottom of the altar." Look. He's doing it exactly as it was written in the Old Testament! The blood was scattered this way over the stones and over the tent containing the Ark of the Covenant! It's here, Marillian. I know it's here!'

Marillian found himself agreeing inwardly. Jennings-Bankhurst was right, he was sure of it, as sure as the old man was that his life's dream was here on the island. It was a shame; Marillian had come to like the archaeologist; more than that, to respect his unswerving diligence in rooting out his objective from its hiding place in history. It was simply unfortunate for Jennings-Bankhurst that the Ark was not something his Chapter wanted to be found.

At Jennings-Bankhurst's excited words, the figure they were watching set down his bowl and turned to face them, sweeping aside his cowl in a single gesture with damp fingers. The face that greeted them was ageless despite being wrinkled, scarred and bleached by exposure to the sun and the elements. Twin bunches of short, translucent tentacles writhed like anemones where his eyes should have been. They changed colour in the sunlight as he looked at Marillian. Straight at him.

As if it were a signal, Yariam copied the gesture, revealing his own, much younger face, containing similar tentacles.

The figure spoke, his voice deep, almost sepulchral.

Ondemwu said, 'The Abbot Menghist Fisseha greets us.'

'Ask him. About the Ark. Ask him if it is here. Ask him if we can see it.' Jennings-Bankhurst's voice was an eager blur of words.

Ondemwu spoke to the Abbot in rapid Amharic. Then the Abbot turned to Jennings-Bankhurst and held out his hand. The skin colour shifted much the same as did the tentacles at his eye-sockets. Closer inspection showed the skin to be covered with a thin layer of hair-fine cilia. Jennings-

Bankhurst stepped forward, hand extended to clasp that of the monk who, surprisingly, made no matching move.

The expedition leader looked in puzzlement at Ondemwu, who said, 'It is not a greeting. He wants money. As much as you can afford, I suspect.'

The Abbot claimed money for candles, incense, tools, insect repellent and electronic components to repair a solar-power array whose main dish had been damaged during a recent storm.

Marillian stopped Jennings-Bankhurst as he prepared to negotiate a fee for the story of the Ark. 'They are old men, Henry. Hybrids. Who knows what damage has been done to their minds already. How do we know that they will speak the truth?'

The expedition leader impatiently shrugged off the younger man's concern. 'You saw as well as I the Abbot's actions at the altar stones. In the Mishna there is also a record of a similar ceremony. In the tractate known as Yoma there are detailed descriptions of the sacrificial rituals carried out by the High Priest within Solomon's Temple in front of the curtain that shielded the Ark of the Covenant from the gaze of the laity.'

Marillian watched as Jennings-Bankhurst transferred a large sum from his own account to the Abbot's credit-chip. The Abbot shook his head, uttered a complex mouthful of Amharic. Ondemwu said, 'I suggest you pay him more.'

Another sum changed accounts; another shake of the head, together with a single word in Amharic, which Ondemwu had no need to translate.

More.

Jennings-Bankhurst sighed, detached his credit-chip and handed it to the Abbot who, after checking the account rating, smiled for the first time, revealing that his yellowed teeth all pointed in different directions, as if trying desperately to escape his cavernous mouth. The smile added nothing to the wrinkled ageless quality of his face; if anything Marillian felt it imbued the man with an even more surreal, almost sinister, quality.

The Abbot nodded, his tentacles swaying gently in the wind blowing across the cliff. Behind him, a bright flash of colour against the white sky, a kingfisher folded its wings and dropped silently towards the water. Seeing this, Marillian wondered how long it would be before he would have to kill someone.

The Abbot spoke. Ondemwu said, 'The Abbot invites you to the church.'

The Abbot directed the expedition members to precede him to a room which served from appearances as a kitchen. Blackened pots and pans were distributed unevenly around the room, together with other implements. The centre was dominated by a large programmable oven, its controls spattered with grease and dust. The Abbot produced chairs and the expedition members sat down. Marillian tried not to wrinkle his nose; the kitchen stank of the preparation of ancient food.

There, among the paraphernalia of day-to-day living on the island, Jennings-Bankhurst asked the questions his money had bought answers to, and listened intently to the answers, as translated by Ondemwu.

Nearly three thousand years previously the Ark of the Covenant had vanished from the Temple of Solomon, amidst a cloud of mystery. Some said the Ark had been looted by soldiers of warring factions; others claimed the Ark had simply decided to leave of its own accord, or by the will of God. Marillian listened as, in sepulchral tones, the Abbot claimed that Solomon's son, the Emperor Menelik I, had stolen the Ark and brought it out of Israel and into Egypt, from Jerusalem to Gaza, from there across the Sinai Peninsula to Egypt, then up the Nile to Ethiopia, where he had hidden it on Debra Makeda – or Tana Kirkos as it was now known.

Jennings-Bankhurst interrupted with another question.

'According to your dates the Ark was brought here four centuries before the birth of Christ.'

'Yes,' Ondemwu answered for the Abbot.

'You do know that 400 BC was a long time after Solomon's death – five centuries in fact. And yet you claim Menelik was Solomon's son?'

'Yes.' The word was identical; needed no translation.

'How do you explain the discrepancy?'

The Abbot spoke again, this time in broken English. 'I explain nothing. I have told you the tradition as it is recorded in our holy book and in our memory.'

There was a long silence. 'May we see this book?'

'You may see the book – but not the pages concerning the Ark. They were removed.'

'I don't follow.'

The Abbot sighed and slipped back into Amharic. Ondemwu said, 'About five hundred years ago a woman came to the island asking to see the book. She cut some pages from the book and took them with her. They were the pages in which the story of the Ark was told.'

Jennings-Bankhurst was almost frantic. 'She took the pages? Was she Ethiopian? European? Why did she take the pages?'

The Abbot spoke. Ondemwu said, 'She was white. A white woman. But not from Earth. Nobody knows why she took the pages.'

'But the Ark. That is still here, right? We can see it, can't we?'

A long silence.

'I have no more money.'

The Abbot listened to Ondemwu's translation and then spoke. Ondemwu said, 'In AD 959 Queen Gudit overthrew the Solomaic dynasty. Gudit was a devil, burning many churches in Tigray and other regions of Ethiopia. The Abbot's forefathers were afraid she would capture the Ark, so they took it from the island.'

'Where is it?' Jennings-Bankhurst's voice held more than a hint of desperation.

The Abbot spoke; Ondemwu said, 'The Ark is not here. It was taken to Axum more than fifteen hundred years ago. If you seek the Ark you should seek it there.' The Abbot spoke again. 'The Abbot suggests you contact the Church of St Mary of Zion, where the main records are kept.'

Jennings-Bankhurst stood, agitated, practically tearing out his hair as he paced furiously across the kitchen. 'No. This cannot be. Not Axum. Does he know?' – this last comment directed at Ondemwu and Marillian – 'Does he know about the infestation? About the sterilization? The Military Red Cross?'

The Abbot's expression indicated clearly that he did not understand.

Jennings-Bankhurst took hold of the Abbot and almost lifted him from his seat. 'The town is infested with infectious hybrid bioforms. The Military Red Cross are here to rescue and purify. They're going to nuke Axum the day after tomorrow! If the Ark is there it will be destroyed, and neither you nor I nor St Mary of blasted Zion will make any difference whatsoever!'

The Abbot struck aside Jennings-Bankhurst's clutching hands and regained his balance. Marillian had no difficulty interpreting the angry glare even though it came through organs other than eyes. Neither man was able to sustain that look for long. The archaeologist was first to drop his eyes in shame at the way he had treated his host. Marillian hesitated long enough to see his mentor humbled and then followed suit. His gaze came down the length of the Abbot's face, his high cheekbones with their writhing shadows, the sharp nose, the angular jaw and chin . . . and lower . . . to the neck . . . the chest . . . to the glint of light there.

Marillian looked closer; he saw a medallion dangling from a leather string, one disturbed by sudden movement from its usual position of concealment. The medallion was old beyond thought, battered, inscribed with a design partly erased by time, but wholly familiar to Marillian from his father's study in London. It seemed that the past of his

Chapter was catching up with him. The design of the inscription was of two knights riding a single horse.

The Seal.

The Abbot Menghist Fisseha wore the Seal of the Knights Templar.

3

ARGINY: 2595

It was at least a hundred kilometres to Arginy. At an average rate of progress of ten kilometres per day, it was clear the journey would be a slow one.

The expedition started out in two explorer class land-rovers, designed and built some years previously by Françoise for the National Tourist Board Rescue Service. Sara and Bernice manned the first rover while Marillian drove the second along with the equipment. The rovers were not large, for large vehicles would have become tangled within the first hundred metres of jungle. Instead the rovers were streamlined, the smooth bodies charged with anti-static fields which repelled the tangling, sometimes intelligently motivated undergrowth. There were no wheels; instead the vehicles hovered on a powerful cushion of air.

Patience opted to run beside the vehicles, moving back and forth at her own speed, hunting, exploring, gauging, assessing, sometimes playing with the trash blasted aside by the vehicles' lifters. At least once per day something would attack her and then the rovers would stop so the crews could load their next meal into the stasis block. At mealtimes, and whilst pitching camp at night, Bernice continued to teach Patience the subtleties of sign language. Patience had picked up the basics within a few weeks of being decanted in London, but the more sophisticated gestures were proving a little difficult to articulate. For her own part, Bernice had become passingly familiar with a range of barks, whistles, grunts, hisses and scents, although she was quite unable to reproduce any of them – at least not and feel like anything other than a complete idiot.

Patience was proving to be quite fascinating. Only once before had Bernice encountered dinosauria of terrestrial origin. There was something about them that was different from the many other life forms she had encountered on alien worlds. It was something she couldn't quite put her finger on. A feeling of *connection* almost, as if . . . well, as if she had more in common with this four-hundred-pound bundle of muscle, claw and brain than she had even with some people. She wondered whether it was the fact of Patience's intelligence which drew them closer. Maybe the sympathy of another soul who was essentially little more than a stranger in a strange land. Then again maybe it was nothing of the kind – maybe it was sheer scientific fascination. Patience was the nearest thing anyone would ever see to a real dinosaur. Here was a chance to see evolution in operation; the laws of chance and mutation. Did the dinosaurs die out because they couldn't compete with more intelligent creatures? Were they themselves in fact the more intelligent creatures? How did they communicate? Build? Run their society? Were they nomads? Single entities with no social cohesion? Did they have extended families as had been extensively theorized about their animal relatives?

So many questions. All she got in answer were barks and whistles; if she was lucky, the occasional scent.

Sara Beaujeu led the expedition with the skill of a natural-born explorer. A small woman with a dusting of blonde hair and Daniel's dark green eyes, she was not much given to smiling. She was deft, decisive and considerably more than passingly familiar with the terrain and life forms. When the rovers broke down it was Sara who fixed them, unclogging the lift filters or using Patience's strength to straighten a bent loudspeaker mounting. It was she who vetted Patience's kills for food value and chose the most appropriate music with which to beat back the inevitable snakevines. When the expedition inadvertently strayed into giraffe territory it was Sara who calmly gunned down the five winged hybrids who chose to attack. The only real surprise – as far as Bernice was concerned anyway – was that Sara elected not to wear a hat or carry a bullwhip.

Nor did her conversation consist of laconic Hollywood one-liners. In fact she did not speak much beyond issuing instructions to Bernice or Marillian on a moment-by-moment basis. In the moments when she thought of it at all, Bernice could not decide whether Sara was being rude, enigmatic or simply laying the foundation for a future conversation. It seemed crazy that after having admitted that she had sent the Templar journal to Bernice, she now chose to say not just nothing about it but almost nothing at all.

Bernice wondered briefly on this as she erected the perimeter sound system around the tents as they set up camp on the fourth night. She loaded a thrashmetal disc into the player and tested the motion sensors. Perfect. The chorus of 'Rip Yo' Head' would serve not only as a deterrent to the vegetation but also as an alarm to match the most strident security system.

She was about to set the next post when a sound behind made her turn.

'I'm not sure I like your choice in music.'

Bernice sighed. 'Marillian. Let's hope the weeds agree, eh?'

'When I was a boy, Father fitted the very first sound system at Kew. The gardeners thought he was balmy; the palms loved it. Especially classical. They particularly liked Sibelius's Third Symphony. They said it reminded them of being in a storm.'

Bernice grinned. 'The palms said this?'

'Yes.'

'To your father?'

'Oh yes.'

'You're teasing me.'

'Only because I like the way your cheeks dimple when you smile.'

'Oh good. I was starting to think you were going to wax lyrical about the negative psychology associated with the confrontational qualities of thrashmetal music as used as a deterrent.'

'Wouldn't dream of it.'

'Good.' An uncomfortable moment came and went. 'You want to know about the Masons, don't you?'

Marillian shrugged, turned away to face the jungle surrounding the clearing in which they were camped. Bernice followed his gaze, seeing for the first time the way the claret sunlight lingered on restlessly shifting vegetation, trying not to react to the various animal cries from the interior – some of which were too human for comfort. 'Do you blame me? It's been weeks and you haven't said a word.'

'Is there any reason I should?'

'I would have thought simple gratitude would have –'

'*I am grateful!*' Bernice caught her breath, allowing her sudden anger to subside. 'I'm sorry. I am. But you should know that what happened to me back there in Scotland was . . .' – *Something moved at her hands; a hammer blow; a silent shriek of pain* – '. . . intensely . . .' – *More blows fell. Her hands! What were they doing to her* – '. . . personal.' Marillian waited. Bernice said, 'I'm not sure I could talk about . . .' – *the awful violation of freezing metal piercing her side* – '. . . even if I did understand it.' A hesitation. 'I can't even work out if it was real or not. How much of it was down to the drugs they gave me.'

'Benny, those drugs they gave you caused your heart to stop beating for more than fifty seconds. You're lucky to be alive.' Marillian pinched the bridge of his nose. He sighed. Frustration. Impatience. When he spoke his voice held more than a little anger. 'You're stupid if you don't talk about it.'

Bernice felt herself responding to his arrogance with anger of her own. 'Why don't *you* talk about it? You're quick to ask me what happened but you certainly never explained how you came to find me there. You never told me anything about what happened when you rescued me. Did you? How did you even know I was there? How come you waited so long before reviving me?'

'As if I had a choice. As if I stood there thinking, "Oh well, I suppose she's been dead long enough – I'll just zap her with some adrenaline and atropine and perform open heart massage if required?" ' Marillian looked at the branches of a nearby tree. Several monkey skeletons were clutched in its curling tentacles. After a few minutes it was clear he was not going to provide her with a more precise response.

'You see? How can I be honest with you if you won't be honest with me?'

'There are things . . . there are things it's dangerous to know.'

'Oh crap! Now you sound like Zayad in Egypt – and you shot him!'

Marillian's face twisted, as if with a painful memory. 'You have to tell me what you saw at the initiation ceremony.' Another hesitation, then, more calmly, 'You know it's always for the best to talk about these things. About things that scare us.'

'And I will.' *Take a breath. Hold it. Try to erase the vision of yourself being crucified; try to forget everything you said, everything they told you, everything you know. Try to forget your fear of the truth, or even your fear of dying.* 'But I'll do it in my own time, OK?'

'But I'm not sure that you –'

'*And I'm not sure it's your place to be sure about anything to do with me!*'

The expression on his face was absolutely indecipherable. 'I'm only asking because I –'

'Don't say it. I married you because an absurd law denied me an alternative. But don't think that because I obeyed that law I subscribe to it.' Bernice tried to catch her breath, failed, then said, 'And don't for one minute make any assumptions about my feelings for you because you'll only hurt yourself if you do.'

Marillian was silent.

Bernice bit her lip until she tasted blood.

Of course I don't love you, don't ask me for that. We hardly know each other. You're interesting. I like you. I don't know what might happen between us. But don't push it or you'll push me away. Just wait. Be patient. Take me on my own terms. Do that and . . . who knows? Maybe it will grow into the love you want.

Bernice found she was crying; she angrily wiped her face on her sleeve. She turned. 'Look. I have to place the last sensor post. We can talk about this some other . . .' She stopped. He was already gone. No – not gone . . . *fallen.*

He had fallen over. Why –

Bernice felt something pluck at her neck. Insect-hybrids? The motion sensors should have . . . She swayed dizzily, felt a sudden rush of heat through her body, and lifted her hand to her neck. The heat turned to cold, freezing cold. Her throat hurt, she couldn't swallow. She managed to lift the thing she plucked from her neck into view. Her arm seemed a long way away. She struggled to draw breath. She struggled to bring her hand closer so she could see . . . that the . . . thing she held was black; a fluff of wings, the needle-shard of . . . of . . . no . . . not wings . . . too fluffy . . . not an insect . . . a . . .

dart

it was a

dart someone had

shot her with a

4

ETHIOPIA: 2575

In Axum the people were rooted in the soil, growing upwards exultantly towards the merciless sun. They did not grow silently. Marillian heard the sound from a distance of nearly a kilometre, a breathless mixture of moans and mutterings blended by distance and the wind echoing playfully from canyon walls. They sounded like excited children playing in distant rooms of an old empty house. It was unnerving, to say the least.

Jennings-Bankhurst had spent almost the entire twenty hours since their return from Lake Tana on a satellite uplink to the Minister for the Interior and, with the aid of polite anger and tactical blackmail information supplied by his own sources, had finally managed to secure a permit to spend six hours immediately prior to the final sterilization within the city limits. Jennings-Bankhurst was overjoyed when the appropriate passes, permissions and visas were downloaded into his palmtop. What he did not realize, however, was that in practical terms all this documentation actually amounted to was permission to find a border guard who would accept a bribe and allow them to borrow his hover-jeep.

Fortunately – or perhaps unfortunately – credit was not a problem for Jennings-Bankhurst.

Now the hover-jeep in question was parked a kilometre from the town centre, while Jennings-Bankhurst, Marillian and Ondemwu sprayed themselves with aerosol prophylactic to provide limited resistance to any airborne infections. That done, the journey continued.

As they approached the town Jennings-Bankhurst was silent, overwhelmed perhaps by the enormity of the changes wrought here by the war. It was one thing to read about them, or see simularities in a museum; it was another thing entirely to move among those changes, to gain intimate knowledge of how they affected real, living things.

The noise from the people-trees was overwhelming, not because of its volume or its pain – there was no recognizable emotional content, nor words for that matter – but simply because the sound was made up of a chorus of wind-blown human voices, uttering continuous noise, articulating what little human feeling remained as a coda to the symphony: the expression of feelings and emotions no human being had ever experienced before.

'Is that all they do?' Marillian found himself whispering. 'Just . . . whisper and mutter like that? Nothing else?'

Ondemwu nodded sagely. 'They are trees more than people now. Alien more than human. What should you expect?'

Marillian drove on in silence.

The people-trees grew denser as they approached the town centre. As yet few of them were burning.

The Church of St Mary of Zion comprised two and a half buildings in a city which – architecturally at least – had changed little over the last five hundred years. In fact there were two and a half churches. Both intact buildings were old though one clearly much older. The more recent building, which had a domed roof and a bell tower in the shape of an obelisk, topped now by an uplink transmitter, had been built by Haile Selassie more than five hundred years before. The other, a rectangular building of dressed stone with castle-like crenellations and turrets, dated back to the mid seventeenth century and was the work of Emperor Fasilidas. The church seemed almost to symbolize Ethiopia, embodying as it did the blurred distinctions between the military and the clergy. Marillian studied the building, backed by the sighing branches of the people-trees, and wondered aloud at the apparent coincidence of repeated history. He allowed his gaze to move across to the nearby ruins, which in effect were little more than deeply entrenched foundations. Consulting his palmtop, Marillian found these were the remains of the original Church of St Mary of Zion, built in the fourth century AD at the time of the conversion of the Axumite kingdom to Christianity and burnt to the ground in 1535 by the Muslim invader Ahmed Gragn, whose forces were at the time threatening the complete extinction of Ethiopian Christendom.

By this time, afternoon was wearing on into evening. It was growing dark and a chill was spreading across the highlands. Beyond the church Axum spread out in whispering stillness; a quiet infested only by the sharp demands of the Red Cross Military as they worked methodically from building to building, tree to tree, trying to ascertain whether any part of the population was capable of determining the manner of their own death. To give the Red Cross their due they were at least trying to find out if anyone could be saved. From the tone of their voices and radio messages they weren't optimistic.

Marillian looked round as shuffling footsteps sounded. A figure approached. A monk. He was stooped, leaning on a prayer stick and he shuffled forward out of the shadows of the church. He spoke in Tigrigna, the local language. Ondemwu translated. 'He asks if you have come to join the congregation.'

'The congregation?' Marillian peered closer. The monk had stopped a short distance away and was leaning heavily on his prayer stick. There was something peculiar about his body, the way he stood, a hunched back perhaps, or . . . no . . . Marillian saw that what he had assumed to be a prayer stick was in fact the monk's arm.

Ondemwu said, 'The least sick are inside the church. He says they are there for protection.'

'From the Red Cross?'

'Yes.'

Marillian said, 'Surely he must know there is no protection from the Red Cross.'

The monk inched forward another step as Ondemwu translated. Now Marillian could make out that his body was warped in peculiar ways beneath his habit. The monk spoke. Ondemwu said, 'He observes you are not locals and asks from where you come. Are you Christian? Why are you here?'

'We're not from the Military. We're here to . . .' Marillian hesitated. To help? That was laughable. 'Ask him how his people will be protected.'

'By the Will and Word of God.'

Marillian listened to the translation and frowned. 'Prayers will not save you from napalm and atomics.'

The monk tipped his head to one side and Marillian could see that a spray of bark was forming across his face beneath the hood, in which eyes moved with lively intelligence. He reached out with one hand, moving suddenly to grasp Marillian's. His fingers were strong, the skin coarse and dry like wrinkled paper. The eyes sparkled in the sunset. He spoke; Ondemwu said, 'The people under my care will be protected by the Will and the Word of God.'

Jennings-Bankhurst now approached. Marillian could sense a familiar excitement emanating from him, an undeniable force. 'I have heard the Ark of the Covenant is kept here. I have heard you are its guardian and protector. I have heard this from the Abbot Menghist Fisseha on Tana Kirkos.'

Ondemwu translated. In reply the monk let go of Marillian's hand. 'The Light will come. Tana Kirkos will be gone. Axum will be gone. The Simien Mountains will be gone. Only the people will survive, protected by the Word of God.' Jennings-Bankhurst began to speak again but the monk was already talking. Ondemwu said, 'These things are true.'

Jennings-Bankhurst said softly, 'People in other countries say they are lies.'

'People may say what they wish. The truth will not change for them.'

'Then it is here. The Ark.'

'It is.'

'And that is what will protect your people from the Red Cross, the atomics?'

'It is.'

'May we see it?'

'No.'

'Why not?'

'Because you are impure.'

'If we purify ourselves?'

'No.'

'Why not?' This time Jennings-Bankhurst's voice was a shout.

'Because there is turmoil in the land. The conflict comes closer every day. And even in times of peace you would not be able to see it. It is my responsibility to wrap it entirely in thick cloths at all times.'

'Why?'

It was a simple enough question; the answer was dumb-founding. 'To protect the people from sight of it.'

There was a long silence, during which the sun slipped below the horizon. The sky above was clear and bright with stars. The monk spoke; Ondemwu said, 'If you wish to be purified then you too may be protected by the Ark. Do you wish it?'

Ondemwu hesitated. Jennings-Bankhurst did not: 'We do.'

'All of you?'

'All of us.'

'Then enter.'

The monk turned and limped heavily towards the church.

5

ARGINY: 2595

Bernice lay near death and watched events unfold with perfect clarity. She didn't feel drugged. She didn't feel like she was dying. But she couldn't move. Sooner or later the paralysis would close about her chest and then she would simply stop breathing. And die.

She waited for panic. It did not come. Was that due to the drug? A side effect designed to quell any last minute flight-or-fight responses which might have saved her? Maybe; unlikely though: she was still cogent enough to ask questions, even if she was unable to articulate them.

All she could do now was think – and watch.

Perhaps it was her misfortune that she couldn't move her eyes or close them. She had to watch it all.

The first thing that happened was that she fell; her line of sight took in the camp and part of the perimeter – it was only partly obscured by Marillian's arm. The camp was motionless. Sara slumped half in and half out of the nearest rover. Patience was also present, kicking feebly beside the second rover. Bernice became aware that parts of the scene were blurred. The parts nearest to her. Marillian's arm was a dark blur before her. Bernice realized why. She had been looking at Sara and Patience – and just as she was unable to move her eyes she was now equally unable to change focus. That was unfortunate because something was moving along the ground at the very edge of her vision. Something that undulated with infinite patience across the ground towards her face. A tiger-willow root? A snakevine?

At the same moment the perimeter alarms cut in and thrashmetal blasted out into the jungle. Bernice jumped – or rather wanted to jump; her body remained unmoving.

A shadow moved at the edge of her vision. Something poked her leg, hard enough for her to cry out. She didn't of course.

The shadow stepped over her, and turned into a pair of legs. Two more pairs joined the first. Men. Two of them. And a woman. She couldn't see or focus on them this close. They moved warily towards the rovers. Sara was still motionless. Patience had stopped kicking now.

One of the figures took a blowpipe from a pocket and blew another dart into the raptor's flank. Patience didn't move. Bernice heard words echoing as if from a long distance through muddy water. She couldn't make them out. Maybe it was laughter.

The creeping blur had moved even closer to her face. She thought she could detect the movement of . . . fingers? Rootlets? Cilia? She shuddered; but remained perfectly motionless.

One of the figures stood over Marillian, another stood beside Sara. Both drew knives.

Murderers.

But why weren't they going to kill her?

Maybe they were. Maybe there was someone standing over her even now, out of her line of sight, with a knife, waiting for the order to open her throat. Maybe they were waiting for the drugs to finish the job. Maybe they wanted her alive. Maybe –

A blur of motion, feathers bright on jungle dark.

Patience.

Shout of alarm, stilled by the sound of splitting flesh.

The killer standing beside Sara fell, mouth and stomach gaping. The undergrowth moved closer interestedly.

Screams. Claws. Teeth. Screams.

The second figure, the one beside Marillian, had time to straighten, to pull a gun, to fire one wild shot. The gun-arm fell close to Bernice, forearm severed at the elbow, trailing blood and strips of muscle, finger still convulsively jerking at the trigger, pumping rounds wildly into the jungle until the gun clicked empty.

Now there was movement near by. She felt someone grab her hair, jerk her head upwards. Cold steel touched her neck.

More movement, too fast and close for her to follow. Another scream. Something fell across Marillian. Her face slammed back into the ground. A handspan from the creeping shadow which had been stalking her. The shadow reared; she saw blotches of darkness which might have been open mouths. Then a clawed foot stamped hard in front of her, grinding – whatever it was – into the ground before lifting and throwing it away.

Bernice found she was terrified. She tried to gasp. Nothing. Now her breath was coming in short gasps. Her chest felt curiously numb. The paralysis had reached her lungs. It would be a matter of moments now, and then, despite Patience's actions, she would die.

She waited. Her view had changed now. She could see less. She felt claws at her body, turning her, positioning her so she could see. Patience growled and signed to her. *Poison. How mend?*

Bernice stared straight ahead at the nearest of the attackers. He was wearing a pouch. Perhaps there was antitoxin in it. She tried to move, to nod or blink – nothing. Total paralysis.

Patience was growling even louder now, a sound Bernice could hear above the thrashmetal perimeter defence. The raptor stalked the clearing, back and forth, poking Bernice, Sara, Marillian. Nothing. No response from any of them. What was she to do?

Poison. How mend? Poison! How mend?

Patience stopped. One of the killers was alive. Patience

bent slowly over the woman. Bernice could see the raptor's breath ruffling the woman's hair. Patience opened her mouth. The woman saw the teeth and moaned; she struggled to push herself away. Her arm was shredded and she fell to the ground. Patience leant even closer, her clawed feet upon the woman's chest and stomach, instinctively moving to the place of maximum vulnerability. Bernice tried to close her eyes. No luck. The raptor was gearing herself to disembowel the woman.

The claws flexed. The woman screamed. The teeth snapped shut –

– and Patience stepped delicately away, leaving the woman still alive.

Patience waited, head cocked, studying the fallen human, then lowered her head and nudged something on the ground near by. The blowpipe. Patience had found the –

Then the raptor was moving again, plucking one of the darts from her own flank with clawed digits, clumsily holding the dart towards the woman, then plunging it into her shoulder. The woman screamed again and tried to move, her struggles noticeably weaker this time. Patience stood back and waited, head cocked, crest-feathers fluffed with anticipation. The woman moaned and yanked the dart from her shoulder; she held it up so she could see the poison still smearing its tip. She slumped back on to the ground.

Patience studied her for a moment longer, then bit through the pouch strap on the dead killer and nudged the pouch towards the woman. The woman grabbed at the pouch, opened it one-handed, and clumsily extracted a loaded syringe.

Antitoxin.

Patience watched as the woman injected herself. Then she stepped closer, took the syringe away from the woman and managed to stick it clumsily into Bernice's leg.

Two hours later she managed to sit up; she was ravenous, thirsty, her body aching from the effects of the toxin. Marillian was already standing, Sara beginning to stir. Bodymass made a difference sometimes, it seemed. The killer was still alive, though delirious from the wounds Patience inflicted. Patience was prowling the perimeter.

Marillian fished in the rover for a bottle of water and they drank, then moved Sara into a more comfortable position so that she could recover properly. Then, waving aside Marillian's questions, Bernice crouched clumsily beside the killer.

'Why?'

'To . . . protect . . .' The woman's voice was a whisper. She had lost so much blood it was hard to see how she could still be alive. 'To . . . protect . . . eternity . . .'

'From who? From us? Are you Templars? Are you here with bloody Newton and Kepler? Tell me!'

The woman reached feebly towards her neck. Bernice saw a glint of metal there, a medallion, a familiar seal. She had taken one similar from Zayad when he tried to kill her in Cairo. 'You . . . *are* . . . eternity . . .'

It was as much as Bernice could do not to shake the woman in sheer frustration. 'No! You don't understand! I –'

'. . . protect . . . from . . . GebMoses . . . and –' The woman suddenly jerked. 'No. Not him! Not –!' The woman slumped in death, her eyes wide open. A blurred patch was reflected in them, a shape which moved, which came closer as Bernice turned.

'What did she mean, "You are eternity"?' said Marillian. His voice was hard, gravelly, a by-product of the toxin, his face frozen at the sound of the woman's dying words.

Bernice shook her head.

'You don't know or you won't tell me?'

'You're raking over old coals.' Bernice gently laid the woman to rest. 'We'd better bury them, don't you think?'

They buried the bodies of their attackers – the parts Patience did not breakfast upon – and drove on. Nobody showed the slightest inclination to discuss the incident. Marillian clearly did not approve of Bernice's continued silence, while Sara simply shrugged the attack aside as if it were no more or less than any other surprise the jungle had thrown at them. In a way she was right. Bernice too, tried to put the incident from her mind, though with less success.

During the afternoon of the sixth day of their journey the rovers were attacked by a tiger-willow, a rogue whose blasted limbs indicated that it had been struck by lightning sometime in the past decade, and which was now merely enraged rather than frightened off by their audio defences. Sara got enough warning to burn some of the vines; Patience made a meal of the creature's brainroots. Patience was sick for the whole of the following day but the tiger-willow finally took the hint and ambled erratically back into the jungle. The downside to this attack was that rover two blew a fan when the intake was invaded by the tiger-willow's vines. The rover sank two metres into a bog and they were unable to drag it free. Sara marked the machine with an ownership buoy and sealed it. They moved on, what supplies they could retrieve crammed into the first rover and everyone taking turns to walk.

A week passed without further serious incident. On the evening of the eleventh day of their journey they made camp amidst fog and heavy rain. Bernice and Marillian slept fitfully in the rover, Sara and Patience prowled the campsite. Since the attack Sara had been spending more and more time with the raptor, studying her, learning the sign language which the raptor was by now almost fluent in. Bernice detected a closeness between them, a meeting of, if not minds, then at the very least experiences. She wondered briefly at this, prepared to push any mission-complicating feelings aside, only to find to her surprise that she actually had no opinion.

That night Marillian sat hunched in the driver's seat for two hours, fidgeting and mumbling in his sleep, before finally getting up and leaving the rover. Bernice sighed. She hadn't slept properly for more than a week. God only knew when they would reach the castle. Sara's GPS fix on the geographical location depended solely on the fickle weather – none too good at present – and what little sleep she had managed to get was invariably plagued by dreams that afterwards she had trouble remembering.

The door of the rover irised to allow someone to enter. Bernice recognized the confident movements immediately. Sara. *Great. So much for another good night's sleep.*

Sara got into the driver's seat, stripped off her wet poncho and shoved it into a plastic sack. She shivered, turned the heating up and blasted the driver's compartment with hot air. In the back seat, Bernice sighed and rolled over, trying to ignore the stream of air and get back to sleep. No luck. Well, that was a surprise.

'Too hot for you?' Sara's voice was quiet. Bernice could detect the stress in it. The journey was taking its toll of everyone.

'I've been in worse situations.'

'I meant the heater.'

'Oh. Yeah. A bit.'

A click; the stream of hot air dissipated, leaving her deliciously warm. *Beats a mutant sea-lion any day.*

'What?' Sara again. She must have spoken out loud.

'Nothing.'

'Oh.'

Another silence – just the thud of raindrops the size of golf balls dancing a samba on the rover's canopy.

'Bernice?'

'Yes.'

'Is there anything you want to say to me?'

Bernice sighed and struggled into a sitting position. 'You're very direct.'

'I'm like Mother in that way.'

'Life's too short to mess about with tactful fripperies.' It was a push; Sara did not bite.

'Basically.'

Bernice drew her blanket more tightly around her

shoulders. 'So. Care to tell me what it is you want me to say to you? Only, you know, then I can say it and we can both get some sleep.'

'You're married.'

'Yes.'

'Tell me about Marillian.'

'What do you want to know? He's a bloke. They follow trends. Certain . . . characteristics. You know.'

'Like Daniel?'

Bernice hesitated. 'Yes.' She waited. Sara said nothing. 'Like Daniel.' She waited again; again nothing. 'Look, what do you want me to say? I loved Daniel? I only married Marillian for his museum pass? Both of those things are true. Neither of them really has anything to do with you. And in any case I can't do anything about them now, can I?' Nothing from Sara. *I should shut up now and try to sleep.* 'Why did you send me the Templar journal?'

Sara put her hands on the steering wheel and joggled it absently. Bernice heard fans knocking in the drive system beneath the seats.

'You wanted to be direct. You wanted to talk. Let's talk.'

A push, and this time Sara responded. She lifted her hands to her face, and rubbed tears from her eyes.

Bernice blinked, feeling her own eyes sting; she held back the tears with an effort. She licked her lips, lifted her hand to Sara's shoulder, aborted the movement before making contact. The arm fell back to her side.

Rain drummed on the roof.

Bernice took the Templar journal from her rucksack and placed it on the front seat beside Sara. She tried to imagine what she was thinking, what she was feeling.

Impossible.

'I've tried to remember what it was like,' she said eventually. 'When I lost him. Hearing him cry out as he was carried off into the dark. I –' Her voice caught for a second, then she said, 'To tell you the truth I . . . I'm finding this whole journey difficult. Not because of how clear the memories are but . . . because of how easily they fade.'

Sara burst into tears. She reached down, grabbed the journal, and flung it at Bernice. 'Don't you think I don't know? Are you really that stupid? That's why I sent the journal to you. *I wanted to forget.* To move on. But you came back! You were stupid and you came back, and now both of us have got to go through it all over again!'

Bernice felt her face burn with shame and embarrassment. It was true. Oh God, it was true. How could she have been so stupid? She tried to think of something to say; there was nothing. No words. She wasn't even sure what she felt any more; a terrible mixture of relief and hatred and anger, something she was unable even to name, let alone understand.

She drew the blanket more tightly around herself, feeling she might go mad without its scratchy solidity bound tightly around her. In the front seat, Sara hugged herself and cried openly.

Neither woman moved until dawn, when the sun rose and the fog burnt off to reveal Castle Arginy looming above the tree-line like a circle of broken teeth bared in a sinister grin, upturned to catch the driving rain which poured continuously into its stone-shrouded throat; a puppet master who had played them both for twenty years and who now waited patiently for the final act to be played out among its elusive secrets.

6

Ethiopia: 2575

The interior of the Church of St Mary of Zion resembled a cross between a refugee camp and a greenhouse. There were people – lots of people; some with children, some alone, but all changing, slowly, into forms which were disturbing as much for their familiarity as for their alien qualities. The noise was disturbing too – even frightening. Marillian heard people crying, praying, begging the Lord to spare them punishment for a sin they did not know they had committed. Unlike the people-trees beyond the church, these people had not completed transformation and were clearly terrified of what was happening to them. The monk – whose name they still did not know – limped awkwardly among the congregation, touching his one good hand to the heads of crying children, comforting the adults where he was able. Candles – hundreds of candles lit the interior of the church. The light painted an image of warmth, but brought little comfort to the congregation.

'Whatever we're going to do here, we'd better do it fast,' was Marillian's spoken thought. Ignoring his companion, Jennings-Bankhurst began to ease his way through the congregation towards the monk, now almost out of sight in the candlelit interior of the church. Marillian stopped him with a hand on the older man's arm. 'The prophylactics have a limited life span. Another hour, no more. If we enter the church we may be open to infection. In any case we do not have much time. According to my uplink the atomics are being placed now. Detonation is set for five a.m. tomorrow morning, local time.'

Jennings-Bankhurst turned, his face shining. 'The Ark is a holy relic, the Word of God. It's supposed to be able to inflict cancer, level mountains, stop rivers, lay waste to cities. But it is more than that. Much more. We're talking about the cornerstone of the Jewish faith. The most important religious icon in history. The Ark is that which implements history. History. God. Who is to say that they are not the same thing? If the Ark is there we will know, once and for all, do you see?'

Marillian almost gasped with the simplicity of his sudden realization. 'You're going to stay.'

'How else to test the faith of the laity?'

'We're talking about atomics!'

'Your father would understand. What a pity you do not.' Jennings-Bankhurst stepped away from Marillian and continued towards the church.

'Wait.' Marillian glanced at Ondemwu, then both followed, pushing more urgently between people who seemed unable to accommodate their movements. 'Henry, wait!'

The older man turned, an arm's length from the monk. 'You do not need to stay here. You should go.'

'I can't leave you here. You do not believe.'

'That's not the issue. I will be purified. I will see the glory of the Ark and hear the Word of the Lord with my own eyes and ears.'

'They won't be your eyes and ears if you're infected. You won't see or hear anything – as a human being anyway.'

Jennings-Bankhurst smiled, the old, tired smile of one who has travelled long and who believes the end of his journey is in sight. 'You really should go now. You won't like it here when the prophylactics wear off.'

'Come with us.'

'I don't think so.' The old man sighed; a deep breath of

candle-scented air held and expelled wearily, but also with some joy. 'You see, I find I am compelled to stay.'

'By what? Belief in a religion whose Bible has the laity responsible for the death of the Son of their God?'

'That was a popular theory centuries ago. Things change.'

'How?'

Jennings-Bankhurst smiled again. 'The Timkat ritual takes place every year. We know that. A wooden replica of the Ark – a tabot – is displayed in the streets for the laity, to confirm their faith and purge their sins, albeit symbolically. There have been expeditions all over the world for centuries trying to find the Ark. Even Adolf Hitler. All these years it has been hidden in plain view of anyone who cared to look. Every church under the sun has its own tabot, its own replica. Who could have guessed that this one was the real Ark? Who but us?'

Marillian was on the point of responding when, from beyond the church, came a terrifying sound – the whispered chorus from the people-trees had risen to a choir of screams. The congregation became even more nervous, sighing uneasily, some bursting into tears. Monks moved among them, offering comfort in the form of communion bread and sips of wine.

'They're burning the trees.'

'Why?'

'To protect the atomics? I don't –'

Another blast of noise had the nearby congregation on their feet. A child ran screaming for his mother, an adult moved, knocking another; a wave of motion which had seven people on the ground, including Jennings-Bankhurst. By the time nearby people had pulled the old man to his feet the damage was done – the left side of his face was bruised beneath the protective film and his hand was bleeding, the prophylactic seal there broken. Jennings-Bankhurst stared at his hand wonderingly, then looked up at Marillian. He did not speak.

Marillian sprayed the last of the prophylactic over the old

man's hand. 'We have to go. Now.' His voice was terse, brooking no argument.

'The Ark –'

'– will rest in eternity, as it was always meant to.'

'No! It was not made only to be lost forever in man's fire.'

'I'm not arguing.' Marillian grabbed Jennings-Bankhurst and tried to pull him back through the congregation towards the entrance to the church. The old man was much stronger than he looked, and the pressure of people all around prevented movement.

Jennings-Bankhurst cried out suddenly, wrenching his arm from Marillian's grip, and held it before him. Marillian could see the skin discolouring beneath the prophylactic shield. Infection had set in. Marillian saw a moment of pain in the old man's eyes; then he turned and was forcing his way through the people towards the monk.

From outside the sound of burning and the screams of the people-trees were growing louder. Orange light beat at the windows of the church. Marillian smelt smoke. The people were openly panic-stricken now; it was as much as the monks could do to calm them. There came the sound of smashing wood. Someone had overturned one of the pews.

Marillian turned to Ondemwu. 'Get out. Get the hover-jeep, bring it as close to the entrance as you can. Then stay with it as long as you can.'

Ondemwu nodded slowly. 'And if you do not come?'

Marillian did not reply. Ondemwu turned without another word and began to force his way back through the crowd towards the entrance. Marillian turned to follow Jennings-Bankhurst and the monk. He found them near the altar. Jennings-Bankhurst was on his knees, head bowed while the monk dabbed holy water on his brow. The monk finished the ceremony quickly. As Marillian approached the old man stood. Both looked at Marillian.

The monk spoke; Marillian did not understand the words but the intent was clear. Was Marillian offering himself for purification? Seeing no alternative Marillian knelt before the altar. Outside the church came the sound of an explosion. A lorry? A house? How much ground needed to be cleared to place a few suitcase-sized bombs? Had it got out of control? What if it had? Would the soldiers care?

Marillian felt a hand lifting him to his feet; the ceremony was over.

Jennings-Bankhurst was smiling broadly at him; the skin of his hand now resembled bark more than human flesh.

Marillian felt a scream building inside his head. How long before his own protection failed and he too became infected? How long before the fire reached the church and everyone burnt to death?

The monk turned to the altar, to a bulky shape there, and began to peel away layers of cloth. As he did this he spoke to the congregation, who became instantly silent. Suddenly the church was filled only with the sound of whispered breathing and the voice of the monk, rolling solemnly among the people. Even the crying children seemed to draw enough comfort from the voice to be still.

The monk unwrapped the final layers of cloth. His voice reached a crescendo. The people began to pray. Jennings-Bankhurst stared, transfixed as the last layer of cloth was peeled away.

Marillian remembered the monk's words: ' "to protect the laity from the gaze of the Ark . . ." '

And there it was, an arm's length from him: the most potent symbol of the Christian world.

A wooden box, lacquered, lidded; blackened by time and worn by generations of worshipping hands.

The Ark.

The Symbol of God.

Marillian waited. He waited for the miracle. He waited for the Word of God.

The wall of the church shook, then burst apart; burning timber rained upon the congregation.

Soldiers stood in the gap, Red Cross insignia glowing

upon their helmets, flamethrowers levelled at the interior of the church.

The monk threw up his hands – one human and the other transformed – and his voice thundered above the flames. The congregation were utterly silent. The soldiers moved closer. Jennings-Bankhurst swivelled his head from the monk to the Ark, to the congregation, to the soldiers, a jerky dance of sudden indecision. The soldiers came closer. The monk prayed louder. Now the congregation joined in, a hymn that reached into Marillian's ear and squeezed even as it pushed back the flames for a few seconds longer.

The monk stepped towards the soldiers. His voice carried even above the song of the congregation. Was he offering them salvation? Absolution? Or telling them to get the hell off God's doorstep while the Miracle happened?

It didn't make any difference to the soldiers; they had their own ideas about purifaction.

Flame burst from the blackened nozzles of over-used weapons, engulfing the nearest members of the congregation, engulfing the monk; the church was suddenly alive with capering demons of flame, screaming incendiary supplicants; the Miracle of God was nothing more than death.

Marillian turned quickly back to the altar – then stopped in amazement.

The Ark was –

– was –

It was gone.

Jennings-Bankhurst was running with it towards the rear of the church.

7

ARGINY: 2595

Bernice listened to the rain thunder along the passages beneath the castle as she moved with Patience into the dark, stone-tunnelled labyrinth. Marillian and Sara had stayed with the rover. Each had their reasons; Bernice hadn't asked what they were. Instead she had packed a rucksack with useful items, including the journal and a fresh can of aerosol prophylactic, and then, together with Patience, she had climbed across the crumbling castle walls and into the courtyard.

The ground was overgrown; centuries of growth slick with rain, the ground turning to mud and full of time-slashed stone blocks that waited to turn the ankles of the unwary. Trees pushed out of the walls, splitting them until little remained except piles of rubble. The inner courtyard was little better: more walls were intact, though the roofs had collapsed where the stables and soldiers' quarters had been. The main castle building was still intact, the single crenellated tower defiantly reaching up towards the beaten-metal sky. Windows were dark slits blurred with foliage. Bernice heard eerie movement where once soldiers had loosed arrows. Birds? Snakevines? Vines eating birds? It didn't matter. She had to go in. She had to retread the road that had brought her here so long ago. The road to Daniel. The road to the Finger of John the Baptist. The Templar treasure upon which the past and the future now rested.

If she were to believe what the Masons had told her.

The route into the castle interior had not changed, though there was twenty years' more rubble to negotiate before gaining the stairs which led down to the dungeon levels. She moved warily from hall to hall, passage to passage, careful to avoid loose blocks of stone. Patience moved quickly but no less carefully, picking her way in a series of inquisitive movements from one point of interest to the next, her snout and feathered crest quivering as she examined everything from torch holders rusting in the walls to the rotted remains of furniture.

The stone staircase leading to the dungeons was wet, as was the entire ground floor of the castle, the risers worn and slippery with lichen. The lichen moved, peering at Bernice with tiny, near-human eyes set into elastic stalks, blinking in the beam from her torch as she descended. She ignored the lichen – not an easy task when every step blinded fifty or so eyes.

Patience followed her, snuffling the air, and making the rhythmic *chugging* cough which Bernice had come to learn meant the raptor was curious about something. Her crest was rigid, the feathers along her spine standing out like bright beacons in the darkness. The scarlet mottling at her throat ballooned in time with her staccato breaths. Once she scraped a clawful of lichen from the wall and tasted it. She chewed, considered, swallowed, then found some more. Eyes weeping, she waved a clawful of the stuff at Bernice, and uttered an interrogative bark.

Bernice signed back in the negative; Patience uttered a humorous growl followed by a complex set of snorts and whistles.

'Oh yeah? Let me see you say that at the next spicy-chicken drive-through.'

The labyrinth was as she remembered: infested with rats, snails and overgrown with roots through which they pushed and in which she occasionally became trapped. On these occasions, Patience sliced her free with humorous barks. Patience didn't get caught anywhere being smaller, heavier and generally more powerful.

Half an hour's work brought them to the first of the trap chambers. Bernice remembered this from her earlier visit. The passage widened into a circular chamber whose floor rose in a small hill covered with roots and creeping vegetable debris. *The Mountain of God* – that was how the journal referred to this chamber.

Patience coughed impatiently, then uttered a series of ear-grating screeches.

Bernice frowned. 'I know all about that. Just wait on a bit.' She placed a hand on Patience's shoulder to caution her to stay put, then took out the Templar journal. ' "For with God nothing shall be impossible," ' she read aloud, shining her torch on the yellowed pages. She closed the journal, repeating the words to herself quietly. Then she took from her satchel a second book, one given to her in London. She held the book reverently, inhaled, smelt the aroma of ink and old paper. She opened the book, found a page, hesitated, then drew breath and read, ' "And the Mount of Olives shall be divided in the midst thereof to the east and to the west with a very great opening." ' So saying, Bernice carefully took a step into the chamber. The roots began to move, slithering aside to reveal a hill of stone which split along its longitude, the stone hemispheres rumbling as they moved apart, rotating back and down like opening clamshells into the floor of the chamber. ' "And half the mountain shall be separated to the north and half thereof to the south." ' Another step. The hemispheres split into halves, four quarters of stone now moving, grinding, rumbling aside to leave a clear passage with one entrance and three separate exits. Patience agitated beside her, head moving to and fro, nostrils flared to catch a hint of danger, eyes bright as she fixed her gaze on the moving stone. Bernice signed her to wait, adding aloud, ' "And it shall come to pass in that day that there shall be no light. And in the time of evening there shall be light." '

Bernice took another step. Stars came out above the cloven mountain of stone – or rather tunnels opened through the stone which allowed shafts of dim sunlight to lance down into the chamber. A maze of light. A mountain of stone. '"In that day there shall be one Lord and His name shall be one."' Bernice folded the book away. '"His name shall be *one*." Now listen to me.' She took hold of Patience's arm and signed carefully as she spoke. 'Do not break the light beams. If you do the "mountain" will slam shut and we'll be crushed. Get me?'

Patience barked softly. Bernice let the raptor's arm go and took a step forward. Patience cocked her head quizzically, watching Bernice move carefully between the stones, slipping sideways between the beams of light, ever careful to touch none of them. Once her satchel slipped, but she caught it before it could break a beam. She stood still, wiped sweat from her face, then moved on. Daniel had been much better at this than her. He'd been thinner, more wiry. He seemed to bend around the light. And she'd put on weight during the years between then and now. Another step. Patience was still waiting, gauging Bernice's steps, feathers ruffling as she watched, considering.

Bernice reached the intersection of the quarters. After ten minutes of back-breakingly controlled movement she sighed and stopped for another rest. There was no doubt about it; this was a game for the young – and *fit*.

Bernice tried to ease a cramp building in her calf. A sudden twinge made her yelp. Patience looked up sharply and coughed a warning. Bernice felt warmth on the back of her hand. She looked down. A patch of sunlight was creeping across her fingers. She'd broken the beam. Her breath caught in her throat. *She'd broken the beam.*

Things happened very quickly after that.

Stone gave voice around her, sweeping upwards, deflecting the beams of sunlight as she leapt forward, running as never before, turning sideways as the stone closed on her from four sides, rose to cut off her view of the chamber, of

Patience, to fence her in with swiftly moving beams of light reflected from the polished rock; rock she could now see was stained ochre with ancient blood.

She leapt clear of the hemispheres a second before they slammed shut with an awful concussion, shaking loose rubble from the roof, jerking Bernice to an abrupt, painful halt by trapping the strap of her satchel with a perfect, unbreakable grip, alive because of simple luck and the retarding effect of more than a thousand years of undergrowth.

Bernice shuddered, drawing breath in scalding gasps. Every muscle in her body was screaming.

And where was Patience?

Had she started to move? She couldn't remember. Was she between the stone when it moved? What if –

A gurgling screech cut short all speculation. Bernice jerked her head upwards in time to see Patience finish a leap that took her clear over the mountain to land in the passage some metres in front of Bernice. She skidded to a halt, legs flexing, arms and neck outstretched for balance, claws striking sparks from the stone blocks of the passageway, then she turned and headed back to Bernice uttering a series of demented, delighted barks and snapping her teeth together in a humorous rhythm.

Bernice showed Patience where her satchel was trapped; the raptor cut through the leather with a simple movement of her finger-claw.

Bernice caught her breath and grinned at the raptor.

'Able to leap tall buildings at a single bound, huh? Where'd you hide your cape, buster?' She gathered her wits to lead the way forward and then realized that the way was not familiar, not what she remembered from her time here with Daniel. Somehow she'd got turned around while running from the Mountain of God. She'd left through one of the other exits.

From now on the labyrinth was unknown territory.

Bernice flipped through the Templar journal again, running

her fingers along what she felt were appropriate routes, then they moved off slowly, exploring each passage with torch and eyes before setting foot in it.

There were other traps of course. Her mind blurred with them; a maze of stone and death and old memories. *The Wall of Knives*, *The Well of Spears*, *The Tower of God*. The Journal provided clues and the Bible she carried provided the answers, albeit couched in the most obscure terms. Her respect for De Beaujeu and his fellow Knights grew as each trap was successfully negotiated.

She did not think of Daniel much during this part of the journey. This had the effect of both calming her and making her feel guilty. In a way it was good that they were covering new ground. The distraction caused by thinking of her former lover had nearly killed her before. He'd never been in this part of the labyrinth so it was easier not to link them in her mind. But still, she could not quite shake the last residual images of his face from her memory, no matter what she had told Sara in the jungle during their journey here. It was her fault he died; all she could do was hope not to suffer his fate.

Her memories of Daniel were driven home savagely in the moment when she realized the path ahead was blocked by a stone wall. A wall covered with damp slime. Turning quickly to retrace her steps she discovered a similar wall dropping into place from a slot in the roof of the passage. She screamed at Patience – who sprang forward and slipped underneath the wall in a flurry of feathers a second before it crashed into the floor, separating them and trapping Bernice in a space which, too quickly for comfort, began to flood with riverwater.

She looked around. No way out. Obviously. But if this flood chamber followed form there should be a stone platform and a pile of rocks to trip the release mechanism. OK. There. She'd passed it twice without noticing it. Stupid.

The water was up to her knees, halfway up the block.

She splashed around, trying to find the expected pile of stones. She found a handful, some marked with carved pictograms of birds or animals. Were there enough? Why shouldn't there be? She gathered all she could find, mostly located in niches in the walls or strewn around the floor, gathered armfuls and dumped them on to the stone platform. By now the water had reached her thighs and movement was difficult. And it was cold – near-paralysingly cold.

'Patience! Can you hear me?'

A distant bark.

'Get to the reliquary chamber. The traps will reset! Can you hear me?'

More barking. Inquisitive. *She doesn't understand me.*

Bernice piled all the rocks she could see on to the platform.

'The reliquary chamber!'

Nothing this time. Just the gush of water falling into the chamber, the bone-numbing cold in her legs which was like a scream itself.

Bernice cast about for more stones. There were none. Taking a breath she dived into the waist-high water, now lapping about the top of the stone platform. She managed to find a few stones which had been dislodged from their niches. She retrieved them and dumped them on the platform, gasping from the cold, her breath almost stilled in her frozen chest.

She scraped at the stones, turning them, peering at them, discarding those without pictograms, and those with pictograms beyond the required number. As she worked she imagined Daniel in a similar position twenty years before. Cold, frightened, but excited, confident. They had the key. It was a puzzle, an intellectual stimulation, nothing more. An adventure, maybe. Not real.

How had he felt when the water had covered the platform, then risen towards his face? When he realized the rocks were eroded, the key to the lock of his life was broken? How did he feel when the water reached his chin, when he could no longer try random combinations of rocks because he had to tread water just to breathe? How did he feel as he counted away the centimetres of air between his mouth and the roof of the chamber, hoping against hope the water would stop or drain? How did he feel when, all hope finally gone, cheeks pressed against the unyielding rock, the water finally poured into his mouth to silence his desperate screams for help? To silence her name – the last thing he had called out before the silence had come.

Water slapped her face. *What had she been doing? Stupid!* The water had covered the platform, the current disturbing the rocks. Her torchlight rippled beneath the surface, the reflections making an accurate assessment of their position and number impossible.

And his voice came out of the darkness again. First joking, then desperate, then fearful, finally terrified, all control gone, driven aside by the realization that his life would soon be over, and that it had all happened, turned almost, on a whim. Of hers.

Bernice! Don't leave me here! I love you!

Daniel. Oh, Daniel. I know. I know. I'm sorry.

She took the breather mask from her satchel and put it on, blew away the water and gulped sweet air.

I'm sorry but I can't die like you.

Her mask could last for twenty hours. More than enough time for Patience to figure out on her own what had to be done. In the event it took only five. Five hours alone in the freezing dark, kicking and punching the water to keep her circulation going, accompanied by rumbling silence and twenty-year-old accusations.

Then the water fell away and the stone doors rumbled open, and she ripped off the breather mask to lie gasping and shivering on the stone floor of the passage, her teeth chattering like machine guns as she struck her own body to keep the blood flowing in her veins.

Twenty minutes later Patience appeared in the doorway

and led her from the chamber. Half an hour after that they entered the reliquary chamber.

There were two coffers in the chamber. One small, one large enough to hold a human body. Opening the smaller, Bernice was shocked at the sense of anticlimax. A shroud of rotted linen covered a crystal sphere in which rested a scrap of mummified flesh. The Holy Finger of John the Baptist. She lifted it carefully, wary of a final lethal trap, but there was nothing. Just silence and dust and the smell of damp earth.

She moved to the second coffer, touched the lid, then hesitated. If what she had been told was correct then contained within this coffer was something human science had never known before. An artifact capable of producing miracles. Maybe even the Word of God.

Bernice took hold of the lid, hesitated, signed to Patience to help her. Patience did not move. She shivered instead, hackles raised, feathers quivering. Bernice frowned. Patience was scared. She signed quickly. 'It's OK. It's all dead. There's nothing here that can hurt you.'

After a moment Patience shook her head, screeched and took hold of the lid.

They lifted together. The lid opened then slid to the floor with a thud. Dust rose into the air. Bernice waved it away, peering into the coffer; eyes widening with anticipation, surprise and finally disappointment.

The coffer contained a dead body, mummified. A knight, with shield and armour. The only sword was the sword sheathed beside his rotting skeleton.

The Sword of Forever was not here.

Bernice began to laugh. 'It must be the wrong coffer,' she said, sitting on the floor. 'Bugger me if the silly old duffers didn't bring *the wrong coffer* all the way from Paris!'

Which meant of course that the coffer supposedly containing the Sword of Forever was still in the Templar Mausoleum – in Paris – even deeper within the Alien Jungle.

Still giggling, Bernice packed the Finger into her satchel

and together they began to make their way out of the labyrinth. It took almost four hours. When they emerged they found Marillian and Sara trapped in the rover, under attack from a tribe of *ghosts*.

The *ghosts* retreated as Patience sprang towards them, slower than normal but still fast enough to be hard to follow with what organs they possessed that passed for eyes. Now that reinforcements had arrived, Sara emerged from the rover, gun loaded, aiming careful shots into the mass of creatures. They squealed piteously when hit and crawled away. In ten minutes the area around the rover was clear enough for Bernice and Patience to climb aboard. Sara then gunned the engines and the rover managed a truly dramatic seven kilometres per hour.

'What do they want?' Marillian asked.

'I have no idea and no intention of finding out.'

'What did you find in the labyrinth?'

'That we need to get waterproof clothes.'

8

ETHIOPIA: 2575

Marillian forced his way through the burning congregation in the wake of Jennings-Bankhurst and the Ark. All around people were screaming. The church was alight, burning fiercely towards the nave. Timbers popped and sizzled; mortar exploded from the walls in crumbling shrapnel which scraped at his face and hands. Breaching the prophylactic seal? Maybe – there was no time to worry about that. With any luck the fire would eradicate any bio-infection before it reached him through any minor breaches in the skinseal.

He was more concerned with Jennings-Bankhurst. He ran, trying to move even faster against the flow of people also trying to escape. Their voices were a wailing chorus of despair and terror. He could well imagine why.

Where was their promised miracle? Their monk deliverer was dead and the method of their deliverance looted. The ancient fear had come true and he himself had helped. He had brought Jennings-Bankhurst here. With his father he had facilitated and financed this expedition. He was to blame as much as the older man.

Marillian stumbled as a child grabbed hold of his leg. The child sobbed, begging for something Marillian didn't need to understand to divine the meaning. *Help me! Save me! I'm scared!*

Marillian scooped up the child and continued to run,

pushing everyone else aside, though it tore at his heart to do so.

Jennings-Bankhurst was at the entrance to the church. Marillian saw him move outside, knocking aside the beseeching arms of the congregation who clustered around him trying to touch the Ark.

Marillian increased his own speed, bursting from the church amidst a crowd of supplicants, some burning, others transforming into biological visions he could not begin to name. It was hell. He was in a hell he did not even believe in.

The hover-jeep stood foursquare among the confusion, its black bulk ignored so far due to the Red Cross insignia painted on its sides. Ondemwu was at the controls; Marillian could see him standing up in the driving seat, head and shoulders above the crowd, scanning the people for signs of himself or Jennings-Bankhurst approaching.

Marillian waved and yelled but Ondemwu's attention was caught by the arrival of the older man with his precious cargo. Marillian turned to run, found his way blocked by a family of four clinging together and screaming, dodged past a man rolling the flames out of his burning clothes in the dust, found himself caught between two suited figures, two boiling jets of flame. He flung himself to the ground, rolled, clothes smoking, skinseal crisping and peeling away. If he wasn't open to infection before he most definitely was now. Protected by the corner of an outhouse, Marillian dodged around the church and ran as fast as he could through the graveyard towards the hover-jeep. By the time he rounded the building the entire ground floor was alight and flames were creeping relentlessly along the gables and crenellations. Plaster popped and burst, fragments stinging his exposed skin, the noise of screaming obscured by the roar of flame and shrouded in a maze of smoke.

Marillian turned the last corner, a voice crying out inside his head. He stopped suddenly, heart hammering. Where was the kid? Where was the kid he had been holding? When had he let her go? Where was she?

He looked around. The hover-jeep was thirty metres away, a dark silhouette against the roiling flames from the people-trees drifting gently in the heat, Ondemwu standing tall and thin in the driver's seat, Jennings-Bankhurst a black figure loading the lumpy shape of the Ark into the cargo-space.

Marillian cast his eyes around for the child, hesitated, started for the jeep, then was arrested by the sound of sobbing from behind. He turned. The child was less than twenty metres away, a soot-streaked ghost emerging from a pall of smoke. Marillian turned back to the jeep. He took a step. Hesitated. How could he leave this child to burn? He turned, ran, scooped the child into his arms, felt her hot, infected tears splash against the side of his face as he turned back to the jeep.

It was gone, a wraith vanishing into the smoke as if it had never been.

Marillian yelled, waved, ran after the vehicle; stopped when he stumbled over a body lying prone upon the ground. Jennings-Bankhurst lay still, a neat bullet hole puckered the skin of his forehead, white hair splashed with his own blood.

Ondemwu, the jeep, the Ark – all were gone.

9

PARIS: 2595

The *ghosts* followed them all the way to Paris. The journey was even slower because of the lack of one rover. The *ghosts* wandered near by all the time; even the presence of Patience – who proved several times how easy it was to disembowel even a hybrid human – could not dissuade them from their attempts to infect the travellers.

In the end they stopped and Sara held the *ghosts* at bay with the flamethrower while Bernice and Marillian made a platform from non-aggressive wood, lashed it to the rover's canopy, and stacked the remaining provisions and equipment there. Then with Patience taking up the rear passenger seat, Bernice sitting on Marillian's lap in the front passenger seat, Sara driving, and all five lift-fans protesting at the extra load, the expedition continued.

From then on the journey went much faster. They reached Paris in less than a week. Cross-referencing the Templar journal against a download from an orbiting geosat made locating the precise latitude and longitude of the Templar Mausoleum if not easy, then at least much less hard than they had expected. It took them only two days to find.

With the crumpled remains of the Eiffel Tower emerging, Mayan-temple-like from the motile jungle, they set about hacking their way into the Mausoleum itself.

* * *

That the building still existed was miracle enough for Bernice.

Inside she marvelled at the workmanship; the architecture and imagination which had created this place; the beauty of the stone, now crumbling; the stained glass, now blocked by the crawling jungle. It was like being underwater; the depths of an ocean glimmering with dim phosphorescence, with murky shapes swirling in the rippling darkness. It smelt of damp earth, old bones and older gods. Or one God, anyway.

They set up the only remaining portable light. The shadows it threw were angular and harsh, the colours revealed as drab greens and browns. Yet beyond the spiky puddle of light, in the glimmering shadows, some of the magic remained.

Without stopping to eat, they began to explore.

Bernice and Marillian found the reliquary chamber. It was long, rectangular, with semicircular ends and a vaulted roof composed of mated arches. Columns supported the roof, and an upper gallery of crumbling stonework. The walls were overgrown, the roof and floor missing blocks, the gallery collapsed in some places into stacks of rubble. Light streamed through a jagged hole in the roof, the hole knitted by time and vines. Rain dripped steadily into the chamber, staining the floor and adding to the feeling of being underwater. Arches debouched from the main chamber into rustling darkness.

The entire chamber was filled with coffers.

Bernice had to concentrate in order to stop herself leaping up and down in delight. Marillian was wandering around the chamber, moving carefully on the slippery floor, eyes moving restlessly over the architecture, the tombs, the stonework, the blocked glass of the windows at each end of the chamber.

Bernice felt a sudden flush – in the excitement she had forgotten about Daniel. How could she have done that? She leant her head against the damp wall for a moment, letting his memory soak away into the cool stone. *I'm sorry. I have to get on with my life now.*

She lifted her head when she became aware that Marillian was watching her, and made her own circuit of the chamber, stopping frequently to examine the walls or coffers, her mind a snow-flurry of speculation and wonderment. She moved slowly, a smile playing about her lips, her fingers touching the stonework, lost in a dreamlike montage of images, passages from the Templar journal mixing with scenes from old movies; a mating of reality and romance, the juxtaposition laying bare the truth of two cultures.

Husband and wife met beneath the hole in the roof, and Bernice tipped her face up to the fine drizzle of rain, letting it splash across her brow and down her neck. She closed her eyes and tried to imagine just for a moment what the water would feel like were it not kept from her skin by the layer of protective bioseal. Probably horrible. Dank and slimy. She grinned, opened her eyes and found herself face to face with Marillian.

'What now?'

She reached out, took his face in hers, and kissed him softly on the mouth.

He blinked. 'I thought we weren't –'

She waved aside his words, closing his mouth by gently pushing her finger against his chin. 'It was just the moment.' She dug into her rucksack and produced the King James Bible given to her in London. 'I've been doing some reading.'

Marillian half smiled.

Bernice frowned. 'What?'

'Nothing. Just . . . well, you said you'd read the Yellow Pages before you read that particular book.'

'Did I? Well. A girl can change her mind. Anyway. This is a kind of directory too. If you know how to read it.'

'Do tell.'

Bernice flipped pages. 'Luke, Chapter 9, verses 18–19. "And it came to pass as he was alone praying, his disciples were with him: and he asked them, saying, Whom say the people that I am? They answering said, John the Baptist; but some say Elias; and others say, that one of the old prophets is risen again." '

Marillian chuckled. 'Herod beheaded John the Baptist.'

'Don't you believe in the Resurrection?'

Marillian seemed almost to overreact to her words; his face abruptly became very serious. 'It's an old story. The verse you quoted contradicts itself even on the most superficial matter of claiming Jesus was "alone with his disciples". If it does that how can you see a truth in any of it?'

'My point exactly. With so much conflicting evidence who's to say my theory isn't the more likely?'

Marillian rubbed his chin; the blue patterns on his cheeks shifted subtly. 'So you're saying Jesus Christ was really John the Baptist brought back from the dead?'

'It's as good a theory as any other.'

Marillian looked away.

Bernice sensed a change come over him; the set of his body was less relaxed. He seemed almost angry. She reached out for him. 'What's up?'

'Nothing.' He brushed aside her hand. 'What now?'

Bernice took the crystal sphere containing what the journal called 'the Holy Finger of John the Baptist' from the leather pouch and dangled it before him with a grin. ' "Let your fingers do the walking"?'

It took ten minutes to sample genetic material from the Finger. Five minutes to set the parameters into the detector. Seven hours to find the right coffer.

Inside the coffer was a shape wrapped in the rotting remains of cloth. The shroud broke as they lifted the lid, fracturing like old cobwebs as Bernice reverently preserved and lifted the relic from its resting place.

It was a head. A mummified head. The scalp was so old it had the texture of parchment dusted with talcum powder – but two things were immediately clear.

First – there were marks engraved upon the skull.

Second – there were a number of wounds consistent with

penetration by several hundred tiny sharp objects pressed cruelly down into the flesh of the scalp. The wounds penetrated to the bone.

Thorns.

Or maybe nails. Or . . . she frowned. No. They didn't have neural samplers then. Did they?

Mind whirling with thoughts, Bernice set the head carefully down inside the stasis cube prepared for it and then sat down. She was in a slimy puddle and didn't even notice. Her head was filled with lightning, the thunder of screams.

– the hammers rose and fell –

– her hands what were they doing to her –

Christ. Possibly.

The Templars thought their treasure was nothing less than the mummified head of *Jesus Christ.*

On it was engraved the Map of Forever.

It all happened peculiarly slowly after that. She supposed she should have expected it. Just for once she felt safe; safe with a man she was coming to have feeling for, maybe even love.

Big mistake – as usual.

Marillian took the gun from his pocket and the stasis cube from her hands in one smooth movement. He put a bullet into Sara's arm as she drew her own gun. He held the gun to Sara's head until Bernice told Patience not to disembowel him. He walked out of the reliquary chamber. He pushed Sara back into the chamber as he left; shot the roof as she sprawled bleeding on the floor.

Stone blocks crashed down, blocking the entrance, trapping them inside.

From outside, she heard his voice. It was warm, intimate, as she had imagined it often lately in her dreams. 'As an archaeologist and historian I respect you, Benny. I probably love you too. I hope you don't die.'

'Why!'

Her voice was a scream. The only answer was the whine of the rover's lift-fans as Marillian gunned the engine and drove away. Only afterwards did she think to wonder if she had overplayed the surprise and anger. She hoped not. She was taking a big risk letting him get away with the head. Things could get very awkward if Marillian knew what she knew. Oh well, there wasn't a lot she could do about it now. She had to put a tourniquet around Sara's arm and try to work out how to get all three of them out of there.

The tourniquet was in place and she had decided the best way of leaving the chamber was through the broken roof, when she realized the hole was already in use.

When the *ghosts* began to climb in through the broken roof, the first to push aside the creeping vegetation and drop silently into the reliquary chamber had the body of a nightmare and the face of Daniel Beaujeu.

10

KAMPUCHEA: 2577

Marillian studied the temples of Angkor Wat through old-fashioned binoculars from his position among the trees. He rubbed old scars at his shins; the newly knitted bone there still ached in the damp. It had taken him a year and a half to track down Ondemwu and the Ark. A year and a half spent in the hell of which Axum had been only the outermost region.

The girl had died of course – not in the flames which had taken their lives, nor even by the torches of the Red Cross soldiers who had tried to purify them both as they fled first Axum and then Ethiopia, stealing a boat and following the White Nile from its tributaries into Egypt. The girl had transformed fully while on the boat journey, the lack of food which had brought him to the edge of death no longer affecting her body, which was now able to photosynthesize sunlight. The child-tree bore fruit – the first of the people-trees to do so in his experience, and perhaps due to mutation from the minor fallout accompanying the purification of Axum – fruit which Marillian avoided for many days until hunger had driven him close to insanity. Then he had plucked and eaten as much as he could.

He had been sick for a whole day and had fully expected to die, yet had not. The sickness had clearly been due to his prior starvation rather than the fruit itself.

So the river journey continued, he making sure the child-tree was well watered and exposed to maximum sunlight and she, in return, providing fruit for him to eat. In this manner they had kept each other alive for weeks, until reaching Egypt.

His own infections were secondary, consisting in the main of minor skin motility and discoloration upon the exposed areas of hands and face. He sometimes wondered whether eating the fruit of the child-tree had blocked further infection, providing immunity or at least greater resistance. If this were the case Marillian knew he had the future in his hands – the future of the human race. In any event he was never to find out. Egyptian bandits found and burnt the child-tree while he was foraging for normal food almost a month into the journey. They took his palmtop (damaged in the escape), all his disks and his clothes. It was only by convincing them his credit cards were gene-coded that he was able to avoid death at all. They kept him prisoner for weeks, shooting him carefully once in each leg to avoid escape; taking him occasionally to nearby towns to draw cash for them. He did this gratefully, for each coded bank statement was a message revealing his location.

A month later the bandits were killed by a sniper as they drew money on his last card. The sniper was English; she worked for his father.

The rest of the year was spent in research in London while his wounds healed. The physical wounds healed in a matter of months; the psychological trauma took longer. But throughout it all, Marillian maintained his drive and focus. He frequented the museums, the libraries, spent more time on the Net than he did in the real world. He was looking for signs of Ondemwu; rumours of the Ark. Anything that would provide a trace, a direction, a scent to follow.

When his father died in a transport accident later that year Marillian was devastated. He withdrew even further from life, if that were possible. He did not attend the funeral in Trafalgar Square, paid no respects to the monument erected in his father's honour beside the restored Nelson's Column. Though he had technically inherited his father's businesses, he paid them no heed either. They were maintained by various boards which had always governed them, only now with slightly more autonomy they did even better business.

Eleven months after his escape from Egypt, on the anniversary of the death of the child-tree he had rescued from the fires of Axum, Marillian found the clue that had brought him to Kampuchea, to the Palace of the Arch-Regent Gebmoses III, self-styled (and unacknowledged by any existing world power) Emperor of the Third World.

Marillian had watched as the Emperor – a ridiculous vanity for one of the lesser sons of a near-fatally inbred line – had posed and postured before his people, openly defying the world powers to intervene, politically or militarily. They had chosen to ignore him; after all what power did the man, clearly insane, have over them? His army consisted of three hundred peasants, his technology little more than slave-run factory-mills. Only the year before he had declared himself a descendant of Egyptian kings and therefore immortal. He was no more capable of posing a threat to the civilized world than he was capable of performing simple arithmetic.

But Marillian knew better. He knew something no other government official in any country knew. He knew Gebmoses III possessed the Ark of the Covenant. Even Hitler had known there was more power in that relic – even if it was nothing more than a rotting wooden box containing only dust – than in all the armies of the world. Because of one simple factor.

The power of belief.

Marillian had tracked Ondemwu down to a bar on the borders of Rangoon. The translator had been three fourths drunk when Marillian entered the shack and dead when he left. Marillian had taken a crate of vodka with him and spent the next week in a drunken stupor. He had caught a terrible chill from sleeping outdoors in the annual rain, because he was too frightened to find lodgings or claim his sub-orbital where it was parked at the local airport. Killing a man had not been as easy as he had thought it would be. Or rather, the killing had been easy, but the aftermath, the feelings, had not been easy. Oh no, not at all.

Another week passed in fever. He was found by a rice-picker and nursed back to health by her husband. He repaid their kindness by stealing food and clothes as soon as he could walk and getting the hell out before they downloaded a newscast which might contain news of the murder. Sure his sub-orbital had been impounded but unable to check without revealing his presence, Marillian had no recourse but to join the community and earn his own food. This he managed by the simple expedient of convincing the locals that he was a wandering simpleton on the ragged edge of starvation who could work with his hands but whose intellectual processes were more than somewhat impaired.

It wasn't actually that far from the truth.

Another six months passed and Marillian began to forget why he had come here. His mind bowed to the pressure of work and his hands hardened to the task. Slowly, by a process of social osmosis, he was absorbed into the farming community.

And then one day came the ritual.

The Timkat ritual.

The Emperor Gebmoses III had decided to show his Ark to the laity.

Marillian had bought the binoculars and an old-fashioned Colt revolver three months previously from a vagabond trader. The weapon and its six bullets had cost him a month's food. He had not even dared to test-fire it. If the authorities found he had it the penalty was removal of the hand used to fire it. If someone was actually killed by its use . . .

Nonetheless Marillian knew he had to use this gun. Not to kill a man – his mind still held enough instinct for self-preservation to prevent that madness – but to perform an even greater function.

Though his original mission had been to secure the return of the Ark to his Chapter, it was clear to Marillian that destiny had decreed the Ark would be destroyed in the fires of Axum. It was clearly what God had wanted. Therefore it should equally be what his Chapter wanted. Jennings-Bankhurst had prevented that through a mixture of eager curiosity and greed. Now it was time to correct the event. To put destiny back on track.

To destroy the Ark – once and for all.

He watched the military cavalcade leave the Palace of Angkor Wat and thread its unsteady way through the local farms and villages. He saw the flatbed load-lifter on which the Ark had been placed. He saw the altar which had been constructed there to hold the Ark high above the heads of the curious watchers. He watched. Waited. Carefully loaded the gun. Moved slowly into position. Worked his way closer through the farmer-workers as the cavalcade approached, humming across the ungathered summer crops.

And as the load-lifter drew level he took out the revolver and drew a bead on the Ark.

He pulled the trigger.

The gun exploded.

He lay upon the ground, his right arm missing from the elbow, feeling slow blood pulse into the rice crop. Half his face was gone; he knew that because he had no sight in his right eye and heard nothing but a continuous cannon-blast of noise in his right ear. Beneath his shredded skull, his mind ached. He felt grainy and tired. Maybe he would sleep now. Yes. That would be very good.

Then he felt hands lifting him. Pain beat against the shore of consciousness, driving him ever further from sleep. He blinked, felt hot blood run down his face. He couldn't turn his head –

He was lifted, positioned before the Ark. A figure swam into view. The Emperor. He was talking. Spouting words at the crowd. Marillian was forced to his knees. It did not take much effort. He saw blood fall from his face to stain his knees and the ground.

The Emperor Gebmoses III had finished his speech; the words, little more than dull firecracker noises, echoed away into the distance. The military escort stepped close to Marillian. He drew a gun – a modern pistol. He placed it against Marillian's remaining temple.

The Emperor signalled for him to wait, and then turned to the Ark. He carefully peeled away the layers of cloth protecting the laity from its gaze.

He lifted the lid.

Marillian did not hear the shot which opened his skull and emptied the life from his body. He did not feel the damp breeze whistle past his face as he fell to lie prone among the rice fields. He did not think of his father, or of the child-tree he had saved from the fires of Axum; he did not think of anything at all. He simply died, quickly, without any fuss or bother, there on the ground among the ungathered summer crop.

His last – and first – vision was the open Ark.

And when some time later the Emperor Gebmoses III offered him the life he had recently lost in return for his eternal loyalty, Marillian was simply too terrified of dying for a second time to refuse.

11

PARIS: 2595

The *ghosts* fell – perhaps *dripped* might be a better word for they undulated and shuddered as they moved into the reliquary chamber. They squatted and scuttled and quivered, slinking into the clinging shadows. Ten, twenty, a hundred of them, all different sizes, all different shapes, yet all one shape: not-human.

Bernice held Sara, and Patience moved in close as the room filled with soft noises: slithering of flesh, crackling of limbs, the swish of tentacles, eyes and teeth and glistening sense-organs invisible in the rippling darkness, but watching. Oh how she knew they were watching her.

And Daniel. Was he watching too? Was there any human intellect left in that hybridized shell of flesh he now called a body? If there was, how would it regard her?

She waited, the sounds and visions coming close on the heels of her discovery and betrayal, driving her close to the edge of madness. She gripped the Finger of John the Baptist in one hand, the King James Bible in the other. Both arms were wrapped around Sara, to keep her from the damp ground. Patience was growling. The growls grew steadily in volume, becoming coughs and then barks, interspersed with hissing breaths. The raptor stamped from foot to foot, muscles bunching in her legs, alternately lowering and raising herself, her toe-claws grinding across the damp stone.

Every bit of fur and every single feather adorning her body rose, like the hackles of a cat, until she seemed to double her size and her body appeared to ripple in the darkness, with no defined edges beyond her burning eyes and frequently bared teeth and claws, scything repeatedly at the damp air before her as she moved.

They waited.

Sara reached awkwardly for her gun-holster and took out her gun.

They waited.

The apparitions, the *ghosts*, waited too.

Sara turned awkwardly, put the gun against Bernice's chin and said, 'I didn't come here to be nursemaided by you.'

'You didn't come here to die either,' Bernice whispered back. Her head jerked as the gun dug into her neck. She shrugged, let Sara go. The younger woman moved away, feet sure amongst the wet stone and earth.

Bernice watched her while simultaneously trying to keep everyone – every*thing* – else in sight as well. 'You led me here. You knew he was alive. You wanted him to find me, infect me. It's your revenge.'

Sara laughed. 'See how the mind latches on to the first plausible suggestion? Your words say more about you than they do about me. And no. I didn't want you here at all.' She glanced towards the *ghost* that had been her cousin. 'But you see . . . he wouldn't come for me. Oh no. But he'd come for you. Because he loved you. He didn't love me; he wouldn't come for me. But if I brought you here he would come. And then I could ease his pain. The pain you brought him because he loved you.' She swayed, loss of blood making her dizzy, but the gun arm remained rock steady. Only now she turned it so the gun was aimed directly at the apparition with the face of her cousin.

Bernice felt her body grow rigid, every muscle tight as rope hauling against unyielding blocks. 'No.'

'I saw him . . . a year after you left him for dead. But he wasn't dead. I saw him at the edge of the jungle. He came to see us. To say goodbye. He was hybridized by then. Beginning to change. He couldn't leave the jungle, not and stay alive. But he came. To see us. I saw him for a moment. A moment that has haunted me . . . oh . . . so long. It was the pain, you see. On his face. The pain of leaving us. The pain of betrayal . . . But beyond that it was the pain of transformation, the physical pain and the uncertainty, of not knowing what he would become. I was seven then. Mother was with one of the calving cows. I ran for her gun. Even then I knew what I had to do. But when I got back he was gone. Now . . . now . . . thanks to you . . . I can finish what you started.'

Her finger squeezed the trigger.

Patience moved, limbs a blur, claw striking sparks from the gun as she hooked it from Sara's grasp and sent it clattering away into the shadows. The bullet went wild, struck stone, shattered part of the stained glass in one window. Coloured glass rained into the chamber.

Sara sank to her knees, cradling her hand, sobbing openly, as much with pain from the finger she had lost with the gun as her failure to spare her cousin the pain she perceived was his.

As if the sound of the shot were a trigger, the *ghosts* began to move closer.

Sara huddled into a small shape on the floor, her back pressed against one of the stone tombs. Bernice moved in closer as well. The *ghosts* hadn't moved until Sara no longer had the gun. Was that action deliberate? Premeditated? Or were all these once-people acting on some animal – alien? – level she did not understand? It didn't matter. There was no way out. The shadows were full of movement; the nearest limbs were already just metres away. Whatever they wanted to do to them they were powerless to stop it. Patience leapt and ran around the two women, slashing with claws and teeth, not to kill so much as discourage. She could tell there was no percentage in killing. Not when the odds favoured the *ghosts* so well.

Nothing Patience did stopped the advance.

Then Daniel stepped out of the shadows. His face was warped by time and alien DNA, half shadowed and backlit from the hole in the roof. He took a step on legs which had no feet, just chitin points, which clicked as they hit the stone blocks.

His mouth stretched, an unfamiliar organ performing an unfamiliar task.

He spoke.

'Benny.' The voice was soft, oddly beautiful, a product of who knew what changes to his vocal chords. His throat resonated with the word, ballooning gently to allow a dozen echoes to emerge from flapped openings.

Bernice shivered. 'Dan . . . Daniel. You remember me?'

'Book. Want . . . book.' His voice was a rippling chorus, a solo choir of aching remembrance. 'Wanted me . . . to steal . . . book.' Limbs moved, scooping dusty parchment relics from nearby coffers. 'Here books . . . Here . . . *all*. . . books.' The limbs deposited the relics at Bernice's feet. 'Here all books of Templars . . . all books want . . . all books, Benny . . . all books for *love*.'

Bernice felt her heart banging in her chest as the parchments banged against her feet. She tried to think of something to say. Tried and failed. He was pathetic. A pitiful, mewling creature. And she had loved him. She tried not to feel the disgust welling in her chest. She tried not to feel the guilt.

That didn't work either.

Daniel left them at the edge of the jungle. Bernice looked around. Fields. Trees. Small buildings. A farm. A tractor was garaged under a sheet metal roof near by. Bernice left her credit implant on a small log in its place. Twelve hours later they were in Arginy.

They took Sara to hospital. Her wounds were treated and both she and Bernice were examined for signs of DNA corruption. The doctors told them it would take a while for the test results to come through. In the meantime they were both to remain in bioseal to prevent the spread of any possible infection to others in the town. It was a nuisance but considering the only alternative was the cleansing flames of a *ghost*-pyre, it was an acceptable one.

Bernice stayed with Françoise in the farmhouse. She tactfully ignored the sobs emanating from her room for the rest of the night.

Sara came home from the hospital. She showed Bernice how to muck out the stables and groom the horses.

Patience learnt there was great fun to be had teasing sheep.

On the third night there were visitors. Françoise brought them to the parlour and left them with Bernice. She frowned when she saw the identical grey suits, grey smiles, grey lenses. 'If it's not the dynamic duo. How perfectly bewitching to see you. Can I offer you a glass of wine?' Her voice hardened. 'Or perhaps a punch in the eye for nearly getting me killed?'

'Thank you –'

'– a glass of wine –'

'– would be lovely –'

'– it was a long journey –'

'– and though we're not exactly tired –'

'– the country is quite rough –'

'– and we do have rather a lot to discuss.'

Bernice's gaze flipped from one to the other like someone watching a tennis match. Her expression hardened to match her voice. 'Now you listen to me, both of you. I did what you wanted. I got your precious Head back for you. It's not my fault my blasted *husband* made off with it at gunpoint – during which jolly jape, I hasten to add, three people nearly got themselves killed. I think you owe me some answers. More specifically you owe me the answers you promised me in Scotland.'

A thoughtful exchange of glances between the Masons led to, 'Well, you might have a point –'

'– especially since your actions were particularly selfless –'

'– and may we just say that what we are about to reveal –'

'- that is to say what Anson the pig has discovered for us –'

'– is far too *sensitive* –'

'– not to mention *dangerous* –'

'– for the ears of those such as the woman and the reptile –'

'– outside the Order.'

Bernice sighed impatiently. 'Three points. First, she's neither a mammal, nor a reptile; don't show your ignorance. Second, if anything's happened to my favourite pig you're in *big* trouble. Third, would you please just get on with it before I have to resort to transplant surgery so I can live long enough to hear the punch line?'

Newton and Kepler exchanged looks – not quite smiles, but somewhere teasingly close. Bernice poured three – large – glasses of Françoise's own wine, then settled down to listen to what the Masons had to say. She listened closely and carefully, and as they talked she felt her anger, already at breaking point, grow even further.

Her only satisfaction came after they had offered to help her break into the Royal Palace at Angkor Wat and steal back the Head of Christ from 'Emperor' Gebmoses III, when she had the immense satisfaction of watching both Masons get so drunk so fast she could swear she saw their eyes cross behind their grey contact lenses as they leant drunkenly together on the sofa and began to snore.

'Revenge,' she observed succinctly while undressing the two Masons, entwining their arms about each other, placing a can of aerosol prophylactic between them and finally covering them with a thick woollen blanket, 'is clearly a dish best served mulled.'

Bernice's amusement at seeing the expression on the Masons' faces when they woke up the next morning wrapped around each other was livened first prior to breakfast when Newton found a moment to be alone with Bernice long enough to ask circumspectly how much Bernice knew about what had happened the previous night because, she added candidly, she somehow found herself unable to remember the precise sequence of events which led to her waking naked, wrapped around her fellow agent; and again an hour later when Kepler had diligently created an opportunity to ask exactly the same question. To both Masons her answer had been the same – an enigmatic smile and a zipping motion of two fingers across her lips. When pressed on the point, Bernice admitted she might be able to remember events proportional to the amount of information the Masons were first able to provide for her.

That information was more readily forthcoming.

'The IFB have known about Marillian's connection with Gebmoses III for some time since –'

'– we've been watching the so-called "Emperor" carefully –'

'– not because we're frightened of *him* –'

'– though fear itself is a useful tool –'

'– but because we fear the power he is gaining. You see –'

'– it's been clear to us for some years that Gebmoses was little more than a harmless imbecile –'

'– but now since he has gained access to Marillian's inheritance –'

'– that is to say, his *money* –'

'– the trend of events has been both more predictable and less containable –'

'– and he has become –'

'– unofficially at least –'

'– the third richest man in the world, so –'

'– when you couple that with a –'

'– bent, a definite *bent* –'

'– towards the religious purity found hitherto only in such figures as Adolf Hitler and Margaret Thatcher –'

'– you can see why his long-term –'

'– *obsession* –'

'– with the accumulation of Christian religious icons –'

'– such as the Spear of Longinus, the Crown of Thorns and the Holy Grail –'

'– together with his desire to become Emperor of Earth –'

'– attain the alarming proportions that they currently have –'

'– and why we must ourselves stop at nothing to make sure –'

'– that he's stopped before he gains enough political power –'

'– to achieve his goal.'

Bernice had long since found staring at her wine glass to be less painful on the neck than watching each agent speak in turn. Now she looked up. 'Which is?'

The Masons exchanged looks but said nothing.

Bernice sighed impatiently. 'All right, let's cut to the damn chase. I ran interference for you guys because you told me you'd let me in on some big secrets about the Sword of Forever. I did that and almost got three people – including myself – killed. OK, so the guy wants a few mouldy Christian icons. So what? It's not like he's going to open the Ark of the Covenant and destroy the world, right?'

Newton and Kepler exchanged glances.

'Is he?'

The Masons licked their lips, both at the same time. Top lip, bottom lip. Perfect mirror images. She waited. Neither spoke. She sighed, 'Well, if you're so worried about this maniac why let him get into a position where he can steal the head of Christ in the first place? I mean, you're Masons, right? Descended from the Knights Templar. The most powerful organization since the Inquisition. Keeping secrets is practically a genetic trait with you guys, am I right?'

The Masons simultaneously rubbed their eyebrows, Newton her right, Kepler his left. They said nothing.

Bernice shrugged. 'OK. I've had it with you two. I'm going to saddle me up Françoise's prime Appalachian in the stable there and I'm out of here.'

'No –'

'– please, Bernice –'

'– we'd be very grateful if –'

'– you wouldn't do that.'

Bernice frowned. 'Well. You know what I want.' She waited. The Masons shuffled uneasily. 'I'm waiting.'

Newton said eventually, 'We really don't want you to go.'

Kepler added, reluctantly, 'What do you want to know?'

Bernice thought for a moment. 'All right, let's start at the start. Tell me about the Sword of Forever. I thought we were coming here to Arginy to find an artifact, not some mummified head-shaped pencil holder. Please tell me I'm not going to have my skull engraved and then be eaten alive for the sake of a metaphor.'

Newton and Kepler halted the movement of identical knifefuls of jam towards their croissants.

'No –'

'– The Sword of Forever is not a metaphor –'

'– it's real enough –'

'– although we never had proof until we were able to access your marriage records –'

'– and confirm your own DNA was a perfect match –'

'– for that associated with certain relics our Order has knowledge of.'

Bernice dunked her croissant in her orange juice and took a big bite. 'Tell me something I can't figure out. What is it then, if it's not a mouldy old head?'

'Our records tell us the Sword is an artifact –'

'– a Holy artifact –'

'– a force placed at the gates of Eden to protect it from the impure –'

'– a force capable of carrying out the Word of God Himself.'

Bernice offered round the coffee. There were no takers. 'Oh, come on. You don't really believe in all that nonsense about the Ark, do you? That it could level mountains and rot armies and what have you?'

Kepler said, 'And lay waste to cities and send forth plagues and dry up oceans and change the face of the world –'

Newton said, '– Of course not –'

'Oh good, because I thought for a moment I was going to be dealing with a couple of raving –'

Kepler interrupted, '–The Ark itself is merely the *control mechanism* –'

'– it contains the operating instructions –'

'– the user manual, if you like –'

'– to the Sword itself.'

Bernice raised a sceptical eyebrow. 'I get you. Like a computer, right, with peripherals and bolt-on hardware?'

'And a human operator –'

'– directing the power of God Himself.'

Bernice broke into a sudden grin. 'This is a legpull, right? A little game to make up for last night?'

'I can assure you it is no game –'

'– the Sword is real –'

'– the Ark is the control centre, the *operating system* if you like –'

'– and the Crown of Thorns, the Spear of Longinus and the Holy Grail are the –'

'– bolt-on extras –'

'– as you put it yourself, so succinctly.'

'So . . . let me get this straight . . . You're trying to tell me the operator of the Sword has to be crucified in order to use it?'

'As far as we know.'

'Doesn't that rather defeat the object?'

'That depends what the objective is. For example –'

'– if the objective is the creation of a myth figure powerful enough to change the world, then –'

'– death and resurrection would seem to be a more than adequate way.'

'But you're talking about cloning . . . We have it already.'

'The resurrection of Christ was a symbol that changed the world. Clearly the world has outgrown such symbols. Power is no longer vested in metaphor. Power is vested in accomplishments.'

'Are you telling me the Sword has the ability to . . . remake . . . the world? Physically change it?'

'The texts are unclear –'

'– though we believe that to function properly no other alternative is possible.'

'Does the Emperor know its capabilities?'

'We believe so.'

'How?'

'Through Marillian.'

'Your husband was a second order Mason before he joined the Emperor.'

'Was that one of the reasons you tried to kill me? Because of my association with Marillian?'

'And your search for the Sword, yes.'

'We know now it was a mistake, of course.'

An embarrassed clearing of throats and then, 'We're actually quite –'

'– sorry about that little misunderstanding –'

'– and hope it won't prejudice you against –'

'– working with us in the future.'

'You guys are impossible, you know that?' She sighed tiredly. 'I assume Marillian knew all your dirty little secrets.'

'Some of them.'

'Did he know how the Sword worked?'

'Detailed information about the Sword is known only to the head of our Lodge –'

'– at least it was –'

'– until we were authorized to impart that information to you.'

'Hadn't you better tell me then?'

Twin hesitation – a mirror glance. Concern? Fear? Bernice wondered if the Masons were supposed to be telling her all this.

'No record exists of the precise means by which the Sword functions –'

'– we only know what it is capable of –'

'– how it is used –'

'– and the use to which is was supposedly put.'

'And that is?'

'To build worlds –'

'– by creating time itself –'

'– since without time, matter cannot exist.'

Bernice needed to think about that one for a moment. 'You're saying this thing can *create* time?'

'Oh yes. Create time –'

'– change its direction –'

'– recreate life from a supplied pattern –'

'– turn energy into matter –'

'– build worlds –'

'– and populate those worlds.'

Bernice felt her head spin. 'You're talking about the power of creation. Resurrection. Biblical miracles.'

'Yes –'

'– we are.'

Bernice shook her head wonderingly. 'Then . . . you're not talking about an artifact *belonging* to God. You're talking about *God Himself.*'

'You might think that.'

'We couldn't possibly comment.'

'Well, OK . . .' Bernice struggled to find a way of expressing the intensity of emotion she felt. Hopeless. Best to dive straight back into more comfortable waters. 'How does it do all this? Perform these miracles?'

'Again the texts are less than precise –'

'– though it would appear that the one who operates the Sword does so through an act of faith –'

'– for no reward comes without sacrifice –'

'– and as to the mechanism –'

'– we suspect that what happens is that the operator is subjected to a life-ending experience –'

'– and a chemical record made of the neural patterns within the brain at the moment of death so that –'

'– if the subject is of sufficiently pure intention, the last recorded thought will be the objective they wished to achieve via the Sword.'

'There is of course a complication –'

'– a safeguard, if you like –'

'– and that is that the operation of the mechanism would appear to be invariably fatal –'

'– you could say that he who wields the Sword of Forever will be killed by it, even as it achieves his aims.'

Bernice chewed thoughtfully on her lower lip. 'A neat way to ensure that anyone with psychopathic tendencies won't live to enjoy the fruits of their desire.'

'Actually we suspect this side effect is incidental –'

'– and that the Sword was simply never designed to be wielded by anything more fragile than a god.'

Bernice uttered a humourless laugh. 'Why am I not surprised?' She hesitated, afraid of asking the obvious question. In the end, of course, there was no choice. 'So break it to me gently – what's my involvement?'

The Masons exchanged brief looks.

'We would have thought that was obvious, Bernice –'

'– especially to a scientist of your experience and imagination –'

'– because you yourself have found evidence to suggest that –'

'– when the Sword of Forever is finally used –'

'– and a culture is created travelling backwards in time –'

'– the human operator who dies creating that culture –'

'– will be you.'

And the two Masons smiled; simultaneous grey smiles that told Bernice if she thought she was in trouble before, it was quite clearly nothing to the trouble she was in *now.*

Part Four

The Blood and the Flame

1

ANTIOCH: 2595

Bernice tied back her hair and stared up at the crumbling stone edifice that was the Church of St Peter. The high walls had clearly once been smooth and, though plain, must have exuded a measure of calm and strength. Now the walls were shored with a layer of concrete which itself was wearing away, and the illusion of power was revealed to be just that – an illusion. The church was just a building. The town just a town. Bernice glanced around at the streets and people and cats and thought that, despite the number of download antennae, nothing very much had probably changed in the last six thousand years.

She glanced down at the guide book she held, acquired for an extortionate amount of money from the local tourist office. The picture of the church must have been taken several hundred years ago, judging by its condition. Bernice flipped pages and began to read.

Three days after the Muslim army under command of Kerbogha, the Turkish ruler of Mosul, invaded the city of Antioch and retook it from the Crusaders, a thief named Bartholomew had a vision. The vision was of the blessed Apostle Andrew who, he claimed, appeared to him one night as he slept in a cloud of light and told him to announce to the struggling people that a source of consolation had fallen from Heaven for them, through the finding of the Lance which opened the side of the Lord. Bartholomew claimed that the Lance lay hidden beneath the earth within the church of St Peter. And it waited there for the Crusaders to find and use to defeat the invading army.

For three nights the visions continued, while Bartholomew tossed and turned upon a rack of indecision. Should he speak? Would he be believed? What if the Lance was not there? Was he going mad?

On the sixth day after the army of Kerbogha retook Antioch, Bartholomew was sought by Raymond of Toulouse who had heard rumours of his visions. Bartholomew admitted the truth. That same day men began to dig. The Lance was found on 14 June 1098, exactly seven days after the invading Turks had retaken the city. Three weeks and four days later their entire army was destroyed, and the Lord Jesus Christ transferred the entire city of Antioch and a thousand Muslim men also to the Roman religious faith.

Bernice closed the guide book and walked up to the entrance to the church. The wooden door was open and through it she could see the interior was shrouded in parchment-coloured light. She closed her eyes for a moment and imagined the church as it might have been, walls smooth but doused in the blood of Turk and Christian alike, screams and the sounds of fighting done but new fear arising from starvation and the knowledge that to survive the famine, the Crusaders were going to have to drink the blood of their own horses. That was his world. His life. Bernice opened her eyes and was confronted with the infinitely more tranquil present-day reality. And she smiled. Because Bartholomew had been a liar and a thief. What the guide book hadn't said was that his claims were false and that he himself had secreted an Arab spear into the area of the dig and that was what had been found by the Crusaders. The ironic thing was that it hadn't made any difference when, with the 'Spear of Longinus' at their head, some few hundred of them took on the entire Turkish army and kicked some serious arse.

The even more ironic thing, Bernice thought to herself, was that if they'd dug another few feet they'd have found the real Lance. Because according to the documents she'd retrieved from the Templar Mausoleum in Paris, the ones offered to her by Daniel shortly after Marillian had taken the Head of Christ, the Spear was exactly where Bartholomew the thief had said it would be. Under the ground behind the altar.

All she had to do was go in there and dig it up.

Three hours and a considerable number of bribes later she was back in her hotel room. She placed the Lance (just the head, the wooden shaft had long since rotted away) into a stasis cube and tossed it on to the bed beside the Grail and the Crown of Thorns, poured herself a very large drink and settled down in the somewhat dilapidated armchair to watch the sunset, and try to figure out what to do next.

While she watched the sun slide gradually around the orbital mirror, she thought. It was inevitable really; the hotel room her own little Gethsemane. Her moment of reflection before the altar of choice. Because that was what it all boiled down to in the end. Choice. Her choice to believe or not believe. Her choice to be herself or like herself or change herself if she didn't.

She drank deeply as the sun sank across the pale stone town, its last dusty fingers creeping slowly up the grimy hotel walls as if to pinch off all choice with the light.

Why was she here? Why was she doing this? Why had she taken this self-destructive course? OK, so she was unhappy, but why was she unhappy? She had a good job, quality friends; her life had been an adventure Tom and Huck would have robbed Injun Joe blind to experience.

So what was it then?

Why this feeling of guilt? Of fear?

Why this obsession with the Sword? The relics? With God?

She tipped back her flask and guzzled more booze; felt the old fire dig into her stomach though, to her surprise, she took no comfort from the familiar sensation.

Maybe that was it.

Whatever else you might say about her life it was comfortable. It fit her like an excavating waldo. It was tight, familiar – comfortable. Except . . . well, now it wasn't.

Why?

What had changed?

She sighed, tipped the flask again, blinked when she discovered it was empty. She rang room service and had a bottle of Bolivian Red delivered. It arrived later, a slightly cold but nonetheless very acceptable substitute for the contents of her flask.

She drank.

She drank some more.

She was happy with herself, wasn't she?

She was happy with her life, wasn't she?

Well – wasn't she?

Another bottle of wine followed the first. By now the moon was up, painting the town with ghostlight and faerie shadows – shadows she had last seen in London. London. Marillian. Husband. Jason. Cock-up.

There *were* things in her life she was unhappy with, of course there were. Everybody had them, didn't they? Everybody had something they felt guilty about, or shied away from thinking about, or –

– wanted to change?

Was there something about herself she wanted to change?

Surely not now. Not this late in life. For God's sake, she was . . . well, she was old enough to know that she ought to be happy with her life – not regret the things she hadn't done, even if she had once thought they were for boring people. For Heaven's sake! Of *course* she didn't regret not having a family. Children. Even a steady bloke who she could respect and be comfortable with. Her? The ace adventurer, Benny the bolt Summerfield? Surprise was her middle name. She liked it. Craved it. She lived for the moment. Time was her enemy. Experience her prey.

She needed an average life like a . . . well, like a . . . hm, well, like something she didn't need very much, anyway, *that* was for sure.

Bernice realized the second bottle of wine was empty when it slipped from her fingers and didn't splash when it hit the carpet.

All right. Be honest now. You're upset about something. There's something missing from your life. Family, car, penguin, something.

That was true enough. But here was the clincher.

Are you sure filling the gap with God is going to make it right?

She stayed awake until sunlight made a rosy reappearance at her hotel window, but it was two days before she found an answer.

When she did she unfolded her palmtop and keyed in Marillian's address.

Marillian arrived later that day. His knock upon the door was polite but firm.

'It's open.'

He came in and closed the door carefully behind him. Bernice tried not to stare. His clothes, his face, nothing had changed. Why had she expected they would?

'Hello, Bernice.'

'Hi.'

'You're not dead then.'

'I v-mailed you, didn't I?'

'So what do you want?'

'Got a present for you.' She hesitated. 'Three presents actually.' She nodded at the bed. He followed her gaze, his expression carefully neutral. When he saw the relics his jaw dropped like a ten-pound sledge.

'Four if you count this.' And she crossed the room, took him in her arms and kissed him.

He pulled away almost immediately. ' "I'm not having sex with you." '

She looked up at her own words. 'Oh, that's cruel.'

'So's stealing the Head and leaving you for dead.'

She stepped back, considering. 'I suppose so.'

'Then why?'

'Because . . .' She hesitated, then went on with sudden resolve. 'Because the Emperor knows more than the Masons about the Sword of Forever. Newton and Kepler have led us all up the garden path. You've never lied to me. Omissions I can deal with – it's just a matter of asking the right questions. In a way it's my own fault you betrayed me in Paris. But I can get beyond that . . . if you can answer one question.'

'Ask it.'

'When you said you loved me . . . did you mean it?'

His answer did not come straight away. 'Not when I first met you, no. But then I realized who you were. Your significance.' Another hesitation. 'You think I rescued you from the Masonic Lodge in Scotland.'

Bernice wondered if her expression was as out of control as she felt. 'I don't understand. How else could I be . . .' She stopped.

He said flatly, 'When I reached Loch Ness you were dead. They'd killed you.'

'*That was an accident!*'

'No.'

Bernice closed her eyes, remembered the pain, the drugged drink, knew he was right.

'Why else would they tell you the truth if they weren't planning to kill you afterwards?'

Bernice found herself sitting down suddenly. Her mouth worked but no words came out.

'You asked me if I loved you. Not then, though I thought of us as friends. But after. After I brought you back. Then I loved you. Because in all the world you were the only one who knew what it was like to die and be reborn. You were the only one. Because we were the same.'

'I . . . don't . . .'

Marillian crouched beside her, taking her hand. He had to hold it tightly to stop it from shaking. 'I have died and been reborn through the power of the Ark.'

'That's utter . . . I need a drink.'

'Think about it. Me. Patience. Now you. All three with essentially the same experience. A Holy trinity. We have been blessed, Bernice, blessed by the Word of God. He took our mortal remains and remade them in His image.'

'Oh yeah?' Her voice was hoarse, her body shaking so hard her teeth chattered. 'How . . . how do you acc-ccount for the fact that Patience . . . is a bloody . . . bloody *raptor* then?'

Marillian just smiled. 'It's a metaphor. We're all alive. Alive as God is alive. In our hearts. And in the Ark.' His smile was radiant. 'You asked if I loved you. If all I have said is true how could I *not* love you?'

Bernice found herself shaking angrily. 'That's tosh and you know it.'

Marillian sighed. 'I know.' The blue patterns on his face swirled agitatedly. 'Funny how things never turn out how you expect, isn't it?'

'What do you mean?'

He sighed, moved to the window, looked out across the sea of stone, the flapping washing, the eye-achingly bright sunglare. 'I'm going to tell you something you probably won't believe.'

'You'd be surprised at some of the things I've believed.'

'I'm sure. Well, here it is. I used to be a Mason. Second Order. I worked with your friends Newton and Kepler. My Chapter had what you might call special responsibilities. We were supposed to maintain the status quo if anyone ever made a discovery.' Somehow the word *discovery* came out in huge capitals. 'Then we got word of an expedition. A man called Henry Jennings-Bankhurst had supposedly found evidence to suggest the final resting place of the Ark of the Covenant. Well, of course, he couldn't be allowed to find it.

It would change the world. I was placed on the expedition to make sure he didn't. By whatever means was necessary.'

'You killed him?'

'No. I did try to destroy the Ark though, because by then it had been stolen by agents of the Emperor.'

'What happened?'

'I was caught trying to destroy the Ark with an old handgun. I was – and this is the bit you're not going to believe – I was executed.'

Bernice uttered a humourless laugh. 'The other one's got bells on.'

'I'm serious. The Emperor shot me. There were several hundred witnesses to my death . . . and to my resurrection, when he let the Ark look upon my dead body.'

Bernice felt her head spinning. 'That's crazy. It's nonsense. You Masons are all round the ruddy bend!'

'It's true. The Ark remade me. I served the Emperor. How could I not? I have experienced death. It is indescribable. The terror in the moment of knowing immediately prior to the end of life is something that would change your life forever, if you ever survived it.'

'So you joined the bad guys.'

'Yes.'

'Willingly.'

'Yes.'

'Why?'

'Because . . . because . . . Gebmoses gave me life. He took it away and then gave it back. Try to understand what that could be like for someone fundamentally Christian in their belief.'

'You think the Emperor is God?'

'I did for some while.'

'And now?'

'No.'

'Why?'

'Because of you. Because I know now how you fit into things. I know about the Ark, and what it does. And because I know the Emperor is a madman.' A momentary hesitation, then, 'He's a madman, Bernice, with the power of God at his fingertips. He wants to change the world.'

'We all want to do that.'

'Not like him. You don't understand, Bernice. You don't know him like I do. You see . . . I thought he was right for a great many years. Right to want to cleanse the Earth. Right to want to banish the evil in man from Eden, right to want to clone an army from the DNA of the Templar Christ in order to accomplish it. He thinks he's purifying the world, Bernice. But he's simply going to remove every bit of uniqueness and individuality from it by destroying everything and everyone in favour of his perfect race. The People of God. Literally!'

'I have to stop him.' It wasn't a question.

'Yes. I'll help if I can.'

Bernice realized she was crying. 'They said I would have to, and they said I would have to die. Sodding Masons! *Don't let them be right. Marillian, I believe in free will. I have to or my whole life's a lie. Don't let them prove me wrong. I don't want to be a puppet or a sacrificial lamb or a metaphor for anyone's damn religious icon.* Don't let Gebmoses kill me. Promise me!'

Marillian nodded. 'I promise.'

Two hours later they and the relics were aboard Marillian's transport, heading East into Kampuchea for a meeting with the man who would be Emperor of the Earth.

2

PANGAIA: 80 MILLION *ANNO QUINCUNX*

And the days of the Lord grew long and the people fell from their great heights many times. And always when they fell there came among them the Saviour, bringing love and death among them to strengthen them against adversity.

But the last time She came among them She saw with great sadness that their lands and cities and farms had fallen to weeds and ruin, and she spake unto them, saying, 'Why do you lie humble like beasts when the Lord hath given you the knowledge of the Stars?'

And they made no reply to Her, and She spake again, saying, 'Live you so close to the beasts of the land in manner that you cannot speak?'

And one among them said, 'We toil not for the world turns younger with each day. And what future have we who know that future is not the boundless Heaven which the Lord promised us but which, instead is naught but a fire in which the world shall end.' And the people rose in fear, saying, 'It is said that the Lord has forsaken us and this fire is the fire of Hell and it shall swallow us all.'

And the Saviour smote her own forehead and furiously spake. 'You stupid, ignorant buggers! That's not the end of the world, that's its birth. Why else do you think you were supposed to develop spaceflight? Heaven ain't infinite, but it does run to billions of years yet – assuming you can get your asses off this sorry rock.'

But the people understood not the Saviour's words, and instead they smote themselves upon their foreheads in emulation of Her divine action and went back to their mud fields and their crumbling cities and their wasted lives.

And the Saviour, knowing Her task with Man was at last done cast about the Land for another to annoint with the knowledge of the stars.

She searched among the beasts and fowl, among the fish that swam in the sea and the birds which flew upon the wing. She searched among the crawling things and flapping things which dwelt within the earth. And so She came, after many years had passed in despair of finding that which She sought, to the Land, and there she waited.

And it came to pass that her gaze alighted at length upon other life. Heathen, true, and godless, but she could change that. She could lift them from their destiny of extinction and give them the stars forsaken by once-chosen Man. She could give them God. But first She had to give them Life.

She waited in the hills of the Cold Lands for many more years, until one such came among the struggling animals that had been Man. And she called that one to her in her temple within the hillside and said unto it, 'What manner of creature are you? For you seem familiar to me, yet I have no knowledge of you.'

And the visitor spoke weakly, for she perceived it was wounded, and it replied in its own voice, 'I am Old and I am dying.'

And she said to it, 'Shall I make of you a Man to have knowledge of life and stars, and to go forth from this place unto your people and teach them of things which I shall decree and which shall make them stronger and wiser that they shall inherit the earth where others have failed?'

And Old said, 'You speak of that which I crave like life itself. You speak of knowledge.'

And the Saviour said unto him, ' "And the Angel of the

Lord appeared to him in a flame of fire out of the midst of a bush; and he looked, and behold, the bush burnt with fire, and the bush was not consumed." '

And Old understood the Saviour's words, saying, 'You speak of life and death.'

And the Saviour replied, 'I speak of life *from* death. I speak of worlds and stars. All this I offer to thee and more. All I ask in return is worship and obedience.'

'Knowledge is its own master.'

'Then I shall gift you with that which you seek.'

And the Saviour took Old, of the race of Raptor and remade him in Her own image.

And later, she died with no regrets, for her task was done, and the *Sword of Forever* had a new guardian, and she came to the Lord with open eyes and heart and was seen no more in the Land.

3

KAMPUCHEA: 2595

Bernice stared at the woman. She was a dancer, an *apsara.* Her left elbow had been shattered by gunfire and both legs had severe bullet wounds. Her left temple was missing, hollowed by yet more gunfire into a gaping crater which began at her brow and continued up into her headdress. Her face was aged yet ageless, still beautiful. At least the bullets hadn't touched her there.

Bernice shook her head. The woman may have been only a relief, one of many thousand figures carved from stone upon the walls of the temples of Angkor Wat, but that did not diminish the tragedy of her injuries, inflicted by Khmer Rouge weapon-fire more than five centuries before Bernice herself had been born. She stood now as an endless monument to the one thing an archaeologist dreads – not wind or acid rain or organic rot but the apparently eternal folly of human nature.

Beside Bernice, Marillian told the load-lifter which had brought them from the spaceport to go to the garage. The vehicle immediately took itself off to park somewhere out of sight. Bernice ignored its movements, instead tracing the outline of the stone dancer's face with her finger, trying desperately not to let the stone maiden's fatal injuries bring back to life the still-too-vivid memories of her own death.

Marillian said, ' "The one who goes through the water of the clouds." '

Bernice felt her hands tremble as she touched the stone. She imagined gunfire, screams, the death of many who were not made of stone. She imagined mass graves, barren fields, a people trying to claw their way back from a hell on earth. Just as she was. 'Twelfth century Khmer.' Her voice was a whisper. 'She lived untouched for eight hundred years. Survived wars, storms . . . the twentieth century took her from us.' She took back her hand, still feeling the grain of the stone impressed into her skin. 'Time took her from us.' She looked at her husband with carefully neutral eyes. 'I'm ready to go in now.'

If Bernice had expected Marillian would take her straight to the Emperor she was mistaken. The first thing he did was bring her to a suite of rooms located in a summerhouse within the ornate temple gardens, which he told her had been provided for their use. He asked if there was anything he could get her to help freshen up.

Bernice grabbed her toothbrush from her satchel and waved it at him. 'Travelling light has become rather a forte. You could find me something to wear though. Somehow all this' – she looked down at her grubby trousers, boots and shirt, torn in France and recently patched, then out of the window of the suite, which overlooked the south-eastern corner of the moat, and the irrigated fields beyond the temple wall – 'seems a little out of keeping with the general atmosphere.'

Marillian nodded. He turned to leave, hesitated, seeming to want to kiss her. Bernice waited.

'Benny, I –' Marillian turned suddenly and left the suite. It was the last time she saw him before she died.

Bernice took off her clothes and made a bee-line for the shower. The water washed over her and she couldn't help thinking of the people she had seen working in the rice fields, protected from the sun by the checkered cotton *krama* bound like a loose turban around their heads. She remembered the thousands scrambling aboard the daily train to Battambang as she and Marillian had entered Phnom Penh. What lives did they have here, she found herself wondering. What quality of life? At least they were still human – she supposed that must count for something – with the 'Emperor' at least.

Now she was here. But what would she do now? Was she capable of carrying out the one thing she knew she must? If Newton and Kepler were telling the truth, she had little choice. It was her life balanced against the survival of an entire culture. But she was still very scared. As scared as she had ever been.

Finding herself shivering, Bernice turned up the shower temperature. The water poured down on her in steaming torrents; for a short while she could forget what she had to do.

Not for long. When she emerged from the shower wrapped in a large towel, a man was waiting for her. He was armed; a soldier. Bernice didn't need to ask why he was there. 'I'll need to dress.'

The soldier nodded; surprisingly politely, she thought.

The soldier led her from the suite and through the grounds of the temple. By now it was afternoon; the sun was high and hot, stretched in its mirror-arc across the sky. The soldier led her through carefully tended gardens to the eastern wall and then left.

Ten minutes later Bernice was still looking at the temple wall, unable, quite, to decide whether it should more properly be considered architecture or art. She supposed in the end it didn't matter. The wall was a symbol as well as a defence and in a historical sense the two were indistinguishable.

Depicted on the wall, as on all the stone surfaces of the temple, were carved reliefs. The one which she was looking at now stretched for more than fifty metres. She tried to count the figures – the stone *apsaras* – depicted there but could only estimate their number at several hundred, at least. She tried to retrieve any scrap of knowledge about the carvings. In truth it was not so much out of scientific curiosity as a desire to put off thinking about what was inevitably to come.

In any event she had no further time to consider. There came the soft tread of sandals on grass. She turned. Gebmoses III was a slight man, but tall. He was dressed in a conservative cream linen suit. His face was thrown into sharp relief by the high sun. His eyes were deeply shadowed, his lips a slash of flesh-colour in his pale skin. Bernice shivered as she looked at the thin face, the fine-boned hands. This was the man who had taken her husband. Taken him before she had ever met him, taken him and made him his own. The man who could snuff out her life at a whim. For the first time she felt fear. She became aware that her hands were clenched into fists, the nails digging painfully into her palms. She unclenched them with an effort, then wiped them on her trousers.

He moved towards her, unsmiling, and now she became aware of other movement. More soldiers. His guards. In case she tried anything? Bernice thought about allowing herself a smile but didn't, afraid it might come out wrong and betray her real feelings.

Gebmoses III moved close to her – too close – before stopping. His eyes held hers. Why did he want to meet out here? In the open? Why the soldiers? Was he afraid for his life even here in his own palace? Could *he* be frightened of *her*?

He smiled; she wouldn't have believed the transformation had anyone else told her of it: the face which only moments before had been a disturbing mask now radiated comfortable familiarity and benevolence. He nodded towards the carving on the wall. 'A Hindu creation myth. *Churning the Sea of Milk.*' He moved closer, hands moving elegantly to outline details of the stone relief. 'The central figure is Vishnu, closely associated with the builder of this temple, King Suryavarman II.' He waited. Bernice waited too. He continued, 'To the left are the *asuras*, or demons, led by Ravana. To the right, the celestial gods led by the monkey god Hanuman. This between them is the serpent, Vasuki, a most important figure. Vasuki, you see, creates the ambrosia of immortality. It is a symbol of the king's beneficence.'

Bernice nodded without speaking.

Gebmoses touched the stone with his bare hand, almost seeming to sense the story being told within the rock. 'Immortality. A hard gift to attain, I am sure you would agree.' It wasn't a question. 'Originally this wall was protected by a vault – a roof. It has been missing for several centuries. Here, you see these dark patches? That is damage caused by water evaporating through the stone itself.' A finger moved, scraping residue from the stone, rubbing it away against a palm. 'The residues are destructive. The stone dies, slowly, inevitably.' A minute hesitation. 'Time. Some call it the great healer. I prefer to think of it as a tireless predator. The ultimate predator. Wouldn't you agree?'

Bernice shrugged.

Gebmoses' thin lips narrowed thoughtfully. 'You have questions. Ask them.'

'For a man who professes an obsession for Christian symbols you seem remarkably well acquainted with the Hindu religion.'

'I am familiar with many religions. But I believe in only one. Only one faith will purify this earth. Only one God will provide forever for His chosen believers.'

Bernice shivered.

'My belief frightens you?'

'Oh yes.' There was no point in lying.

'Good. Purification can only be achieved through fear.' A moment, then, 'There are many things here you would find interesting. I could show you a selection. Would you like that?'

Bernice shrugged. 'Under normal circumstances.'

Gebmoses said, almost bleakly, 'The world being the way

it is you may be properly thankful these circumstances are not normal.'

Bernice shrugged. 'Whatever.'

Bernice was led into the temple proper through a vaulted entrance. The tour was unhurried, Gebmoses an ingenuous host. Frequently they stopped to examine this relief or that statue, some recovered from museums or private collectors over the last twenty years. Gebmoses would give a small commentary about each. The stops punctuated a tour which consisted of a bewildering array of laboratories, special research units, prayer rooms. The temple, clearly refurbished to Gebmoses' own unique vision, was a strange combination of science and religion.

The tour continued, moving away from the temple in a small convoy of military load-lifters, wafting along the impressive walls of the Eastern Baray, one of four artificial reservoirs designed to irrigate the fields with collected rain-water from the monsoons. Bernice could not help but be impressed. The Barays were more than a thousand years old yet still provided a perfectly adequate irrigation system. The skill and beauty of its construction would have easily placed it among the Seven Wonders of the Ancient World.

'The Khmer were gifted with an integrated view of the universe.' Gebmoses spoke with a dreamy half-smile playing about his lips. 'A powerful political organism, a strong, centralized and uniform society, and fabulous technical organization.'

' "And a partridge in a pear tree." '

Gebmoses frowned. 'Not precisely. No partridges here, you see. Wrong sort of climate.'

Bernice's expression did not change. 'How silly of me.'

'Well.' Gebmoses signalled the driver and the load-lifter ground to a halt at a small temple to the south of the Baray. When Gebmoses took her hand to usher her from the vehicle it was as much as Bernice could do not to break his arm.

* * *

The interior of the Temple of Pre Rup was unlike any she had seen previously. She recognized it straight away from descriptions she had read during the research she had conducted into the Egyptian culture while in London, and also from her Masonic sojourn in Scotland.

'An interesting combination.' Bernice gazed interestedly at the faced stonework, the pillars, the precise design as familiar to her as the patterns of a snowflake.

'You recognize the influences?'

'The Temple of Solomon. The Pyramid of Unas.'

'The place from which the Ark of the Covenant vanished from living memory.' Gebmoses seemed pleased she had recognized the styles. 'The Pyramid of Kings.' A moment, then, 'The Pharaohs thought they were the embodiment of Horus while a man, and that they would be reborn into eternity as the god Osiris when they died.'

'And you expect to do the same?'

Gebmoses' face explored the boundaries of another thin smile. 'That would be a convenient cliché, wouldn't it? Fuel to the fire of your own scepticism? No, Bernice. I do not seek the wisdom of ancient gods. My own God has already offered me immortality. I have a more important task to achieve.'

'Oh yes, I'd forgotten. "Nobody expects the Spanish Inquisition." ' Bernice did not smile.

Gebmoses moved into the centre of the stone chamber, raised his hands, and said loudly, ' "Forgive them, Father, for they know not what they do." ' He drew back curtains concealing a space behind the altar and beckoned Bernice forward. It didn't take much to figure out what the cloth-covered, box-shaped object sitting on its stone dais was.

Gebmoses waited for the echoes of his previous words to subside then continued, 'They seek to forgive. To accept. To embrace. They seek to pollute the purity of Earth with the seed of the heavens. They do not realize it is time to cast out the Serpent. Time to build a new Eden. And you, Bernice. You will help me in this. You will be my architect. The

Architect of Eden. Together we will purify Earth.'

'Just don't ask me to carry any bricks – I'm useless with a hod.'

The somewhat desperate humour was lost on Gebmoses. He smiled; a mindless killer's smile she had last seen on the face of a shark.

'It won't be that sort of Eden.'

4

THE ORIENT: 4500 *ANNO QUINCUNX*

It was a time of miracles but the people did not rejoice.

What should have been harmony was disharmony; what should have been unification was diversity. Whims and passions were indulged; Man prayed for intellectual pleasure – and preyed for visceral pleasure – upon Man.

So it was when the Saviour came for the third time and, walking among the people She spoke to them, saying, 'The knowledge that I have brought among you is gone, scattered as your people were scattered generations since by the Word of God. You failed Him then as you fail Him now. You do not remember the wrath of the Lord or your promises to his Saviour.'

And the people, fearing the wrath of the Lord rose up against the Saviour and cast Her from their midst, saying, 'Go thou from this place of intellect and decision lest your Master, who is no longer our master, visits his vengeance upon us and lays our wombs and lands barren and scatters us as once before.'

And the Saviour spake unto them, saying, 'Fools. In your ignorance you are scattered. You simply do not know it.'

And She travelled for many years throughout the wilderness, and strove mightily, seeking a solution to the ignorance of the people that they would accept, lest the knowledge of the *Sword of Forever* be once more lost to time.

And it came to pass after some years that She came to the Land of the East and there She spoke with learned Men who maintained the Way of the Lord, and bade them use their skills to preserve forever the knowledge that was hers by inscribing it unto her shaven head that even in death she might be its progenitor.

And the wise men made a gift to her of their ability and so she was Marked, and by her Mark would she be forever known, and the Mark was this:

'That whomsoever beareth the Crown and spilleth blood by the Crown and by the Spear, and holdeth that blood within the Grail and placeth that matter within the Ark of the Covenant, and obeys the Law of God as written therein, so shall they wield the Sword of Forever, the Sword which can kill death, the sword which can bear time itself as a child.'

And so the Saviour passed again from living memory though Her gift of knowledge remained.

5

KAMPUCHEA: 2595

The Temple of Ta Prohm, a mile to the west of the Ark's resting place in Pre Rup, held a complex genetics laboratory. State of the art facilities and personnel; mid to high level computer operations performed by pigs servicing a serious AI. Bernice did a double-take as she noticed one pig staring at her. Was that Anson?

Hooked up to a gene-sequencer via a computer interface was the relic described by Templar lore as the Head of Christ. As Bernice watched, Gebmoses bent forward so that his face was on a level with that of the mummy. He blinked, wriggled his eyebrows and set his mouth into a number of different positions, trying to match his expression to that of the relic. Bernice had to stop herself from smiling. It was as though Gebmoses was pretending to look in a mirror; his reflection the mummified face.

Gebmoses turned suddenly, straightening to fix Bernice with a direct gaze. He smiled, a blink-and-you'll-miss-it expression of humour. He nodded towards the Head. 'Ugly fellow. But powerful. Had the world in his hands. Gave it all up for his people. They killed him for it. And he let them.'

Bernice did not have to feign interest. 'A mistake you are not going to repeat, I presume.'

'On the contrary. Look at what he achieved through his

death and resurrection. I will achieve all that and more. I will achieve Heaven on Earth.'

'How?'

He shrugged, placed his hands at the scraps of flesh that were the Head's ears and gently tugged. He poked his tongue out at his 'reflection' and waggled his finger reprovingly. Bernice bit her lip until she tasted blood.

'Umm . . . I'm not sure I want to tell you. You might think I was mad. Then again, you are part of it, so I suppose it's all right after all . . . All right. I'll tell you. It's very simple. The Sword of Forever is not a metaphor. It is a real artifact. The will of God made manifest as a set of Holy relics.'

'The Ark, the Spear, the Grail, the Crown. Tell me something I don't know.'

'Well, Bernice, let me put it like this. You are born. You grow old. You die. Straightforward enough, correct?'

She nodded.

'All one direction, unchanging, unchangeable, correct?'

Another nod.

A self-important catch of the breath. 'Well, you see, Bernice, that isn't actually true. Everything you've heard about the direction of movement of life through time – well, that's wrong too.'

Bernice felt her head spin. 'I don't –'

'Oh, but you do, Bernice. You do understand.' A beat, then, ' "The Christian Bible tells us God made the world and everything in it: but no *thing* can exist without time to define it. Did God make time as well?" ' Gebmoses rubbed his hands together in delight while Bernice shivered at the sound of her own words, spoken so long ago, it seemed now, to her then-new husband.

'You see?' he said. 'You *do* understand. So simple. God exists outside time and space. He *made* time and space. He wrote the rule book for the universe. He made the dice. Every so often he gives the tumbler a shake and – *whoops!* –' he mimed rolling dice, '– sometimes they come up sevens.'

Bernice folded her arms impatiently. 'Meaning what exactly?'

'Put simply, the Ark can create life from death, order from chaos, time from no-time. God made the Earth in seven days, right? Oh, I know it was all supposed to be just a metaphor to allow for the intrusion of evolution into someone's until then neatly reasoned religion. But . . . suppose it was true? How do you suppose He did it? What mechanism do you think enabled the conception of everything we know?'

'Bet your life it wasn't inner-city planners.'

Gebmoses beckoned conspiratorially. Cautiously, Bernice followed him to an observation port set into the length of one wall. Through the port she could see a vast chamber filled with what seemed to be life support systems. Incubation pods. Each was connected to a web of medical and computer systems. They were in rows of twenty. She could not count the number of rows.

'Bernice,' said Gebmoses in a whisper. 'Meet the resurrection.'

She followed his eyes into the room, found herself pulling focus to the image of the mummified Head reflected in the glass.

'You think you're cloning Christ.'

Gebmoses smiled gleefully. 'Yes.'

'Lots of Christs.'

'Oh yes. A considerable number. Tens of thousands.'

'At once?'

'Oh no. A few thousand at a time.'

'An army.'

'The Army of God.' He considered. 'I like that. It has a nice ring to it. Yes. An army. Perhaps. If the need arose.'

'To purify Earth. Kick out the aliens, the non-believers.'

'Mmmm . . . I sense tongues have been wagging . . . no. Not quite.'

'What then?'

Gebmoses touched a control on the wall and the port opaqued. 'It's a matter of symbolism. Christ sacrificed himself for his people. I shall do the same.'

'I see. So you're going to jump up on your jolly old

wooden cross and hold your arms out and say, "Here I am, chaps, bring on the hammer and nails"?'

'Mmm . . . yes, essentially.'

'And the Ark will bring you back to life.'

'As it did your husband when I killed him twenty years ago.'

She shuddered. 'And I suppose you're going to kill me as well?'

'No. Like Barabbas your release is secure. You may leave, or be witness, as you choose.'

'Why?'

He looked at her and his eyes were unfathomable. 'Because I know you'll understand.'

Bernice tried to ignore the moment of connection between them. 'I want to know more. What if this isn't Christ's head?'

He shrugged. 'It is only important what people believe.' A moment, then, 'I have employed teams of scientists to research the relics. They've been working for two decades. The power of the Sword of Forever is the power of creation. Not of space but of time itself.'

'But time already exists.'

'Linearly, yes.'

Bernice rubbed her eyes. 'You're talking about non-linear time. You're talking about . . .' Her mind raced as she grasped the concept. The image of worlds, whole universes existing in parallel, connected only at points of temporal rotation made her dizzy.

He said, 'Think of a data storage crystal. Read by lasers, the information is stored on planes. Rotate the crystal a fraction of a degree and another plane of information is brought into view. How many planes can co-exist in the same block of space? Hundreds? Thousands? I only need one.' His voice took on a poignant tone. 'God made the world pure but now it has become tainted. Eden lies in ashes and the Sword guards its gates from any return. I will therefore create a new Eden. A new world for the pure, for the sons and daughters of Christ the Saviour. A new universe. A new frame of temporal reference. Time,' he added quietly, 'for a new *time*.'

Bernice laughed out loud. 'You're insane if you think that's true.'

'You think so? Then watch.'

After that it happened very quickly. Robed figures (priests? soldiers?) took Bernice from the presence of Gebmoses, took her back to the Temple of Pre Rup, to the reconstruction of the interior of the Pyramid of Unas. There she was given a robe and told to wait with several other robed and cowled figures. More priests or soldiers? Witnesses? There was no way to tell. She tried to talk to them but they all ignored her. Realizing eventually that no one was going to talk to her, she walked towards the temple entrance. No one tried to stop her. She came back. That achieved an equally blank response. She was on the point of exploring the temple further when the main doors opened and a robed figure was brought in. The figure was hooded but she knew who it was. The shape of the body told her it could only be Gebmoses.

Bernice found herself watching the ceremony with a mixture of fascination and dread. Gebmoses was led into the centre of the room and made to kneel before the altar. Now she saw that the altar held a rectangular shape covered in cloth. The Ark. The figure of a high priest stood before Gebmoses and lifted back his hood. His head had been shaved. His face was blank, covered in a faint sheen of sweat. He was frightened! Bernice swallowed hard. She knew from her experience in the Masonic Lodge in Scotland how he must feel.

The priest began to speak.

'Thou standest, protected, equipped as a god, equipped with the aspect of Osiris on the throne of the First of the Westerners. Thou dost what he was wont to do among the spirits, the Imperishable Stars. Thy son stands on thy throne, equipped with thy aspect; he dost what thou wast wont to do aforetime at the head of the living by the command of Re, the Great God; he cultivates barley, he cultivates spelt, that he may present thee herewith. All life and dominion are given to thee, eternity is thine, says Re. Thou thyself speakest when thou hast received the aspect of a god, and thou art great thereby among the gods who are in the estate. Thy Ba stands among the gods, among the spirits; fear of thee is in their hearts. Thy name that is on earth liveth, thy name that is on earth endureth; thou wilt not perish, thou wilt not be destroyed for ever and ever.'

Bernice found herself shivering. Substitute 'Re' for 'God' and it was the same prayer pronounced over her in Scotland. A movement caught her eye. Curtains were being drawn back. The wooden cross she had seen before was carried by seven robed figures into the centre of the room and set into a receptacle in the stone floor. Upright, it stretched as high as two men.

An upholstered footstool was placed before it.

The priest turned to the altar, back to face Gebmoses holding something. The Crown. Bernice recognized it easily. The priest placed the Crown upon Gebmoses' shaved head and pressed down hard. Gebmoses was held tightly but did not move as blood began to run down the side of his face. The crown in place, he was raised to his feet.

Gebmoses was led to the footstool and climbed it without protest, turning to stand with his back to the wooden upright.

Bernice was unable to look away, unable to separate the horror she felt at what was surely a ridiculous and pointless death from the stomach-churning relief that it was not her up there on the cross.

And then, as Bernice watched, unable to look away, his robe was removed and he was crucified.

'Let the Spear be brought forth to open his body.'

A movement; a robed figure took the relic from the priest and raised it to Gebmoses' side.

'Let the Grail be brought forth to hold his blood.'

Another figure held the stone Bernice had found to catch the blood from his wounds.

Gebmoses struggled, his voice emerging in blurting gouts of words. 'Verily I say . . . unto thee . . . today shalt thou be with me . . . in . . . *Paradise.*' The last word was a breath-starved, agonized gasp.

Bernice could stand no more. Unaware she was crying, she turned and moved towards the temple entrance. Three robed figures blocked her path. She tried to move around them. One stepped forward to hold her, removing its cowl to reveal –

'Marillian! What –'

A finger at her lips silenced her voice.

Two more cowls fell back to reveal the grey faces of Newton and Kepler.

'I don't understand –'

'Be silent –'

'– be still –'

'– and wait.'

By now Gebmoses was writhing upon the cross, his chest working, every rib defined, every muscle dripping sweat. His breath came in shallow, pain-filled gasps. Slower. Slower. Until finally he exhaled and did not again draw breath. He slumped. The quivering upright figure vibrated once and was still. He hung silent. Still. Dead.

The priest spoke again.

'Let the sight of God be upon these proceedings.'

He turned and began to unwrap the Ark.

Bernice held her breath, forgotten tears coating her face, her heart hammering at her own ribs, her ears ringing with the precious movement of blood.

The priest unwrapped the Ark. The Spear and Crown were removed from the hanging body and, together with the stone that was the Grail, were placed inside the Ark.

The body was removed from the cross and taken from the temple.

The priest re-covered the Ark and left the temple.

The robed observers slowly left the temple.

That was all.

'I don't . . .' Bernice turned to her companions. 'Is that it?'

'Not quite –'

'– the body will be taken to the people –'

'– so they can see that Gebmoses is dead –'

'– before his resurrection takes place.'

'Here. You've been crying.' Marillian used the sleeve of his robe to wipe tears from her face.

'What now? I suppose we could go to the incubator chamber and stop the machinery cloning Christ. No need for an army when the general's dead. And if we can keep him dead . . .' She tailed off, aware she was probably talking utter gibberish due to the shock.

'No.' Newton.

'Have you forgotten what we said?' Kepler.

'There's something you must do here first.' Marillian, his voice soft, his eyes wet with tears.

Bernice uttered a noise between a laugh and a sob.

' "You are eternity." '

' "You must die so the future past may live." '

'You know, I was wondering when you'd get around to mentioning that again.' Bernice followed both their glances towards the blood-stained cross.

6

JERUSALEM : 3355 *ANNO QUINCUNX*

And it came to pass that there was a war upon the land. For it had been more than three hundred generations since the Lord had created this place, and the people now were arrogant and divided and improperly appointed with weapons and the knowledge of how to use them.

But for one weapon there was more strife; for it alone had been jealously guarded by those defenders of the Temple of Bernice Surprise Summerfield, to the exclusion of those who now coveted it. And it was called the *Sword of Forever*, and it was said that whoever held the Sword held the reins of time itself.

So it came to pass in the fortieth year of the greatest battle, the Temple was sundered and the Holy of Holies was taken by the people from the Place which the Saviour had decreed it be kept.

And while the people lamented there came among them for a second time the Saviour.

And, walking among them, friend and foe alike, She saw what had come to pass and said unto them, ' "And I will execute vengeance and fury upon the heathen such as they have not heard. For a man's enemies are the men of his own house." '

And those that lay seige knew that it was so because they had coveted what was not theirs, but so also did the defenders know that it was so because they had hid from them that coveted what might have belonged to all.

And the Saviour saw that they knew this, friend and foe all, and said unto them, 'God is jealous and the Lord revengeth and is furious. The Lord has His way in the whirlwind and in the storm, and the clouds are the dust of his feet. He rebuketh the sea and maketh it dry. The mountains quake at him, and the hills melt, and the earth is burnt in his presence, yea, the world and all that dwell therein. His fury is poured out like fire and He will make an utter end of this place thereof, and darkness shall pursue his enemies wheresoever they shall be found.'

And the people, be they friend or foe alike, fell to their knees in fear at the sound of Her voice and the sight of Her judgement, but She recanted not and instead bade them unwrap the Holy of Holies and lay themselves and their world bare before their God.

And the Saviour said unto them, 'You've been naughty boys and girls and you're going to get a spanking,' and She threw open the Holy of Holies and God sundered the world and scattered the people to the four quarters, and many died, but many also travelled to the East and many to the West, as the sun rises and time passes, and never did the people meet again for their worlds were different now and their tongues were different and they travelled in opposite directions not only across the land but also in the direction of their lives and in time.

And so the people were scattered and all knowledge of the Sword of Forever was lost. All save the sons and daughters of the Saviour, unto many generations of generations, for they were given a great gift, and that was the gift of knowledge, and a burden was laid upon them and it was the burden of protection of the knowledge of the Sword, and the knowledge of it was signified by the emblem of an All Seeing Eye bounded by a Compass and a Square and these symbols stood for Truth and Righteousness and Compassion, for it was without them that the world had been sundered.

But even this knowledge passed with the generations of the Saviour into obscurity and myth, and unknowing.

7

KAMPUCHEA: 2595

They helped her on to a footstool and her right arm was yanked out in a straight line above her head where it was held in place by a rough nail driven between the radius and the ulna bones just above the wrist and

Jesus, turning unto them said, Daughters of Jerusalem, weep not for me but weep for yourselves, and for your children, for behold the days are coming in which they shall say, Blessed are the barren, and the wombs that never bear, and the paps which never gave suck and

her left arm was pulled out sideways and nailed at full stretch and

verily I say unto thee, Today shalt thou be with me in paradise and

the footstool was kicked away, causing her right shoulder to dislocate instantly as the full weight of her body was transferred to the vertical arm and

a darkness remained over all Earth until the ninth hour and

a third nail was hammered between the second and third metatarsal of the right foot and

the sun was darkened and

the knees bent upwards so that both feet could be pinned flat against the wooden shaft and

the veil of the temple was rent in its midst and

she screamed and

all the people that came together to that sight, beholding the things which were done, smote their breasts and

tried to ease the pain in her arm by standing on the spike which skewered her feet but

all his acquaintance and

the angle of her knees made even this small relief impossible and

the women that followed him from Galilee stood afar off beholding these things and

Marillian pressed the Crown of Thorns against her head and

Patience pierced her side with the Holy Spear of Longinus and

Newton took her blood upon the Grail and

Kepler flung open the Ark of the Covenant and

into thy hands I commend my spirit and

Bernice cried out to the Lord and

cried with a loud voice and

welcomed Him into her heart and

gave up the ghost and

died and

A rain of dimensions.
The word of God.
Time without time.
The moment of creation.

8

KAMPUCHEA: 150 *ANNO QUINCUNX*

The Saviour came first among them at a time of strange peace. Many generations had passed since God had created their world. They were a pitiful people by then, inbred, on the ragged edge of extinction. The Saviour looked at what they had become and shook Her head in despair. In Her image had they been made, yet now they had fallen, their aspirations, hopes, dreams, all dashed as a bottle containing a cry for help might be smashed against unyielding rock by the merciless sea.

They were animals.

Like animals, She culled them; feeding the survivors, teaching them the skills they had lost, yanking them by their bootstraps into a world and a future which had all but forgotten them.

And when She had done this, and saw that it was good, She instructed them in the construction of a place of great worship and learning. And She said unto them, 'This Temple, which shall be named for Solomon, is to have two rooms, one of which shall be a crypt. And the hall shall have fourteen free-standing pillars, twelve of which are matching, but the ones in the southeast and the northeast shall be unique, and these pillars shall be known, the southernmost of them as Boaz and the northernmost as Jachin, and they shall be named, the southernmost of them for Strength and

Patience, and the westernmost of them for Establishment and Stability.'

And so it came to pass. For years the people toiled, and the temple was built. And She looked upon their work and saw that it was good. And She called the people to Her, the learned and the ignorant among them as one, and said unto them, ' "Let the earth bring forth the living creature after his kind, and it was so." '

And in their ignorance they did not understand Her words. But She walked among them and said, 'The fruit of the tree of knowledge shall be yours.'

And still they did not understand Her.

And She said unto them, 'The knowledge of enzyme analysis of DNA shall I give to thee. The knowledge of nucleotide sequencing and messenger RNA and codon signal chain termination shall I give to thee. All these shall I give to thee, in the name of thy Saviour, whose name is, was and ever shall be Bernice Surprise Summerfield, and whose word is the Word of the Lord.'

And still the people did not understand Her.

And the Saviour looked upon them in their ignorance, and verily She said unto them, 'Look here. I'm a scientist. I'm here with a message from God. You've got a bit of a problem in the old gene-pool department at the moment. Not unexpected considering that you were all cloned from the same DNA. But trust in Me and everything will work out just fine.'

And the people, hearing the Saviour's words, were fruitful and multiplied, unto many generations of generations, all across the living earth.

9

QUINCUNX

There were no words to describe what she experienced. How could there be when words were defined by thought and thought by time and time itself was being reborn? She existed, that was all, but without definition; a point, a singularity of conception within the mind of something more powerful than herself. A mind that saw her and knew every detail of her existence right down to her memories of

scooping sand into a plastic bucket, throwing the sand, watching the crumbling lumps scatter across the beach as she leapt, clapping and squealing delightedly, 'Daddy, look, look what I can do I can knock them all down –' and her father said, 'Why don't you build something, Benny? Use the sand and build with it?' And she stopped jumping and clapping at the tone of her father's voice and, crying, she began

brushing dirt from the skeleton, slowly removing the debris, a double O brush working to expose fossilized bones with painstaking care as, in her head she leapt, clapping and shouting delightedly, 'I found one, check it out –' and her teacher said, 'Why don't you learn from it, Bernice? Take the fossil and use it to build on your knowledge of the past.' And her excitement faded at the tone of her teacher's voice as, quietly determined, she began

operating the controls of the gene-sequencer, breaking down the cell sample, watching the strands re-form on the computer screen, incomplete as yet but still enough to make her clap delightedly. 'Look at the DNA, it's forming –' and her professor said, 'Why don't you try to build a whole strand? Take the structure, determine a possible nucleotide sequence to replace the missing sets; use the past to build the future?' And her excitement grew at the sound of her Professor's voice as, mind buzzing with endless possibilities, she began to do as He said.

Epilogue

The Birth of Forever

Kampuchea: 2595

She awoke in a hospital bed. Newton and Kepler were standing next to her. 'Did it . . . work?'

'We don't know.'

'We don't have your frame of reference.'

'But we know that you died.'

'And the Ark brought me back?'

'We can show you the body if you like.'

She shook her head. 'If I don't see the body then I can pretend I never really died. And maybe then my life won't change too much.'

The Masons nodded, twin admissions of sympathy which somehow left Bernice wishing for the threatening hostility of their rare smiles.

London: 2595

She said goodbye to Marillian over a bottle of wine in the same restaurant in which they'd first dined. It was predictably messy; he wanted her to stay and she badly needed a friend. And as he said, they had so much in common. Life. Death. Life.

But as she had told him when, in Antarctica, he asked her why she had come to Earth in the first place, she eventually had to acknowledge that it was time to go home.

DELLAH: 2595

Bernice took Patience with her back to Dellah. As far as Earth was concerned they were both strangers in a strange land. And Bernice was fairly sure she could get the raptor a job on the teaching staff, once she'd had a vocoder fitted and programmed.

The load-lifter from the spaceport got her home as the sun was setting across the Sz'Enszisi Range. She placed the Templar journal on a shelf next to her own diary – a fitting symbol, she thought. And a fitting parallel.

The air was musty so she opened the window. She gazed across the snowy peaks of the Sz'Enszisi Range and thought of Marillian, staring down from his lofty penthouse as a child, watching the people he could see go about their daily lives. She held up her right arm – the wrist was smooth, the skin unbroken. It was as if everything that had happened, somehow had not happened. The sun slipped behind the mountains and she lowered her gaze from the heights to the bustle of the university.

She closed the window, picked up a few stray pieces of homework which had somehow escaped her notice. The first was Stephen's last essay, one she hadn't yet been able to mark. She smiled. Taking out a pen, she opened the notebook and settled down to read.

ACKNOWLEDGEMENTS:
ELEPHANT SURFING

A word of explanation: the quote printed on the back cover of this book no longer appears in the text, though it was very definitely in the original plot (along with many other scenes dragged kicking and screaming from the final typescript). The reason for this is simple: due to the difference in printing lead-times between colour and black-and-white, the back cover copy needed to be set some time before the book was. As a consequence I was required to provide a quote from a book I had not yet written more than twenty pages of. If ever I had need of a time machine this was it!

As ever I am indebted to any number of people, but particularly:

Simon and Peter:	for being so patient (and getting me some cash when I needed it)
Paul Hinder:	for helping to resurrect a terminally crucified plot (and letting me share his internet address for so long!)
Allan Adams:	for providing research, book titles and *Fortean Times* articles above and beyond the call of nature
Roger Clarke:	for providing televisual entertainment above and beyond the call of his VCR engineer
Nige and Debs:	for the loan of Deborah Jennings' Very Important Book
Louise and Paul:	for laptops and rhubarb jam

Special mention for:

Andy and Sue: shortly about to pass a *First Frontier* of their own.

An extra-special mention for the usual cast and crew (in order of appearance): June, Jop and Andrea, Jo and Steve; Trees; Timbo; Kurt; Jon, Alison and Ziggy, Lynne and Lizzie; Audrey and Nakula; The Jolly LightWorX Crew; Alan and Alis, Dave (cheers for the Doc Savage books, meladdo) and Martin.

An extra-extra special mention for Jo who was kind enough to loan me her elephant, her flying saucer and her raygun (all right, hands up, it was a couple of cushions, a drainpipe and a trowel, but that's the magic of Photoshop) and *still* have enough good humour left over to play Benny in the unused alternative cover for this book. Which if it doesn't make it into these pages will be available on my website (which should be sorted by now) – for details check out JimMortimore@compuserv.Com

An extra-extra-extra special mention for Steve Parsons and the Exe-Wing Fundraisers who made Star Wars Day Two go with such a bang. Steve raised more than £1200 for the Exeter Leukaemia Fund, so if there's anyone out there who feels like bunging them a donation they can send it care of: Steve Parsons, 11 Badger Close, Honiton, Devon, EX4 8XG.

For anyone who's interested, a more sensible account of the Templars, the Crusaders, the Pharaohs, the Ark, et al., can be found in the following fun literature: *The Hiram Key* and *The Second Messiah* by Christopher Knight and Robert Lomas, *The Keeper of Genesis* and *The Orion Mystery* by Robert Bauval and Graham Hancock, *Fingerprints of the Gods* and *The Sign and the Seal* by Robert Hancock and *The Chronicles of the Crusades* edited by Doctor Elizabeth Hallam; the creation of Patience owes a considerable debt to Robert Bakker's *Raptor Red* (thanks Anthony!); and the idea for a culture doing what it does in this book first appeared (to the best of my knowledge) in a book called *Collision with Chronos* by Barrington J. Bayley, although in a somewhat more sensible form. Anyone who wants to check out some barnstorming pictures of the temples of Angkor Wat, together with a very good history of the monuments and the country, can find it (if you have a time machine, of course) in the pages of *National Geographic Magazine* 161/5 (May 1982).

In the meantime, remember that the First Frontier to Cross is Not Space (It's Ourselves); and if anyone can tell me where I can get hold of any Doc Savage Novels (and believe me you're going to have to go some to beat Dave's personal best) I'd be very grateful; but until then I'm –

Outtahere –

Jimbo

ALSO AVAILABLE IN THE NEW ADVENTURES

OH NO IT ISN'T!

by Paul Cornell

ISBN: 0 426 20507 3

Bernice Surprise Summerfield is just settling in to her new job as Professor of Archaeology at St Oscar's University on the cosmopolitan planet of Dellah. She's using this prestigious centre of learning to put her past, especially her failed marriage, behind her. But when a routine exploration of the planet Perfecton goes awry, she needs all her old ingenuity and cunning as she faces a menace that can only be described as – panto.

DRAGONS' WRATH

by Justin Richards

ISBN: 0 426 20508 1

The Knights of Jeneve, a legendary chivalric order famed for their jewel-encrusted dragon emblem, were destroyed at the battle of Bocaro. But when a gifted forger is murdered on his way to meet her old friend Irving Braxiatel, and she comes into possession of a rather ornate dragon statue, Benny can't help thinking they're involved. So, suddenly embroiled in art fraud, murder and derring-do, she must discover the secret behind the dragon, and thwart the machinations of those seeking to control the sector.

BEYOND THE SUN

by Matthew Jones

ISBN: 0 426 20511 1

Benny has drawn the short straw – she's forced to take two overlooked freshers on their very first dig. Just when she thinks things can't get any worse, her no-good ex-husband Jason turns up and promptly gets himself kidnapped. As no one else is going to rescue him, Benny resigns herself to the task. But her only clue is a dusty artefact Jason implausibly claimed was part of an ancient and powerful weapon – a weapon rumoured to have powers beyond the sun.

SHIP OF FOOLS
by Dave Stone
ISBN: 0 426 20510 3

No hard-up archaeologist could resist the perks of working for the fabulously wealthy Krytell. Benny is given an unlimited expense account, an entire new wardrobe and all the jewels and pearls she could ever need. Also, her job, unofficial and shady though it is, requires her presence on the famed space cruise-liner, the *Titanian Queen*. But, as usual, there is a catch: those on board are being systematically bumped off, and the great detective, Emil Dupont, hasn't got a clue what's going on.

DOWN
by Lawrence Miles
ISBN: 0 426 20512 X

If the authorities on Tyler's Folly didn't expect to drag an off-world professor out of the ocean in a forbidden 'quake zone, they certainly weren't ready for her story. According to Benny the planet is hollow, its interior inhabited by warring tribes, rubber-clad Nazis and unconvincing prehistoric monsters. Has something stolen Benny's reason? Or is the planet the sole exception to the more mundane laws of physics? And what is the involvement of the utterly amoral alien known only as !X.

DEADFALL
by Gary Russell
ISBN: 0 426 20513 8

Jason Kane has stolen the location of the legendary planet of Ardethe from his ex-wife Bernice, and, as usual, it's all gone terribly wrong. In no time at all, he finds himself trapped on an isolated rock, pursued by brain-consuming aliens, and at the mercy of a shipload of female convicts. Unsurprisingly, he calls for help. However, when his old friend Christopher Cwej turns up, he can't even remember his own name.

GHOST DEVICES
by Simon Bucher-Jones
ISBN: 0 426 20514 6

Benny travels to Canopus IV, a world where the primitive locals worship the Spire – a massive structure that bends time – and talk of gods who saw the future. Unfortunately, she soon discovers the planet is on the brink of collapse, and that the whole sector is threatened by holy war. So, to prevent a jihad, Benny must journey to the dead world of Vol'ach Prime, and face a culture dedicated to the destruction of all life.

MEAN STREETS
by Terrance Dicks
ISBN: 0 426 20519 7

The Project: a criminal scheme so grand in its scale that it casts a shadow across a hundred worlds. Roz Forrester heard of this elaborate undertaking, and asked her squire to return with her to sprawling and violent Megacity – the scene of her discovery. Roz may be dead, but Chris Cwej is not a man to forget a promise, and Bernice is soon the other half of a noble crime-fighting duo.

TEMPEST
by Christopher Bulis
ISBN: 0 426 20523 5

On the wild and inhospitable planet of Tempest, a train is in trouble. And Bernice, returning home on the luxurious Polar Express, is right in the thick of it. Murder and an inexplicable theft mean that there's a criminal on board; the police are unable to reach them; and so the frightened staff and passengers turn to a hung-over, and rather bad-tempered, archaeologist for much-needed assistance.

WALKING TO BABYLON
by Kate Orman
ISBN: 0 426 20521 9

The People – the super-advanced inhabitants of a Dyson sphere – have a problem: to stop an illegal time-travel experiment they must destroy ancient Babylon and all its inhabitants. If they do not, war will break out with the dominant power of the Milky Way, and whole galaxies will be destroyed. Their only hope is that Bernice can travel back to the dawn of civilization, and find the culprits – or Earth history will never be the same again.

OBLIVION
by Dave Stone
ISBN: 0 426 20522 7

A man called Deed is threatening the fabric of the universe and tearing realities apart. At the heart of the disruption, three adventurers, Nathan li Shoa, Leetha and Kiru, are trapped. Their friend Sgloomi Po must save them before they are obliterated, and in his desperation he looks up some old friends. So Bernice joins her feckless ex-husband Jason and her old friend Chris on the rescue mission; but then Sgloomi picks up someone who should really be dead.

The Medusa Effect

by Justin Richards

ISBN: 0 426 20524 3

Medusa, an experimental ship missing for twenty years, is coming home. When one of the investigation team dies mysteriously, Bernice is assigned to help discover what went wrong. But to do so she must solve a riddle. Somehow the original crew are linked to the team put on board – their ghosts still haunt the ship. And the past is catching up with them all in more ways than one.

Dry Pilgrimage

by Paul Leonard and Nick Walters

ISBN: 0 426 20525 1

Thinking she has been offered a blissful pleasure cruise on Dellah's southern ocean, Benny gladly accepts. After all, she has some time on her hands. But trapped on a yacht with an alien religious sect who forbid alcohol, she soon discovers that all is not well. And, as the ship heads toward a fateful rendezvous, she must unmask a traitor or risk the system being torn apart by war.

Should you wish to order any of these titles, or other Virgin books, please write to the address below for mail-order information:

Fiction Department
Virgin Publishing Ltd
332 Ladbroke Grove
London W10 5AH

COMING SOON

Another Girl, Another Planet

by Martin Day and Len Beech

ISBN: 0 426 20528 6

20 August 1998

Lizbeth Fugard, an archaeologist working on the backwater planet of Dimetos, is in trouble. Someone is following her – watching her. Terrified, she calls on an old friend for help. On arrival, however, Bernice becomes involved in politics, gun-running and a centuries-old love affair, and soon realizes that unless she can find the truth a cycle of violence and hate will jeopardize more than one planet's future.